# THE DEVIL SHE KNOWS

# The Devil She Knows

Barbara Ann Martin

La Casa Press

*To my forever supportive husband, Tony.  You are the wind beneath my wings. XO*

# One

The convertible was built for speed, taking hairpin turns with ease. His heart pounded in tune with the pace of the car, faster and faster. The cool night air stung his face, his foot heavier and heavier on the gas pedal as his headlights lit the dark road ahead. This is what he lived for, adrenaline pulsing through his body, blood pumping, breathing quick and short. The martinis he drank only added to his pleasure.

He gripped the steering wheel with one hand and down-shifted with the other in anticipation of the curve ahead. But the curve seemed to be coming too quickly, his reflexes inadequate.

In a slow-motion instant, the road curved right as the car headed straight toward the utility pole. *Downshift, hit the brake!* He tried to will his foot to move from gas to brake while his other foot slammed down on the clutch a moment too late. The grinding of the gears assaulted his ears. Then the sound of screeching tires as he slammed down on the brake in a futile attempt to stop the inevitable. The screeching was replaced by the thumping sound of tires careening off the road into a grassy embankment. Dirt assaulted his face and obstructed his vision.

His body jolted from the impact of the collision with the massive pole. The pole snapped as if it were a twig, causing splinters of wood to rain down on him before finally crashing to the ground.

Despite the excessive amount of alcohol consumed, he had remembered to fasten his seat belt. This one act of clarity prevented him from being catapulted from the car and ultimately saved his life. Like a cat, he had nine lives and he surely had used one tonight.

His unconscious passenger wasn't so lucky. She was thrown from the car on impact. Blood poured from her wounds and turned the ground beneath her black. Fortunately, her level of intoxication prevented any feeling of fear or pain.

*I have to get out of here, now!* His head was pounding. Pain seared through his body. But that one thought came through loud and clear. He cautiously moved his right arm. *Good, not broken.* Then he maneuvered his hand into his pocket. He felt the phone and gingerly shifted his body to allow the phone to be freed. Pain shot through him. *Shit, broken ribs.* He struggled to pull the phone from his pocket, knowing this call was his only ticket out of here.

He tapped the number of the one person who would be key to his salvation. Then he waited and prayed salvation would come. He gave no thought to the body that lay lifeless on the ground beside the wreckage. He only thought of himself. He always had. It wasn't entirely his fault. He was raised to be self-indulgent.

# Two

Laura had insomnia. Again. She mindlessly scrolled through Instagram and Facebook hoping she'd start to feel drowsy, but so far, no luck. It was already after 3:00 am. If she fell asleep now, she'd get about three and a half hours of sleep before the alarm sounded. Another day ahead feeling like a zombie. Her yellow lab, Sam, was sprawled on her bed next to her, looking at her with his sad brown eyes as if to say, "Mom, can we please get some sleep." Laura rubbed Sam's belly and said, "Sorry, buddy, looks like another sleepless night."

A loud bang in the distance startled her and Sam. Sam barked as the bedside lamp went dark and a piercing beeping sound disturbed the previously middle-of-the-night quiet. The beeping was a sound that meant the power had gone out in the home. The alarm had been installed years ago when Laura started her flower business in the little barn at the back her house. It alerted her to power outages so she could insure the generator started, preventing her inventory from spoiling.

"Now what?" she thought. She couldn't imagine what had caused this outage. Storms or car accidents were often to blame, but it was too early in the summer season for severe thunder storms. And it was unlikely that anyone would be out driving at this time of night on the dark country roads surrounding her home. This was a small, sleepy-town in rural Pennsylvania where most places closed by 11:00 pm. If anyone wanted a late night out, they'd have to drive or take the train to one of the nearby cities of Philadelphia or New York. And then they usually spent the night there.

She forced herself from bed to address the annoying alarm. Once again, she was reminded that she was alone when it came to these sorts of things, things that husbands might normally do.

She fished around in her nightstand drawer for the flashlight, then slowly made her way down the dark hallway and stairwell to the alarm panel. She entered the code needed to cease the irritating sound. She was relieved the required lights were lit to indicate the barn generator was working. She paused in the stillness and quiet that comes with the absence of electricity. No humming motors from the various electrical appliances, no air movement from heating or cooling systems, no television or music playing from a distant room in the house — just the sound of silence

She also was aware of the complete darkness. With only the faint glow from her flashlight to lead the way, she decided to check on her daughters. As she walked up the stairs, she shined the light over the pictures on the wall that told her life story. Laura as a baby with her parents. No siblings since she was an only child, born to parents late in life. Her beloved grandmother working in the gardens of her house. Laura's house now and she works in those same gardens her granny cherished. Her wedding with Bill. A wave of sadness washed over her as she remembered they were all gone now. These were pictures of happier times. Laura continued down the hall. The next set of pictures included the birth of her twins, moments from their lives, birthdays and other life milestones. It was hard to believe the twins were fifteen already. She was reminded of the phrase, "The days are long, but the years are short". How true that was.

Sam followed along, his panting interrupting the silence in the hallway outside of the girls' bedrooms. Sam patrolled the hallways each night to make sure everyone was safe, and he took his job seriously, assuming the role of family protector.

Both girls were soundly asleep. The kind of sleep only children and babies can attain naturally. Sleep not encumbered by the demons of age and experience, worry, and regret.

Once back in bed, Laura allowed the demons to intrude, as they often did late at night. Sometimes the loneliness was unbearable. Tonight, she found herself overwhelmed by a sense of foreboding she couldn't seem to shake.

Her thoughts were interrupted by the glow of approaching headlights on the road in front of her house. She watched them advance, assuming they would pass. Instead they appeared to stop in front of her home. She waited for several minutes before giving in to her curiosity and peeking out her bedroom window.

Her house was set back several hundred feet from the road, with a winding drive and thick trees and foliage this time of year, so she wasn't sure she would be able to see anything. As she suspected, nothing but blackness, punctuated by what she assumed were the headlights of the road crew attempting to find the source of the power outage. There was some commotion in the distance, but she was too tired to make the trek to the road to investigate. She hoped they would find what they were looking for and restore power before morning. She returned to bed, hoping for an hour or two of sleep before the busy day began.

# Three

With daylight came the sound of sirens and commotion on the normally tranquil street. Laura awoke to these sounds and the piercing stare of Sam, informing her it was time to be let out for his morning walk.

She fumbled for the television remote, checking if the power had been restored, but the box remained black. It would only be a matter of minutes before her girls discovered this and the complaining began. "Mom, how can I shower and do my hair!?" It was every fifteen-year-old girl's nightmare.

As if on cue, the uproar began. Ella, the oldest twin, was the first to barge into the room.

"Mom, what's with the electricity?"

"There's a power outage," Laura replied, as she shooed Sam off her bed and began making it.

"I know that, but why is the power out and how am I supposed to shower and do my hair?"

"You can still shower. You'll just have to be quick so you don't use all the hot water. Besides, it's going to be warm today so you can..."

Before she finished, Brooke stormed in.

"Mom! There's no electricity in my room!"

"I know, Brooke. There's no electricity in the whole house. You'll need to take a quick shower and let your hair air dry."

"Are you kidding? I have to go to school today, Mom!"

"You don't have a choice. We have no power and the longer you wait, the colder the water is getting in the water heater. So, go!"

"I'm getting in first!" yelled Ella.

"No way, I am! You take too long," countered Brooke.

"You both better go now or you'll be going to school without a shower or clean hair!"

That statement caused both girls to run towards the hall bathroom, still fighting for the shower.

Laura sometimes wondered how she was going to handle the teenage years as a single parent. This certainly wasn't the plan. But life had a way of veering off course. Laura learned that at a young age, finding herself unexpectedly pregnant, then married and the mother of twins in her early twenties. Not exactly how she thought things would turn out.

The commotion from the street diverted her attention. This time when she glanced out the window daylight illuminated what darkness hid last night.

The mammoth utility pole in front of her property had been split in half. That explains the loud bang. Wires dangled to the ground and a white Jeep Wrangler with a flashing light on top was parked at the end of her driveway. She took that to mean that a volunteer firefighter had been summoned to direct traffic around the mishap.

She threw on jeans and a tank top, pulled her blond hair up in a clip, brushed her teeth, and decided she'd take Sam for a walk to investigate the scene.

Sam darted out ahead and beat her to the end of the driveway. He was well-trained and never went through the open gates without permission.

The Jeep was parked on the part of her driveway outside the gates. This section was about fifty feet long and allowed a vehicle to pull off the street and approach the gates should they ever be closed. In all the years she had come to this house, as a child visiting her grandmother and now as its owner, she never remembered the gates being closed. She wasn't even sure they would close.

As she neared the street, the sound of a familiar voice caused her heart to skip a beat. *It can't be him. It just can't be.* Over the years she wondered if she would ever hear his voice again. At times she had hoped she never would. Her heart began beating fast, too fast, as if it would beat out of her chest. She realized she had stopped walking and now debated turning around. *It can't be him.* This was crazy. He would never return here. She was sure of that. It had been a long night and now her mind was playing tricks on her. She took a deep breath and continued down the driveway. And there he was.

He was directing traffic around the downed pole and wires.

"Straight on through ma'am, just follow the signs up ahead, keep moving, please. Sir, please keep your vehicle moving."

Her heart was out of control again and her face felt warm and flushed. *Oh my God, it's him.* How many years had passed? Sixteen? Seventeen? It was before her girls were born, so it had to be at least that long. Would he even recognize her? Of course, she looked a mess. But who cared what she looked like? She had no time in her life for Jake Callaway. And he, as proven, had no time in his life for her.

She would just march down her driveway, inquire about the situation, and explain that he would have to move his vehicle so she could drive her daughters to school. She forced her feet to continue and Sam, after a quick run through the field, dutifully followed.

She was not prepared to be this close to him. He looked even better than she remembered. *Damn him.* Still tall, strong, and lean.

Why couldn't he be short, fat, and bald? He kept his sandy blond hair short, but still a little messy. He had matured well.

She wondered if he would think the same about her. She was a few pounds heavier. A few gray hairs had crept in, but nothing her visits to the hairdresser couldn't fix. Her hair was shorter than he would remember, but her eyes were still that greenish shade of hazel that he always loved.

*Stop!* Why was she doing this? So much had happened. So much had changed. She had changed. She was no longer that trusting young girl Jake would remember. She now knew how the world worked and at times could be cruel and unfair. She had come a long, long way from the girl she once was. Along that journey, she had learned to depend on herself and to protect herself and her girls above all else. She would not deviate from that path for anyone or anything.

He caught sight of her out of the corner of his eye and turned to meet her gaze. She wasn't expecting this and it startled her. Their eyes met and held for too long. So many words left unspoken, so many loose ends left untied. Sam broke the spell by running between them and barking his protective warning at Jake.

"It's okay, Sam. Come here." Laura called.

"Hi, Laura, it's been a long time." Jake moved closer then paused as his eyes held hers captive. She was unable to look away or to speak, so he continued. "I heard that you moved into your Granny's old place. I was hoping to run into you."

She tried to regain her composure and managed to form a sentence. "Hello, Jake. Long time, no see. What are you doing here?" She silently chastised herself. *Long time, no see...really Laura, that's the best you could come up with?*

Jake continued to direct traffic around the downed pole and wires as he replied, "I moved back about a month ago, on and off.

I had some things to settle in the city before I made my move here permanent."

Laura was shocked by this news, "Permanent? I thought you hated this town. Why would you move back here?"

"That was a long time ago, Laura. I've grown, matured." He smiled at that comment. "I realize this town's not so bad after all."

A car approached and lowered the window. The occupants, three elderly ladies, asked Jake for directions to Cody's local flea market.

"Straight ahead ladies and follow the signs."

Jake took advantage of another lull in the traffic and turned to Laura. "Of all days to have a pole down on this road. Wednesday. Cody's flea market day. Normally there'd be half the traffic on this road. Doesn't this drive you crazy? All these fleas coming up here every Wednesday, clogging up your quiet road?"

Laura ignored the question and got to the point. "What happened here, do you know?"

Jake replied, "It seems some idiot took out the pole with his car sometime last night. I got a call this morning to come here and direct traffic."

Another shocker for Laura, "What? You joined the town's fire department?"

"Yep. I did a story on fire departments in NYC when I lived there. It's actually what made me a little homesick. Thinking of my dad running the department here all these years. He's retiring you know?"

Laura did know this, "Yes, I've heard. He's been a good man to do it for so long. The town will surely miss him."

Jake nodded, "I'm sure. Anyway, I signed up when I got back a few weeks ago, and this is my first assignment. I'll be doing some reporting for the local paper as well."

Another car approached and slowed down to look at the downed pole and mess of wires.

Jake used his official voice, "Please move along, keep moving."

"Could you give directions to Cody's?" the car's occupant asked.

"Stay straight and follow the signs," Jake replied again.

Laura couldn't help but chuckle. She had to admit, the flea market could be a nuisance. But it had been operating on the Cody family farm for as long as she remembered and people came from all over to purchase the wares for sale. She used to go with her grandmother at least once every summer. She remembered they had the best blueberry muffins and tons of cheap jewelry and hair accessories. She often would take her girls there in the summer when school was out.

Jake turned and caught her laughing. "I'm glad you're finding humor in my predicament." He laughed with her. "I always did love your smile." Their eyes met and held again. Jake spoke first, "Hey, I'd love to get together for dinner sometime and catch up."

Laura broke the gaze. He was still the cocky, over-confident guy he'd always been. She used to find those qualities in him attractive. Now, dinner with Jake was the last thing she needed.

"Look, Jake, I just came down here to see what was going on and to ask you to move your Jeep because I need to get my girls to school."

"Ouch! Shot down, and so quickly. That hurt." Jake put his hand over his heart and feigned a painful expression.

*Nothing like you hurt me*, Laura thought, but she replied, "Just move your Jeep, please."

"How about I move it and you agree to dinner with me tonight?" he teased.

"I...I...can't." He was starting to fluster her and she needed to distance herself. She turned and started back to her house.

There was another lull in the traffic, so Jake walked closer to her, "Laura, wait. Look, I never got to tell you how sorry I was about Bill. My mom called me when it happened. I wanted to send you a card or something at the time, but it seemed...inappropriate considering our history...the three of us, you know what I mean? I don't want to upset you. If you want me to stay away I will. But I'm not sure that's what you really want."

That last comment landed on her in a bad way. "How do you know what I want? You don't even know me anymore." Her face was burning with anger.

"I did know you, Laura. There's a lot of history between us." He had a way of locking her in his intense gaze, making it almost impossible to look away. Just like he did all those years ago. Now that he was closer, she could see the deep blue of his eyes. They were intoxicating. Old feelings began to stir in her stomach, feelings she forgot she was capable of having.

This, combined with his comment, caught her off guard. She snapped herself back to reality. She wasn't little Laura MacIntosh anymore who would swoon over Jake Callaway. She needed to end this conversation, fast.

"Just move your Jeep so I can get out of my driveway. Please." She broke the intense gaze, and turned to walk towards the house with Sam. Jake yelled, "Only if you promise to have dinner with me."

"I will not have dinner with you," she yelled over her shoulder. "Move your Jeep!"

"Great, I'll pick you up at seven," he playfully yelled as he got into his vehicle and pulled it down the street.

"I am not having dinner with you!" she yelled back, although she knew he couldn't hear her.

# Four

The day was predicted to be a scorcher for June. Even though early in the season, rain had been scarce, meaning the possibility of small brush fires popping up was strong. Jake would keep his cell phone handy and stay in the vicinity.

He also needed to stop at the office to check on a story. He had landed a reporting job with the local paper. Nothing like what he left in New York, yet he felt it was just what he wanted. When he left this town for the city all those years ago, he took with him his dream of becoming a Pulitzer Prize-winning reporter. Now that he had checked that box, he set his sights on more modest endeavors, such as writing for the local paper and marrying his high school sweetheart. By the looks of things, the former was turning out to be a lot easier than the latter. But Jake was never one to walk away from a challenge.

He loved the city at first. It was just what he needed at that time. Eventually, he felt something was lacking. He missed this town and the small-town lifestyle he grew up knowing. The same lifestyle he longed to be free of as a teenager. And he still missed Laura. Sure, he'd had his share of girlfriends over the years, but nothing serious. He tried to get over Laura and move on with his life. Finally he realized he was happier alone than with any woman who wasn't her.

When his parents called with news of Bill's death, he was hit with many emotions. Of course, he felt sadness for Laura, for suffering another loss. He felt sadness for her children, for losing their father. He even felt sadness for Bill, once a good friend, who would no longer be enjoying life with his family. At the same time, he felt hope. Right or wrong, he felt hope that he might get the chance to rewrite history with Laura.

Eventually, he decided to return home. Home to the town he couldn't wait to leave years before. Home to the family who welcomed him with open arms and warm hearts. Home to the only woman he had ever loved. Now he just had to be patient.

***

The Cavanaugh wedding was this Saturday and Laura had no time for a power outage in her shop. She was thankful for the generator. It kept the flowers, the shop, and the greenhouses at their optimum temperature and humidity level.

Laura loved flowers as a child. It was another part of her that her grandmother had shaped and molded. She would help her grandmother in the garden on all her visits and learned about the many varieties, especially roses. They were her favorite. She decided to specialize in them when she went into business and provided many of the local restaurants and bed and breakfasts in the area with all their centerpieces and room arrangements. This enterprise was quite lucrative for her and provided a steady source of business throughout the year.

Newberry was considered a tourist destination. A small river town in Pennsylvania, it resembled a quaint New England village with lots of country charm. Shops and restaurants lined the bank along the Delaware River. Other points of interest included the local playhouse, museums, art galleries, and numerous bed and breakfast establishments to accommodate all the weekend and summer guests. Adventurous visitors could pitch a tent on one of many campground facilities. It was a popular destination for wealthy New Yorkers to purchase a home as a weekend retreat.

Every morning Laura made her rounds delivering flowers to her loyal customers. This time of year was especially busy since it traditionally was considered the wedding season. Many couples chose venues in Newbury for their wedding reception and photos because it had the charm and ambiance brides often desired. When she returned this morning from taking the girls to school and making daily deliveries, she was disappointed to find the power had not been restored.

The utility company arrived and moved debris from the road. They were now in charge of directing the traffic, which had slowed considerably since most of the flea market customers were happily shopping. It would pick up again around noon when vendors packed up for the day and a mass exodus ensued.

Laura decided it would be a nice gesture to take some cold drinks out to the busy workers since it was such a warm day. It would also give her a chance to ask when they thought power would be restored and maybe encourage them to speed things up a bit.

She gathered some cold-water bottles and soda, put them in a basket, and headed out to the road. Sam insisted on going with her. As she approached the scene, she was again shocked at how bad the situation was. The utility pole was demolished, wires were scattered everywhere, and deep ruts were visible in the grass on both sides of the road. It appeared the vehicle had careered from side to side before crashing into the pole.

Apparently, this morning she was too preoccupied with the appearance of Jake to fully digest the appearance of the accident scene. He had some nerve to invite her to dinner after everything that had happened between them. She forced him from her mind and tried to concentrate on the matter at hand.

"Hello. I thought you might like some cold drinks," she called out as she approached the workers.

The men stopped what they were doing, turned and stared at her, surprised that someone was offering them anything. Finally, an older man, probably the foreman, approached her. He looked to be in his late forties, attractive, bald in a good way and tanned from working outdoors. He had flirtatious blue eyes, and she got the impression he used them quite often. Sam barked a few warnings and Laura assured him it was okay.

"Thanks, that's real nice of you." He smiled as he accepted the offered drinks.

"Looks like you have quite a mess here," Laura said.

"Yeah, although I've seen worse. Do you know what happened?"

Laura was surprised he was asking her this question. She was hoping to get this information from him. "No. Jake…ah, the fire-fighter who was here earlier just said that someone crashed into the pole."

Blue-eyes shook his head, bewildered, "Well if that's the case, I can't imagine he or she survived the crash. That pole was hit good. Car must of been flying."

"I couldn't tell you. I wasn't aware anything was going on until a loud bang and loss of power. A vehicle approached at some point in the night, but I didn't think it was an ambulance. No lights flashing or sirens blaring. This morning the fire company arrived, then your utility trucks." Laura got to the point, "Do you have any idea when the power will be restored?"

"It's gonna be a few hours. First, we have to remove the rest of the split pole and install the new one. We're still waiting for that to be delivered. Once that's secure, we can work on the wires. And we're just here for the electricity. You'll have to call the phone and internet companies to do their part. Good luck with that. They might not show up for days."

This was not good news. She needed her business phone, Wi-Fi, and computer.

"Do you think they've been notified?" Laura asked.

"Probably not. And even if they were, it helps to have more people complain. Gets 'em moving a bit faster. Know what I mean?"

"Right. I'll head in and do that now. Thanks for your help. Let me know if you need anything else." Laura turned to head back to the house.

Blue-eyes yelled after her, "You have a nice day now. We'll get you up and running, I'd say by two, three o'clock."

"Thanks so much," Laura replied with a wave over her shoulder.

This was disappointing. She had hoped to have the power restored sooner and had not even thought about the phone and internet. She headed back to the house. She'd need to use her cell phone to make the calls.

Once back at the house, as she was searching for all the phone numbers she needed, the doorbell interrupted her thoughts. Sam began to bark and Laura had to quiet him as she approached the door. She was greeted by an unfamiliar woman standing on her doorstep.

"May I help you?" Laura said.

"Hello, my name is Betty." A middle-aged woman stood before Laura, wringing her hands, with hunched shoulders and a soft, shaky voice.

"I wanted to apologize. I was here early this morning when that accident happened. I'm a cook over at Cody's flea market, so I have to get there real early. I live over in Wadsworth, so this is the quickest way. It was real early this mornin' when I came by and saw the car smashed. I pulled over to see if anyone needed help and my car got stuck in the mud on your property. I didn't know what to do. My wheels just kept spinnin'. Next thing I knew the police pulled up and started yellin' at me."

Laura wasn't sure what to make of this woman. She was probably younger than she appeared, as if a hard life had aged her beyond her years. She was a small, frail woman who looked even more helpless in her blue apron, which was covered in splatters from her day of cooking. Her short, dark hair was frizzing from the heat, and the smell of greasy French fries created an aura around her. She was visibly upset, rambling, and not allowing Laura to say a word. Laura wanted to stop her, to tell her it was okay, but Betty seemed to need to tell her story, so Laura let her.

"He was so mean, and he accused me of just being nosy and just rubber-neckin'. That wasn't true. I wanted to help if I could. I didn't mean for my car to get stuck like that. Anyway, he said the people that live here would be really mad. He took my name and address and said you would want me to pay for the damages. I just wanted to apologize and say that my husband and I would be happy to fix the ruts. We could come this weekend and take care of that for you..."

Laura had to interrupt.

"Mrs..."

"Simpson. Betty Simpson. You can call me Betty though."

"Betty, thank you so much for stopping here to explain this to me. It's not a problem. I think the utility company is probably doing more damage to my property than you did. Don't give it another thought."

At that news, Betty audibly exhaled and dropped her hands to her side.

"Oh, thank you. You don't know how worried I've been all day. I was stuck in the rut and I had to get to work. I don't have a cell phone so I couldn't call no one, and that bastard...ah, cop, left me sittin' there, stuck like that."

"I can't believe he was so rude to you when you were just trying to help."

"I was, I swear. I saw a girl lying on the ground too, but no one was helpin'. Then another man came and the cop told him I was snooping around. I tried to tell him I wanted to help. They both went off talking. I sat there not knowing what to do and thinking I would get fired for sure. Next thing I knew a tow truck comes up and pulls me out. I didn't even thank those bastards, just got on my way to work. But I was sick with worry all day, thinking of you suing me or sending me a big bill to fix that rut. My husband would blow his stack."

"Betty you don't have to worry about that. I'm sorry the police officers were so nasty to you. You didn't get their names did you?"

"No, I didn't. I was too shaken up. Only one was a cop though, I think. The other one drove up in a real fancy car. One of those black Mercedes, I think. Fancy, like the car that crashed. And he wasn't dressed like a cop. But I didn't get either one's name."

"That's okay. I'll ask around. I'm sure someone will know who was out here this morning and I plan on saying something about the way you were treated."

"Thanks so much. I was worried all morning."

"Please don't give it another thought." Laura smiled and sent Betty on her way.

The day seemed to fly by. Laura spent most of it in her shop, a converted barn behind her home. Two greenhouses flanked the shop and this was where she grew her roses and other varieties of flowers. She also had several outdoor gardens beyond the greenhouses. It was between these three areas that she spent most of her days.

She did as much work as she could on the table arrangements for the wedding before heading out for the afternoon deliveries. Before she knew it, it was dinnertime.

The night went smoothly. The girls were happy electricity was restored, but still complained about the lack of Wi-Fi service. They were all in the kitchen and Laura was in the process of telling them about the strange woman who came to the house earlier when the doorbell rang again. Brooke went to answer it, assuming it was someone for her. She returned to the kitchen with a puzzled look on her face.

"Mom. There's some guy at the door for you. He says his name is Jake."

# Five

The injuries he sustained from the crash were minimal considering the extent of the damage to his car. It was too bad about the girl.
Oh well. He'd find others. He realized he had made a huge mistake.
They were all furious with him this time and the effort expended to
cover his tracks was monumental. He had faith they would handle
it, as they always did. However, this was the first time someone
died, at least accidentally.

He was confined to the house until his visible injuries healed.
Most could be easily concealed, which was good, considering his
busy schedule. Unfortunately, his car was totaled. His beautiful
black Porsche. He'd have to wait until they arranged to have an
identical model delivered.

He trusted they would do what they always do and insure he
couldn't be traced to the accident or the missing girl. Nothing would
interfere with their plans for the future. Even if it meant more
people had to die.

# Six

Laura stood frozen in her kitchen, staring blankly at her daughter. Jake was here? Now? She had no idea how to react.

"Mom. Did you hear me?"

"Ah…yes, hon, I did."

"Are you going to go to the door?" Brooke looked at her as if she'd lost her mind.

"Of course."

"Who the heck is Jake, mom?" Ella asked curiously.

"Just an old friend."

"Why haven't you ever mentioned him?" Ella asked.

"I don't know. Girls, can we discuss this later? I need to go to the door, I guess." Laura glanced at her reflection in the kitchen window and smoothed a hand over her hair.

"Do I look okay?"

Her girls exchanged a concerned glance with one another. They had never seen their mom act like this before.

"You look fine, Mom," Ella said.

"Yeah, fine," Brooke added while rolling her eyes.

Laura mustered the courage to go to the door. The sight of Jake took her breath away. He looked different than he had this morning, even better, in his jeans and a button-down bright white shirt. It provided a nice contrast to the faded blue jeans and stood out against his tanned skin. A faint breeze flitted through the door and carried a hint of his clean, musky scent. Jake's scent. Wow! The memories attached to that were overwhelming.

Laura had no idea what she was going to say and felt as if her tongue had swelled inside her mouth, making it impossible to talk. She approached the door, staring at him without saying a word. Finally, he broke the silence.

"You look surprised to see me. We have dinner plans remember?"

His cockiness helped Laura find the words to respond.

"We do not have dinner plans. I told you that was out of the question and would be inappropriate —"

"Look, I can see you're upset with me for showing up at your house. I thought once you saw me here you would change your mind."

"You thought wrong," Laura said with an edge. "Still as cocky as ever, I see."

Jake smiled, undeterred, and chose this moment to present a bottle of wine that he had been holding at his side.

"I was going to bring flowers, but I thought that would be silly to bring a flowers to a florist. Plus, I'd have to buy them from a competitor." He continued to smile. "So, I thought wine would be a better choice." He glanced over her shoulder. Laura turned to see Brooke and Ella peeking around the corner, curiously watching this peculiar scene. Jake had a look on his face that said, "I need help fast!"

Laura was about to launch into a tirade citing all the reasons why she would not have dinner or wine with him, when Ella came into the room.

"Who's your friend Mom? Ah, a nice bottle of wine. It's your favorite. I'll take it and open it for you guys." She took the wine from Jake before Laura could protest.

"Hi. I'm Jake." He reached out his hand to shake Ella's. "Your mom and I are old friends. We haven't seen each other in years. You must be Ella."

Ella shook Jake's hand. "Yeah, how'd you know my name?"

"My parents live in the area and told me Laura has two beautiful daughters. Ella, who's blonde like her mom, and Brooke, who has chestnut hair like her dad."

"Who are your parents?" Ella asked.

Laura interrupted, "Ella, why don't you take the wine in the kitchen and let Jake and I catch up." She thought it wise to choose conversation with Jake over explaining who Jake was to her daughter. Ella did as she was told.

"Your girls are beautiful, Laura, just like their mama. Are you going to invite me in?" Since she was left with little choice, she waved her arm toward the living room and motioned for him to enter.

He smiled victoriously, as he sauntered into the room. This added to her annoyance, but she followed him anyway. He made himself comfortable on the couch as if he belonged. Laura sat in an adjacent chair.

"Why are you here, Jake?" She hated the effect he was having on her. She had to gain control of this situation. But control seemed more elusive, when her daughters entered the room with cheese, crackers, two glasses of wine and the bottle. When did they become so helpful? She shot them a disapproving look, which caused them to smile sweetly. They had been after Laura to "get a life," as they put it, and spend less time meddling in theirs. But Laura didn't think they were serious. She feared her dating would pierce the safety bubble she built around them. They were the three musketeers ever since their dad died. As if on cue, the girls handed Jake and Laura a glass of wine then set the cheese and crackers on the table in front of Jake.

Laura took several hearty, much needed, sips of the wine. Ella was right, it was her favorite — Simi Cabernet Sauvignon. The crisp, dry red glided over her tongue and slid easily down her throat, warming her from the inside out. "Well, it appears your charm has worked on my daughters. I thought I'd raised them better." It was her turn to smile slyly at him. But rather than deter him, it encouraged him.

"I'm glad to see you smile. See, this isn't so bad, right?"

Laura rolled her eyes. Before she could reply, Brooke chimed in, "Mom, tell Jake about the strange woman who showed up at the door today." Both Ella and Brooke made themselves comfortable on the floor as they waited for Laura to tell the story.

"What woman?" Jake leaned forward, helping himself to the snacks.

Laura retold the tale of Betty Simpson appearing at her door and her story of the accident.

Her daughters discreetly slipped out of the room as she told the strange tale.

Laura finished the story and then asked, "By the way, do you know which officer was there this morning?"

Jake seemed to be thinking about her story and didn't immediately respond.

"I'm sorry. What was that?" he asked.

"The officer. Do you know who was at the scene this morning?" Laura repeated.

"That's the strange thing. Sally Cohen was on call this morning. A passing motorist called in the accident around five-thirty this morning, but when Sally arrived the car and driver were gone. I thought that was strange judging by the look of that pole, and now you're telling me this woman saw a car and a possible fatality or injury. Why wouldn't Sally report this?"

Laura was confused by this too, "I don't know. And don't forget the officer Betty reported seeing and the second man. She was sure the first man was a police officer. I assume he was in uniform and driving a police car since she commented that the other man wasn't. Also, the man from the electric company said that the pole was hit hard and he doubted the driver survived. So how did he or she drive away from the scene? I hate to think someone died in front of my house."

"I'll stop in the police station tomorrow morning to visit some buddies and see if they know anything. I'll also keep my eyes and ears open at the *Tribune*. In the meantime, I owe you dinner and I'd love to take you out tonight. Nothing fancy, I know it's been a long day. How about pizza or Chinese?"

It had been a long day. That, combined with the glass of wine, weakened her resolve. Before she knew it, she was agreeing to Chinese food and telling her girls she'd be home soon.

# Seven

The restaurant was packed. Laura hadn't thought about the repercussions of having dinner with Jake in such a small town. She was sure they would be the hot topic discussed over tomorrow's morning coffee.

She was about to suggest another restaurant when Bob Caully, deputy mayor and local postmaster, spotted them. It was impossible to avoid his approach. Bob, whose nickname was Four-by-Four since he was as short as he was wide, had been the local postmaster for as long as Laura could remember and, in addition to the mail, he delivered the daily dose of gossip.

"Well, well, look who we have here. Just like old times, eh? Haven't seen the two of you since...how long has it been? Fifteen years? You look good together. I always said, those two...they look good together."

"We're not together Bob. We're just hungry and both came here for dinner," Laura said while trying to keep the frustration out of her voice.

"Together," he said with a smile and a wink as he sauntered away.

"Jake, maybe this was a bad idea."

"Look, we're both hungry, this is a restaurant, they serve food. Let's eat. It'll be fine." He led her by the arm to a table and pulled the chair for her. She was acutely aware of stares from other diners and refused to make eye contact with anyone. Living in a small town had its advantages, but being known by just about everyone was not one of them. She would get this night over and start fresh in the morning, hopefully with better judgment. They both perused the menu but were interrupted by a loud voice.

"Hey, hey, hey…Jaaake! What's up, man?"

Laura turned to see three of her least favorite men approaching the table, brothers Mike and Matt and their tag-along buddy, Dan. These three had been friends since high school and refused to grow up. They never married and still tried to pick up any woman in proximity just as they did in high school. They had no respect for women, and Laura had no respect for them. She remembered Jake being friendly with them in school, but knew he didn't consider them friends.

"Mike, Matt, Dan. What's up, guys?"

"Not much, man. I see you're up to your old tricks." Mike said as he smirked at Laura. "It didn't take you long. You've only been back, what, a month or so?" Mike tended to respond for the threesome, as he always had. Laura wasn't even sure the other two could talk. She decided to take the high road and continue with her menu. To respond to these losers would be a waste of her time. She'd let Jake handle this one.

"It's been about a month, yeah. Laura and I are just catching up. It's been a while since we've seen each other."

"Right. Gotcha. Catching up, good one. Well you two go ahead and 'catch up.'" Mike leaned into Jake's ear and said, "You can tell us about it in the morning." The trio howled at this and followed Mike out of the restaurant.

"Nice friends you have, Jake. Real mature."

"You know they're not my friends. We both know they're like an annoying mosquito bite – if you scratch it, it just itches more. It's better to ignore them and hope they go away.

"Shouldn't they have grown out of that by now? I mean, they're in their thirties. And you should see the way they treat the women in this town, Jake. You haven't been here for a while, but I have. They still act like sixteen-year-old boys in heat. They're at their worst during the summer when they prowl on women here for vacation. Most people here just look the other way. One of these days, they're going to get themselves in serious trouble."

"They have nothing to do with us, let's just forget them and enjoy our meal."

"It bothers me. You forget I have two daughters. Guys like that annoy me."

"I know. They annoy me too. But your daughters are too smart to get involved with guys like that."

"You don't know that."

"I know their mother. And before you protest that I don't know you anymore, I do know who you were, and a leopard doesn't change all its spots. You may have had some rough times over the years, and I know you believe I contributed to those times, but you are still the same person inside, Laura. We all are. No matter what we go through, we're still the same person deep inside."

She wasn't sure how to respond to this. On some level, he was right. She liked to believe she had changed, become more independent, more street smart, and less trusting of people, but deep inside she was still the little twelve-year-old girl who loved the solitude of working in the garden, as opposed to being in a room full of people. And, like that twelve-year-old girl, whether she liked it or not, she still had a bond with this boy, this man, who was sitting across the table from her and who, indeed, did know her better than most any other person in her life.

Could Jake be right? Do we stay the same child on the inside, afraid and insecure, pretending to be someone we're not? Maybe some people were just better pretenders than others.

Laura realized Jake was staring at her, waiting for a response. She looked blankly at him.

"Have you decided?"

She realized while she was lost in thought, the waiter had arrived. She quickly ordered then turned her attention to Jake.

"You say that, 'I believe you contributed to my rough times.' What do you know about what I believe? You weren't here to know."

The bitterness in her voice was unmistakable. It was there to hide the hurt, but a keen observer could easily see through it. When it came to Laura, Jake was a keen observer.

"Laura, I…"

Jake was interrupted by, of all people, his parents. "Jake. Laura. What a nice surprise!"

"Mom, dad, what are you doing here?" Jake stood and gave his mom a hug and kiss, then shook his dad's hand. Laura noticed how Jake was looking more like his dad as he aged. Mr. Callaway was tall and strong, still in great shape for a man his age. His blond hair was mostly gray now and Jake had inherited his deep blue eyes. Mrs. Callaway was an attractive woman, more petite than her son. Although her hair was still blond, Laura assumed nature had turned it gray some time ago.

"What? We're not allowed to go out to dinner once in a while? Surprised to see you here…and with Laura! Sweetheart, how are you?" Jake's mom leaned in and gave Laura a big hug and kiss which was wholeheartedly returned.

Laura always loved Jake's parents. She had stayed in touch with them over the years, and she remained good friends with his sister, Addi, but it wasn't the same as when she was a kid and would stop by their house regularly.

Laura stood, "Mr. and Mrs. Callaway. It's great to see you."

Mr. Callaway's face lit up as Laura hugged and kissed him too.

"Please join us." Laura moved around the table and sat next to Jake. This left two seats open for his parents.

"We'd love to honey. How sweet of you."

*** 

Later, as Jake reflected on the night, he was disappointed that things didn't go quite as he had hoped. His parents unexpectedly joining his reunion with Laura was not in his master plan. He had waited too many years to talk to her about that summer so long ago. Now it looked like he would have to wait some more.

As disappointing as that was, he could take comfort in the fact that Laura had naturally moved to sit next to him while making room for his parents. The scene they portrayed, sitting at the table, having dinner, was one from his past that he treasured and often had hoped would play itself out again. Indeed, it had.

His goal now would be to insure that it became a more frequent occurrence and not some distant memory he had to dust off from time to time.

# Eight

Laura's day started much better than it had yesterday. She had a little bounce in her step this morning, but she refused to attribute that to the events of last night. Of course, she had a nice dinner with Jake's parents, and it was good to reminisce about old times. The Callaways were like a second family to her growing up. Since she was an only child, she loved feeling a part of their robust family. To be fair, it was nice to be with Jake, too, but she was far too sensible to let all that go to her head.

She had to be careful. He was the one person who could destroy the cocoon she had wound so tightly around herself. She liked her cocoon and had no intention of letting Jake or anyone else unravel it. She was safe and secure inside it.

Her morning routine ran smoothly. The phone and internet had been restored overnight. All of her flower deliveries were made on time, and she had the rare opportunity to sit with a cup of tea and scan the morning news.

She went straight to the local news, searching for any information on the crash. She thought for sure she'd find an article about it and was surprised when she didn't. She continued to search and then something caught her eye. It was a piece about an accident, but not the one she was looking for. It was the driver's name that grabbed her attention.

*Local woman dies in motor vehicle accident*

*A motor vehicle was discovered in the ravine off Pottsgrove Rd. last night.*

*It appeared the driver swerved and lost control of the vehicle, possibly to avoid*

*colliding with a deer. No deer was found at the scene. The driver, Betty Simpson*

*of Wadsworth, sustained severe injuries and was rushed to Cedar Falls Hospital,*

*where she was pronounced dead upon arrival.*

Betty Simpson. Wasn't that the woman who appeared on her doorstep yesterday? Could it be the same woman? Laura was sure she said she was from Wadsworth. The article didn't say how old this woman was. Laura would have to make some calls to find out. Maybe Jake would have some information about the other crash by now and she could ask him if he knows anything about this one too.

She reached for the phone to call him, as if she did this every day, then realized she hadn't called Jake in over sixteen years. She had no idea what his phone number was or where he was living for that matter. She stared at the phone not knowing what to do. She was upset with herself for automatically thinking of him. She had not needed a man in a long time and had no intention of ever needing one again.

This was exactly what she was afraid of with him. If anyone had the power to break down her defenses, it was Jake. She debated what to do. She could call his parents and they would happily provide his number. It wasn't as if she was calling him because her toilet wouldn't flush or some other "female in distress" matter. This was an unusual circumstance. She was concerned about a possible fatality that had happened in front of her home, and now the death of a woman who, just yesterday, may have been standing on her doorstep.

She made her decision and searched through her phone contact list to obtain the number of the Callaways. She hesitated for a full minute before calling. The phone rang once, twice…maybe they weren't home…three times…she should just hang up…

"Hello." The voice of Mrs. Callaway broke into her thoughts.

"Hello," she said again.

"Hi, Mrs. Callaway, it's Laura. Laura MacIntosh-Delaney."

"Oh, Laura, hello honey. How are you? It was so good to see you last night."

"Thanks. You too. I was just wondering if you happened to have a number where I could reach Jake? He was looking into the specifics of the accident for me, you know, the one that occurred in front of my house the other night, and I just wanted to check on his progress."

"Of course, dear. I have his home and his cell. But can you hold a moment? I've got another call coming in on the other line?"

"Okay." As Laura waited, she began to second-guess her decision to make this call. Jake's parents made no secret that they always thought she and Jake should be together. She didn't want them to get their hopes up, and she could tell by the sound of Mrs. Callaway's voice that she would like nothing more than to give her Jake's numbers.

"Hello. I'm back. You still there, Laura?"

"I'm here."

"Well talk about timing. That was Jake on the other line. When I told him I had you on hold and what you were calling about, he said he just happened to be driving by your place at that very second. So, he is going to pop in himself to update you on all he's found out. Isn't that great?"

Laura felt her adrenaline kick in. Jake was going to "pop" in, now?

"Laura, dear, are you there?"

"Yes, yes I'm still here. That's great," she said halfheartedly. With that, Sam began to bark, which meant Jake must have pulled into her driveway.

"Oh, look he's pulling in right now. Thanks so much for all your help, Mrs. Callaway."

"No problem, dear, anytime. You know we're only a phone call away. And Laura, we would love to see more of you. Don't be a stranger now, you hear?"

"Okay, I won't. Thanks again."

Laura disconnected the call. Before she had the chance to analyze her feelings, her doorbell was ringing and Sam was barking and running to the door.

"Okay, Sam, that's enough." She opened the door to find Jake with a grin on his face, and a business card in his hand.

"Heard you were looking for me. Here you go. The card has my name, address, phone, cell, and pager number on it. Feel free to use any and all of 'em to reach me whenever you need or want me." He handed her the card and added the piercing eye contact to the signature grin, which drove Laura over the edge.

She forced herself to break his gaze, which wasn't easy.

"Jake, you didn't have to go to all this trouble. I'm sure I won't be needing or wanting you. I was just wondering if you found out anything else about the accident?"

"As a matter of fact, I did. I was able to review the initial police report. However, what I found out raises more questions than answers. I think you should invite me in for some coffee and we can trade information — you show me yours and I'll show you mine."

Before Laura knew what hit her, Jake was sauntering into her home and patting Sam on the head. Some watchdog he was.

Jake made his way into the kitchen as if he had lived here all his life. In a way, he had. He had spent almost as much time here as

Laura when they were kids. Her grandmother loved Jake and she enjoyed having him and all of Laura's friends over to visit.

Jake shared a special bond with her grandmother, so much so that when she passed away, Jake needed as much comforting as Laura had. They were a tremendous source of strength for each other during that painfully sad time. It was the worst summer of Laura's life. That is, until the summer Jake broke her heart.

"Coffee still in the same place, Lars?"

The familiar tone he took with her sent a pang straight through her stomach to her heart. No one ever called her Lars, except Jake, and she hadn't heard him use that term of endearment in more years than she could recall.

She was so shaken by this, she couldn't form a reply, sarcastic or otherwise. She just stood and watched as Jake made his way over to the coffee pot and opened the cabinet above to find that the coffee indeed was still kept in the same place. She was a creature of habit, not one to embrace change, and Jake remembered that about her. He knew so much about her, whether she wanted to admit it or not.

"It appears that it is. I'll make it just how you like it, so strong it'll make your eyes water." Jake turned to her with a grin, but the look on her face must have said it all. He stopped abruptly from his task.

"I'm sorry Lars…ah Laura, I didn't mean to overstep my bounds. This is your house, you should make the coffee. I didn't mean to… overstep like that."

Laura didn't reply at first, mostly because she wasn't sure how she was feeling. For a moment it felt like old times, as if the years had not come between them at all. The sincerity in his voice softened her reply, "No, it's okay. It's just that it's been a long time since there's been a man in my kitchen. It's just been the girls and me for so long now…and the name…no one ever calls me Lars. It took me by surprise, that's all."

"I'm sorry…I…"

"No, really, it's fine. I'm fine. Go on, make some coffee. I still like it strong enough to make my eyes water. While you're doing that, I'll find the news article I want to show you and we can trade information."

Jake turned towards the coffee pot and continued with his task while Laura searched for the article to share. Then she retrieved mugs, spoons, sugar and creamer for their coffee and set everything in place on the kitchen table. Jake filled their mugs, they both sat at the table and he began updating Laura on the information he gathered so far.

"Apparently, a call came into the police dispatch center around five thirty in the morning. Sally Cohen was on duty, so she took the call. The caller wished to remain anonymous but reported an accident on Wagontrail Road, which had resulted in a downed utility pole.

"When Sally asked for more information, the caller hung up. Upon arriving at the scene, Sally witnessed the destruction first-hand. The pole was snapped in half and wires hung from the pole and surrounding trees, some resting on the ground. Tree debris littered the street. Sally noted various tire tracks all over the road and on both sides of the street as if the car had careered back and forth. The strong odor of gasoline was present, and probably was a by-product of the car colliding with the pole.

"Most upsetting to Sally, was the black-stained grass near the downed pole. Sally said she inspected this with great caution, careful not to disturb the evidence. Most likely it was blood, but from what or whom she wasn't certain. It could be that a deer had been hit and was the cause of the accident. Perhaps the deer collapsed in this spot, lost a lot of blood, and then ran off to die deeper in the woods. That happens a lot in this area.

"The other interesting thing Sally noted was the absence of a vehicle. It was surprising, to say the least, that the person who caused this destruction was able to drive away from the scene."

Laura interjected, "The man from the utility company said the same thing."

Jake continued, "Standard operating procedure required Sally to call the utility company immediately to handle the hazardous electrical situation. Upon doing so, she was informed that a call had already been placed and that a crew was on its way. It arrived a few moments after Sally ended her call.

"Next, she was required to call the fire department to deal with the potentially dangerous gas spill. That's where I come in." Jake smiled and winked. "Finally, she called her department requesting an investigative team to aid her in putting the pieces of this puzzle together by collecting evidence, taking pictures of the scene, and analyzing the blood found."

After Jake explained all this to Laura, they began to dissect the information bit by bit, adding additional pieces they possessed.

Laura poured the last of the coffee into their mugs and added, "We also know that the tire tracks on my property were from Betty Simpson's car. According to Betty, there had been a demolished car at the scene, a male police officer, who was not very nice, an unidentified man with an expensive car, and possibly a fatality or a severely injured person on the ground who may or may not have been the source of the blood. However we must also consider that Betty may have been mistaken about that. I mean, it was dusk so her visibility may have been compromised."

"True. So, what does this all mean?" Jake took a long swig of coffee and looked at Laura.

"It means we need more answers." Laura reached for her laptop at the same time Jake reached for it. Their hands met and then their eyes. Neither pulled away. Laura felt the electricity between them shoot through her body. *This is crazy.* She pulled away, quickly stood, and began to gather dishes from the table to take to the sink. Jake stood and followed her.

"Lars...don't run away. I don't bite, promise." Jake reached for her to turn her towards him.

"Jake, don't...it's just too much, too soon for me." She allowed herself to make eye contact with him. *Big mistake.* That was always her downfall with Jake, those deep pools of blue.

"What is? The information on the accident?" Jake asked as he held her gaze.

"No. You."

"Do you want me to leave?"

"No. Yes. I don't know." Laura managed to break the gaze.

"Hey, remember the time in high school when the school gym was vandalized and we broke the case? Before the cops could." Jake was referring to the year they were on the school paper together and, after much solid research and questioning of fellow students and town members, had gained enough evidence to determine the culprits. They broke the story before the local town paper. "That was quite a rush. We were awesome together, Lars. Good times."

Laura could tell Jake was trying to lighten the mood. She replied, "Yeah, I remember. Everyone thought for sure we'd go into the investigative reporting field. I even thought that at one time. But...life happens." She smiled at this and added, "But things worked out for you in that regard."

Jake nodded, "In that regard, yeah." He let his sentence hang for a bit. Laura knew there was more hidden in that comment, but she didn't want to go there. She wasn't ready.

Laura decided to change the subject, "Well, we have a lot of information we've gathered so far on our current mystery. We both agree we need more and we agree we are good investigators, so what's the next step?"

Jake followed her lead, "I guess we decide what info we need and how to find it."

Laura walked over to the table and showed Jake the article on Betty Simpson's death. Then she grabbed her notepad and said, "Let's make a list and get started."

# Nine

Jake's unexpected visit yesterday put Laura behind schedule, so she had to spend the better part of the afternoon and evening in her shop working on the centerpieces for the wedding. Now here she was back this morning, with only one day left until the ceremony. She would need to spend the day preparing. She didn't mind. Her work was solitary and afforded her the time to reflect on all that had happened in the past few days.

As she busied herself tying ribbons and arranging candles for each piece, she thought of the information she and Jake had learned regarding the accident. As he said, it raised more questions than answers.

None of this made any sense and, for some reason, this bothered her. She couldn't explain why, other than the fact that the accident occurred in front of her home and caused her immense inconvenience for two days. She also toyed with the idea that being inquisitive gave her an excuse to talk to Jake, but quickly dismissed that thought.

The next logical move was to let the police continue the investigation and wait for their conclusion. However, according to Jake, Sally told him she had been removed from the case and, to her knowledge, no one was very concerned about researching it. Laura and Jake were both puzzled by this, so they decided to do some investigating on their own.

Jake was going to snoop around the police department and causally run into some friends he had on the force to pump them for information. He also would check with the local hospitals to inquire if anyone had been admitted that morning, or anytime after, with injuries consistent with a car accident.

Laura would follow up on the Betty Simpson angle. In fact, the obituary indicated that the memorial service was scheduled for tonight and Laura planned on going. She would casually mention the accident as she made her deliveries over the next few days to gain insight into the town gossip. Then she and Jake would meet to compare notes.

She realized she was a bit too eager for that part. She was treading on dangerous ground, but had to admit, it was the most alive she had felt in years. She was fondly reminded of her high school days, just as Jake had said. Of course, they never covered anything as serious as a fatality, but they had their share of interesting stories.

Now here they were, after all these years, falling so easily back into old roles. Perhaps they were making much more out of this than needed. That was a possibility. But if someone had died, didn't people have a right to know? Didn't Betty Simpson deserve to have someone concerned enough about her death to check into it? Or did she simply want the chance to feel like a teenager again? Difficult questions.

She would pursue this with Jake for a few days, see what developed, then go on with her safe, comfortable, predictable life. She felt she was strong enough to handle whatever Jake threw her way. She had to be, she had two daughters to think about.

***

This accident, as strange as it was, was Jake's ticket back into Laura's life. So, if she wanted to play super sleuth with him, he would gladly oblige. At least it gave him a reason to have contact with her. He would do his part, as they decided. He would snoop around the police station and talk to old friends. If it was important to her, he would find out everything he could. Hopefully, by the time her curiosity was sated, he wouldn't need an excuse to be with her. Time would tell.

He decided to stop at the police station before heading to the office. He might as well start his investigation now. He entered the building to find his old high school track buddy on the duty desk.

"Well, well, look who finally showed up. It's about time, ya bum. How long have you been in town…a month or so? Thought you'd forgotten all about me."

"Hey, Jimmy, my man. How could I forget about you?"

Jimmy stood and they shook hands and pulled each other in for a manly bear hug and slap on the back.

Jimmy said, "What have you been up to, man? Heard you bought the old Peterson cabin in the woods and fixed it up. What brings you back to this ol' pile of sticks, as you used to call it?"

"What can I say, Jim, I missed this ol' pile of sticks."

"Hear you did well for yourself in the Big Apple. What could you possibly miss around here?" Jimmy asked.

"Of all people, you should know the answer to that, bro."

"I suspected she had something to do with it. How's she feeling about all this?"

"She doesn't know yet. Haven't had the chance to get into all that. Just ran into her the other day actually. I was out to her place to direct traffic because of that accident. Pretty bad one it would appear. The utility pole was snapped in half. No cars or bodies by the time I arrived. Laura's all bothered by the whole thing. Hates to think someone died right in front of her house. Told her I'd look into it for her, and see what I could find out. I read Sally's accident report but wanted to follow up on the investigation. Thought I'd visit some old friends here and get the scoop. You know anything about it?"

Jimmy replied, "I'm not on the case. A couple of the old-timers are working on it. Haven't heard much otherwise."

"Do you know if there were any fatalities or if the vehicle was found at the scene?" Jake asked.

"Don't know. Like I said, it's not my case, so I haven't been paying much attention to it. Get a lot of car crashes this time of year. Kids with spring fever, end of the school year parties, you know. Combine that with the increase of the deer population being kicked out of their homes by all the new housing, and what you get is too many car accidents. It's not like when we were growing up, Jake. Too many people here now for these country roads. And those city slickers don't take kindly to all the twists and turns and lack of street lights."

"I hear ya, I couldn't believe how built up the area's gotten since I left. Shame. But I guess nothing stays the same."

"You got that right," Jimmy nodded in agreement.

"Well, it sure is good to see you again, Jimmy. Let's get out for a beer one night when you're not on duty."

"Sure thing. How do I reach you?"

Jake pulled out one of his cards and handed it over.

"It's got my home and my cell. Try me at either. Thanks for your help, Jim. I won't keep you. Make sure you call for that beer. It's on me."

"In that case, you can bet on it."

Both men shook hands again, and Jake headed out to his Jeep.

***

Jimmy was left thinking what a coincidence it was that just this morning his boss had given him the odd instruction to let him know if anyone asked about the accident on Wagontrail Road. He'd almost forgotten all about it. Then Jake walks in and asks just that.

Weird. Better do what he was told. He walked over and knocked on Chief Stark's door.

"Come in," the chief barked.

"Hey, Chief."

"Afternoon, Jim. What's up?" Chief Stark was a large man in his early sixties, nearing retirement but refusing to acknowledge this fact. He had a large square head, graying hair and dark, piercing eyes. He could best be described as intimidating and he wasn't someone you wanted to mess with.

"Just wanted to let you know I had someone come in and ask about that accident on Wagontrail."

"Who was in, Jim?" he asked casually as he continued to work on his computer.

"Jake Callaway."

Jimmy thought the man hesitated for just a second before responding.

"Jake Callaway, huh. He back in town?"

"Yeah, came back a few weeks ago. Said he missed the place. But truth be told, he missed a girl. Laura Delaney. Went to school with us. She was Laura MacIntosh then. They were hot and heavy all through high school, then she married Bill Delaney and Jake took off for New York. Or maybe it was the other way around. Now he's back and trying to get in her good graces. She's all spooked that someone might have died in front of her house or something, so he's looking into it for her."

"Laura MacIntosh…knew her grandmother. Don't know her that well though. Lives in the grandmother's house now, right? Don't remember her going to high school here."

"You wouldn't. She lived on the other side of town with her parents. Practically in the next school district over, but right on the border, so she came to high school here. Nice girl, good grades, nice group of friends. That's why you wouldn't remember her. Not one to have a run-in with the law. She moved into the grandmother's house after she married Bill."

Chief Stark nodded, "Right. Now Jake's another story. Seems I remember the two of you in my cell once or twice."

Jimmy smiled. "Yeah. They were the good ol'days."

"So, what'd you tell your buddy Jake?"

"Not much. It's not my case, so I don't have any info on it. Anything I should know about it, was there a fatality?"

"I'm sure Joe's looking into it, so I wouldn't worry about it. We got enough car accidents to keep us busy this time of year," replied the Chief.

"That's for sure. Okay then, I'll get back to the desk." Jimmy left the office with the feeling that something wasn't right about this.

# Ten

Memorial services were not something anyone looked forward to, and Laura probably less so than most. She stumbled over the right words to say to those grieving loved ones. Tonight, as she prepared to go to Betty Simpson's, she realized she wouldn't know a soul in attendance and, to make matters worse, she was going alone. This made her more anxious than usual.

She was putting finishing touches on her makeup when the doorbell rang. Sam began to bark as she called out to her daughters to please answer the door. The bell rang again and Sam continued to bark. Apparently, no one was listening to her. This seemed to be a common occurrence around here lately.

She took a final glance in the mirror, blotted her lipstick, smoothed her little black dress, and headed to the front door.

"Sam, quiet already!" she scolded as she opened the door.

She was surprised to find Jake standing on her doorstep. Even more surprising was the fact that he was dressed, quite handsomely, in a dashing black suit, white shirt, and gray tie. Since she was rendered speechless once again, Jake was forced to speak first.

"Hey. Thought you might like some company tonight. Know this isn't your favorite pastime."

"Right..." Laura wasn't sure whether to be grateful or annoyed by his presumptuousness. She stood staring at him while she decided.

"Do you think it'd be alright if I came in? Or should I wait out here until you're ready to go?" He smiled as he said it and Laura felt her face flush at her apparent lack of manners.

"Of course, you can come in. I'm just a bit surprised you're here. I'm used to doing things alone, Jake. You don't need to babysit me." She decided to go with annoyed.

Sam greeted Jake with a warm welcome and a wet sloppy toy. Jake knelt on the floor, black suit and all, and began to play tug-o-war with the well-worn rope toy, completely ignoring Laura's exasperated tone. Brooke finally appeared from another room.

"Oh, hi, Mr. Callaway."

"Hey. Brooke, right? Call me Jake. Good to see you again," Jake said with a wink.

"Okay, Jake. Two points for getting my name right."

"Don't you have homework you should be doing?" Laura asked, still annoyed.

"Sorry," Brooke rolled her eyes. "Just coming to answer the door like you asked. Guess you beat me to it. You two going out again?"

Laura let out an exasperated sigh, "We are not going out. We have a memorial service to go to. Actually, I have a memorial service to go to and Jake assumed I'd want company."

"That was nice of him, Mom. You hate to go to those, especially alone."

If Laura had hoped for any solidarity from Brooke, she was not getting it. Her daughter, her own flesh and blood, was clearly on Jake's side. This time Laura rolled her eyes and gave Brooke "the look".

Brooke responded, "Soooorry. I'll be on my way back to my room to do my homework."

Laura nodded in agreement, "Good idea. I won't be late. Make sure you let Sam out later and don't forget to let him back in."

"Yes, mom." Brooke replied, as she turned on her way back to her room.

Jake interjected, "Well, should we go? I can drive. My Jeep's right out front."

"Do I have any choice?" Laura asked sarcastically.

"None that I can see." He smiled smugly as he opened the front door and gestured for her to go first.

The funeral home was in the next town. From the look of the parking lot, attendance to pay respects to Betty's family was low. Jake and Laura walked solemnly into the building and signed the guest book, taking a moment to glance at the names before them.

It was a closed casket, but a memory board stood next to it with pictures of Betty from over the years. Jake looked at Laura as if to ask, "Is that the woman you met?" Laura nodded slightly. It was indeed the same Betty Simpson whom she met just a few days before.

They slowly made their way to the front, where Betty's family stood thanking those who came to offer their condolences. Laura tried to surmise how each person was related to the deceased. She assumed the older, angry-looking man was the husband. Next stood three younger people, two boys and a girl, all late teenage years or possibly early twenties. She guessed these were Betty's children. At the end of the line was an elderly woman in a wheelchair, who looked as if she might be Betty's mother.

Jake and Laura made their way through the line, telling each member of the family how sorry they were for their loss. When Laura got to the end, she could almost feel the pain on the mother's face. Laura's eyes began to fill at the thought of having to bury a child. To her surprise, Betty's mother began questioning her.

"I don't recognize you. How do you know my daughter?"

"My name is Laura Delaney. I just met your...Betty was your daughter?"

"Yes."

"I'm so sorry for your loss. I just met your daughter the other day. A car accident occurred in front of my house and she witnessed it on her way to work. She came to my door to apologize for her car getting stuck on my property. She seemed so kind and I was impressed by her honesty. Then I read about the accident in the news and..."

"It wasn't no accident. Police say so, but it wasn't no accident."

"What do you mean?"

"My Betty was pushed off that road. Dents all over the back of the car to prove it." She began to cry as she spoke.

"She was a good driver, been driving these roads her whole life. Somebody pushed her off the road..." She was becoming agitated and attracting attention. The girl, who Laura assumed was Betty's daughter, came over and leaned down to her.

"Grandma, you need to stop getting yourself worked up. Remember what the doctor said." She handed her another tissue and patted her hand.

The girl looked at Laura, "I'm sorry, you'll have to excuse her, she is quite elderly and this has been such a shock to all of us."

"Of course. I can't imagine what you're all going through. Again, we are so sorry for your loss," Laura said as she patted the elderly woman's hand.

Laura and Jake moved away from the receiving line and took seats. They sat quietly, reflecting on the sadness of death, while empathy for the loved ones left behind washed over them.

Laura realized the last time she was at a funeral with Jake was for her grandmother. Jake, as if sensing her thoughts, reached over and took her hand. The mix of emotions was overwhelming. She guessed he was thinking of her grandmother as well and remembered how difficult that time was for both of them. She looked over. Their eyes met and held, both filling with tears. He reached his arm around her, pulled her closer to him, and placed a soft kiss on top of her head. No gesture could have been more appropriate, and Laura was catapulted back in time. Being this close to him allowed her to breathe in his clean, musky scent, so familiar to her at another time in her life. This triggered memories of being comforted in his strong embrace. For a moment, it was as if only she and Jake existed. As long as she was with him, she would be safe and happy.

The moment ended when she was brought back to reality by the sound of crying. A woman was up with the family and hugging the children as she sobbed. Laura released herself from Jake's embrace, and slowly slid her hand from his. She tried to bring herself back to the present.

She was at a funeral for a stranger, not her grandmother. Jake was not her lover or her protector. She was old enough to know that no one could completely protect you from hurt and disappointment.

She sensed that Jake was bringing himself back to the reality of the situation as well. He had resumed the role of reporter, scanning the room for some sort of clue that would guide them to their next step. Suddenly he stopped scanning, gave Laura's arm a nudge, and made a slight nod to indicate that Laura should look to her left.

When she did, she observed a very well-dressed man standing by the door. The fact that he was so well dressed caused him to stand out from the crowd of mostly blue-collar friends and family members. Laura wasn't sure what to make of it, or what Jake was inferring from the situation.

Certainly she and Jake were standing out from the crowd as well. She wondered if Betty's mother had questioned this man like she had Laura. But Laura didn't remember seeing him with the family.

The man turned and quietly left the funeral home. Jake motioned for Laura to stay as he rose, intending to follow the man. Laura, not one to take orders, followed Jake. They entered the foyer of the funeral home in time to witness the man entering his car. Jake shot her an annoyed glance.

"I told you to stay inside," he scolded in a whisper.

"News flash, I don't take orders from you," she retorted, also in a hushed tone.

The glare of approaching headlights diverted their attention. A car had pulled out from the second row and was heading toward the exit. It had to be their man, as no one else had recently left. The car, like the man, stood out from the other cars and trucks in the lot. It was a black Mercedes.

Jake headed towards the exit with Laura close behind. "I know him from somewhere, Lars. I just can't place him at the moment, but my gut is telling me to see where he goes. Let's find out."

Since her curiosity was aroused, she didn't put up a fight but kept pace with Jake back to his Jeep. He wasted no time wheeling out of the lot, while Laura kept her eyes peeled for the shiny black car.

She pointed, "There. He just turned right at the next light."

"Good eyes, Lars, good eyes." Jake signaled to turn right as well. Now he was the only car behind the shiny black one, so he slowed down and hung back. The car continued for a few miles then turned left. They continued their pursuit to an intersection where they would have gone straight if heading home, but the shiny black car turned right. They turned right to follow, still keeping their distance. Suddenly, Jake made a left turn, even though the other car continued going straight.

"What are you doing, he's going straight?" Laura asked in surprise.

"I know a shortcut. This way if he's getting suspicious of being followed, we'll throw him off."

"Or lose him."

"Have faith, Lars!" he said with a grin.

He was driving faster now on these back roads, making turns right and left until he came to a main road. Sure enough, the shiny black car passed as Jake made a left turn behind it. He continued to hang back and allowed another car to pull out between them while keeping a close watch on their target. The car made a right onto a dirt road. Jake debated what to do.

"That's Lower Valley Road," he said. "We'll be the only two cars on it. What's your gut tell you?"

"We've come this far, go for it."

"That's my girl." Jake slowly made the right and found the car up ahead. Just then the brake lights flashed, indicating the car was slowing down, so Jake did the same. The car made a left.

Jake hesitated and slowed his truck, "He must have turned into a private drive. That's not a public road. I don't think we should follow him farther."

"Drive by to check for an address," Laura got her phone prepared to take a picture.

Jake continued, slowing as they approached the turn. A sign was visible at the entrance to the turn.

Laura read the sign and took a picture, "Hallowed Hills Private Community – A Community of Christ. That's the park and campgrounds where that church has its retreats each summer. They bring kids here from the city to experience nature and fresh air. They learn to fish and swim in the lake, things like that. I read an article about it a few years ago."

"It sounds like it's some sort of church as well. Maybe he's a minister? Someone who gave Betty religious guidance?" Jake added.

"I guess that would make sense, his being at her funeral, but wouldn't he have had more interaction with her family? And you would think he would stay till the end, or at least notify someone when he was leaving."

"Again, looks like we raised more questions than we answered." Jake continued to drive as they both sat in silence.

Jake spoke first, "It was nice being with you tonight, even though we were at a memorial service. Not the best place for a date," he joked. Laura was about to protest that it wasn't a date but Jake continued, "I know, I know, it's not a date. But I still enjoyed your company. I don't want to push my luck, it being a school night and all, so I'm gonna take you home. But I want you to know where I'm coming from, Lars. I like being with you. There may be a lot of stuff in our history that needs sorting, but for now, I just like being with you."

Laura didn't respond at first. The emotions swirling inside were unsettling. He was making her head spin and her stomach do flip-flops at the same time. That was more than she was accustomed to and certainly more than she wanted to handle tonight. So she simply replied, "Yes. My girls will be expecting me home soon."

# Eleven

Not one for fancy curtains, Jake's windows were adorned with nothing more than ornate crown moldings. In fact, it was the hand-crafted moldings that he most admired about the old cabin in the woods. Since he was into carpentry as a hobby, he appreciated the lost art and delicate work displayed throughout the place. The cabin was surrounded by woods, so he didn't have to worry about neighbors seeing things they weren't supposed to, such as Jake walking around in his boxers.

This particular morning was a bright, sunny one so Jake was awakened early by a warm beam of sunlight bursting through the glass. His first thought upon waking was of Laura. Going to the memorial service had stirred up some intense and dormant emotions for him and he hoped for her as well.

But now he was concerned he might have moved too fast and that Laura would pull back further from his reach. He had to be patient with her. There was a lot of hurt that needed to be worked through, on both ends. But he was willing to do whatever it took to sort it out and regain her trust.

The best way to do that was to stay focused on the task at hand, which was the mystery surrounding this accident. They didn't get a chance to discuss the comments from Betty's mother. He imagined Laura ruminating over the possibility that Betty was deliberately pushed off the road. Of course, it may just be the crazy delusions of an elderly distraught mother having to bury her daughter, but it was worth investigating and he would be more than happy to help Laura do so. Even he had to admit, the mother's statement, along with the man they followed, had his investigative instincts standing at attention.

He pushed himself out of bed, threw on shorts and running shoes, and prepared for his morning five-mile run. He made a quick detour to the kitchen to start a pot of coffee. Once that was going, he stepped out into the warm sunshine. It was going to be another hot one if it was this warm already.

A flash of white caught his attention and he turned towards it. Taped to the porch railing was a note. He ripped it off the railing and opened it. In scrawled, almost illegible handwriting it said, "Stop poking your nose where it doesn't belong. This is a warning for you and your girlfriend. You don't know what you're dealing with. Signed, A Friend."

What kind of friend issued threats, Jake wondered. This was an interesting twist. His investigative instincts were now on high alert. He abandoned the morning run and hurried back inside to call Laura. He had to make sure she was okay and find out if she had received a note as well.

He grabbed his cell, which had her number programmed, and called her house.

Laura answered on the second ring, "Hello."

"Good morning. I hope I didn't wake you."

"Nope, been up for a while. The girls head to school early these days. What's up?"

"Just calling to check on you…"

"Jake, look, you don't have to check on me. I know last night we had… a moment…"

As he feared, she was regretting last night and trying to pull back. He interrupted her monologue.

"Laura, listen. Something more important is going on here. I woke up this morning to find a somewhat threatening note on my front porch."

"What? What are you talking about?"

"I would feel better if you let me come over to check your place out and make sure you and the girls are safe." He purposely added the girls, knowing she may take risks with her safety, but would never compromise theirs.

"What are you talking about, Jake? What kind of threatening note? From who?"

"All excellent questions and I'd really like to come over now and show you the note and check your place out to make sure you didn't receive one as well."

"Jake, I've already been out to take the girls to school and there was nothing out of the ordinary."

"Good. Just stay put till I get there."

"Jake, I have a million things to do..." But he had already disconnected the call.

***

Well, that was just great. Now she had to wait for Jake before getting started in her shop. The heck with that, she thought. She grabbed a piece of paper and wrote a note explaining that she was in the shop. She taped the note on the front door, then headed out the back.

"Come on Sam, we're heading to the shop." Sam dutifully followed with tail wagging.

The door to the house slammed behind them and they started their walk down the path to the converted barn. For a split second, Laura felt a chill run up her spine and the feeling that she was being watched. She furtively glanced around, but all she saw were the trees and woods that surrounded her property. Then she felt foolish for doing so. She had never felt afraid or unsafe here and she'd be damned if she started now. How dare Jake try to ruin her sense of safety and security in her own home. She certainly hoped this wasn't some ploy on his part just to attract her attention.

As she and Sam approached the barn, she searched on her key chain for the proper one to unlock the door. Finding it, she reached for the door, only to find it already unlocked and slightly ajar. She was able to simply push it open. She fought back the urge to turn around and wait for Jake. She probably just forgot to lock up last night, even though she was usually careful about that. Did someone break into her shop? She was afraid of what she would find upon entering. Unconsciously, she held her breath as she pushed the door fully open and reached for the light switch.

Sam ran in ahead of her and began wildly sniffing around the floor. Laura cautiously scanned the room before entering. Everything seemed to be in order. Nothing was broken or appeared to be missing. She never kept money here over night, so that wasn't a concern. She entered and began to feel relief. She must have forgotten to lock up, after all. She was probably preoccupied with the memorial service she had to attend, as well as everything else going on, and completely forgot her normal lock-up routine.

She did a quick survey of the entire barn and determined that nothing was out of place. The only thing unusual was Sam's behavior. He usually came into the shop and took his spot on the cushioned window seat where he'd lay for hours, occasionally rousing to keep his eye on a wayward squirrel or rabbit that happened by. But today he was still busily running around sniffing the entire floor of the place. Perhaps some sort of animal had wandered in overnight and left its scent.

"Sam, that's enough. Go lie down!" Sam reluctantly obeyed Laura's request and took his usual place in the window.

Laura had another busy day. Tomorrow was the big wedding and she had to put the final touches on the centerpieces and corsages and make sure all the flowers were ready to be added in the morning. She'd be up very early tomorrow, work all morning and afternoon, then relax all evening once her job was successfully completed.

She went into the back room where she kept her work-in-progress jobs. The room was filled with ribbons, decorations, glue guns, scissors, paint, foam forms and anything else she might need to make her arrangements, plus a long worktable she used to make it all happen.

She sat down at the table and continued where she'd left off yesterday, but was interrupted by the sound of the door opening in the front of the shop. Her senses were on alert this morning, so she listened intently. She heard Sam jump down from his perch and waited for the low bark, but it didn't come. She instinctively reached for the scissors she kept on the table. Where were the scissors? She always kept them on the right side of the table. She was annoyed at the fact that her first reaction was fear.

She had worked here for years and was never afraid of the sound of her door opening. It usually meant business and that was a good thing, not a reason to look for a weapon. Damn that Jake! She stood and brushed the debris from the apron she wore while working and made her way into the front room to greet her potential customer.

"Well, speak of the devil." She entered to find Jake crouched down, rubbing Sam behind the ears.

"Can't get me out of your mind, can you?" Jake said with his signature grin.

"Yeah, and not in a good way. How dare you scare me like that this morning. I've been jumpy since your call. I must have forgotten to lock up last night. When I found the door to the shop open this morning, a wave of panic raced through me, thinking the worst.

Now the door opens and again I think someone is out to get me. How dare you do that to me. I have never been..."

"What? Someone was in here last night?"

"No. You're not listening. I must have forgotten to lock up and..."

"Do you do that often, Lars, forget to lock up?"

"No, of course not. I never forget, but..."

"You never forget, but for some reason, you think you just happened to forget last night?"

"Well, yes. I mean I had so much on my mind with everything going on..."

"Exactly, with everything going on, why wouldn't you think that someone else might be involved here?"

"Why would I think that?"

"Let's sit down. I want to show you the note I received this morning."

Sam was scratching at the door to go out, so Laura first opened the door for him, then motioned for Jake to follow her into the back room to sit at the work table.

"Here, take a look at this." He handed her the note he found attached to his porch this morning. She read it aloud.

"Stop poking your nose where it doesn't belong. This is a warning for you and your girlfriend. You don't know what you're dealing with. Signed, A Friend." Laura gave Jake a puzzled look.

"What does this have to do with me? Obviously, you and your girlfriend are into something that's ticking somebody off, so stop it."

She threw the note on the table. She was even more annoyed with him now that he felt compelled to rub her nose in the fact that he had a girlfriend.

"Laura, you're the girlfriend. I mean, I don't have a girlfriend, you're the only woman I've been spending time with and the only thing I've been poking my nose in is this business with you."

# Twelve

He called an emergency meeting of The Brethren. Some would believe him to be an alarmist, but he didn't attain the position of Grand Master, their Leader, by leaving loose ends untied. He was a thorough, organized man and this situation required a thorough, organized plan.

Various cars began approaching down the long dirt and stone drive, so he made his way into the vestibule to greet them.

The old church lacked a decent cooling and ventilation system and during the summer months it become quite hot and humid. He wiped sweat from his brow. It was imperative that he not appear nervous in any way. The complication they were about to discuss was unexpected, and he anticipated some concern.

The leading members of The Brethren, the Elders, filed in and greeted him with a nod as they proceeded into the meeting room and took their usual seats around the long rectangular table. Once all four had arrived, he entered the room, approached the table and took his seat at the head. The Elders were similar in appearance, all in their mid-to-late-sixties, all graying and balding, all wearing similar clothes of shorts and polo shirts. To a casual observer, the gathering would resemble an innocuous meeting, perhaps of businessmen discussing their company's bottom line or a group of concerned citizens discussing community business. In reality, this group had a much different agenda.

"Good morning."

"Good morning," they replied in unison.

"I have summoned you all here this morning to discuss a complication that needs immediate attention. You are aware of the woman, Betty Simpson, who witnessed the accident and how we agreed to handle that situation. It has come to my attention that we have another problem. Before we were able to handle this woman, she spoke with the owner of the house where the accident occurred, Laura Delaney. It is unknown what information Mrs. Simpson relayed to Mrs. Delany. What is known is that Mrs. Delaney, for some reason, has taken it upon herself to do some investigating and has enlisted the help of a friend, Jake Callaway. In the interest of thoroughness, I, personally, attended Simpson's memorial service last night. Both Mrs. Delaney and Mr. Callaway were at the service. To complicate this, Mrs. Simpson's mother, who is quite distraught, informed them of her belief that her daughter's death was not an accident."

This piece of information was met with sounds of discomfort from the group. The Grand Master cleared his throat to regain order.

"This is not something that needs to cause great concern. I have a plan ready to be put in place, with everyone's agreement, of course."

"Is it wise to take action at this point? It may raise more suspicion," one member asked.

The Grand Master replied, "It appears that Mr. Callaway has contacts inside the police department as well, and has already been asking questions of them. We will use this opportunity to assess what information they have and to feed them a few morsels to satisfy their curiosity. Meanwhile, a member from The Brethren will be providing a few distractions to keep them occupied. I feel this is the best course of action for the circumstances."

The member to the right spoke next. He was the second in command, having been a part of The Brethren as long as the Grand Master. He was often a source of malcontent among the group, believing he possessed the better ideas and should be in charge. "I have some concerns with this plan. You are usually more thorough with the loose ends. Why not have them both meet with an unfortunate fate?"

The member across from him spoke next. He was closer to sixty with dark piercing eyes that cut right through a person, and a lack of polish the others seemed to possess. In a deep, menacing voice he supported the Grand Master.

"I agree with this plan. Taking care of the Simpson woman made sense, but these two are different. They are well-known and connected to the community. An accident involving them would bring too much attention. Something we can't afford at this point, so close to our sacred ceremony on July 4th. I think it best to give them some false information to satisfy them, as you said. And if you want to throw in some distractions, that's fine with me."

The Grand Master addressed the group, "Are we all in agreement then?"

One by one each man at the table raised his hand and uttered the word, "I". Except for the second in command. He hesitated briefly, long enough to make the point that he was not in total agreement. Then he slowly raised his hand and mumbled the required, "I".

# Thirteen

"Oh," was Laura's response to the news that she was considered Jake's girlfriend.

Jake continued, "This is why I was so concerned this morning. I thought that maybe you received some sort of message here as well. And now you're telling me someone broke into your shop."

"I am not telling you someone broke in. I just said the door was unlocked. The shop is fine. Nothing was out of place or missing and there was no evidence that anyone was in here, except maybe a squirrel or something since Sam found some interesting scents on the floor. But other than that, nothing."

"So you didn't find anything out of order, no footprints, nothing missing?"

"Nothing...well, except for my scissors," Laura remembered the missing scissors and began to search the table for them as she spoke.

"I always keep them here, on the right side of the table, but when I reached for them today, they were gone. I'm sure I must have misplaced them, or maybe one of the girls had a school project and needed them. In fact, now that I think about it, that makes perfect sense. I bet while I was out last night, one of the girls was working on a school project and needed some materials. They know I have ribbons and glue and all sorts of crafts in here so they probably came here, took what they needed, moved my scissors, and forgot to lock the door."

"Do they come in here often?"

"They're supposed to ask first, but since I wasn't here, they might have just come in on their own. I'll ask them as soon as they come home from school. But that scenario makes much more sense than your theory."

"Okay, we'll wait for you to talk to them. But I still want you to be more careful."

"Jake, I think you're making too much of this. Why would someone want to hurt me just because I was concerned about an accident in front of my home?"

"I don't know, Lars. But some strange things are going on. Maybe I'm making too much out of it all. Maybe my investigative reporting instincts are out of whack here and I'm still thinking like a city dweller. I don't know. But I don't like the missing scissors."

Laura rolled her eyes at the last comment. He really was making too much out of the missing scissors.

Jake caught the eye roll, "What? You're rolling your eyes at me, you think I'm crazy, Lars?"

She wanted to lash out at him for trying to scare her, for calling her Lars, for upsetting her quiet, safe life, but the concerned look on his face prevented her from being angry with him. She had to admit it was a bit flattering that someone was so concerned for her safety. This caused her to choose her words carefully.

"No, Jake, I don't think you're crazy. I...I think it's kind of... sweet that you have taken such an interest in this case for me. But Jake, I don't need you to take care of me. I have been taking care of myself for quite a while now. And, frankly, I wonder what your motives are here. Why such an interest in all this, in me, after all these years?"

This question seemed to surprise Jake. His eyes found hers, then slowly, he reached over and took her hand. She was acutely aware of her heart racing and tried to calm it down while she waited for his reply.

Then, instead of a verbal reply, he unexpectedly leaned in and kissed her. Her body immediately responded, which surprised her since it had been so long since a man had kissed her.

Still, the feelings were familiar, the tingling in the depths of her stomach, the blood rushing to her head, the sensation that her heart was beating too loudly, and the shortness of her breath. All familiar and all so missed and longed for, but at the same time, feared. Laura pulled away, embarrassed that she allowed herself to lose control so easily.

"Jake, I…"

The sound of the shop door opening in the other room startled both of them.

"Laura, are you here honey?" It was the sound of a familiar voice, one of Laura's regular customers. She quickly ran a hand over her hair as if she hoped to brush away the scene that just occurred.

"I'm back here, Mrs. Brenner. I'll be right out."

Her eyes met Jake's for a second, before turning to go and greet her customer.

"Good morning, Mrs. Brenner. What can I do for you today?" Mrs. Brenner was one of Laura's closest neighbors who stopped in frequently for fresh flowers to adorn her home. She had been friends with Laura's grandmother and Laura remembered her visiting often in the summers.

"Hello, dear. I wasn't sure if you were here. I'm used to being greeted by Sam. Where is that darling dog of yours?"

"That's a good question. He was here a few minutes ago, then Jake stopped by so I let him out." Laura walked over to the door, opened it, leaned her head out and called to Sam.

Jake entered the room to greet Mrs. Brenner, "Well, hello, there beautiful."

"Jake, this is a surprise. Honey, how are you?" Jake sauntered over and grabbed her in a big embrace, which seemed to dwarf the elderly woman, as he planted a kiss on the top of her head.

Jake replied, "I'm doing just fine, even better to be running into you on this fine morning."

"How are your parents, honey? Your mother and I keep trying to get a date on the calendar for lunch, but that woman is so busy these days."

Jake nodded in agreement and added, "You know what a control freak she is planning the 4th of July festivities. She won't rest until it's over and everything's gone off without a hitch."

"I know and I offer to help her every year. She barely delegates a thing. I guess I'll just have to pay her a visit in person and demand more responsibilities."

Laura was still at the door calling and whistling for Sam. This got Jake's attention, "What's wrong, Lars, Sam misbehaving?"

"I don't know. It's not like him not to come when I call or whistle. I don't see him in the yard either. He must be back by the woods. I'm sure he's fine, I mean the whole yard is fenced and all, but it's just not like him."

Laura was concerned and she could see Jake picked up on this. He said, "Tell you what, why don't you take care of this lovely lady while I take a walk around the yard and see what ol' Sam is up to? Maybe he has a lady friend he meets in the woods from time to time," Jake winked at Mrs. Brenner, gave her a peck on the cheek and headed out the door.

Laura yelled after him. "He usually goes over to the east side. Sometimes he gets a glance of Mr. Burns doing yard work and feels the need to protect his territory." Laura turned her attention to her customer.

"And how can I help you today, Mrs. Brenner?"

"Well, you know me, got to have my fresh flowers around. Give me the usual for the house. And throw in an extra bouquet for Jake's mom. Think I'll pay her a visit today and see how she's making out with all the plans for the Fourth. She must be thrilled to have Jake back home. I was so surprised to find him here at first, but it makes perfect sense. You two were such a cute couple back in the day."

Laura was familiar enough with small-town gossip to know she should not respond to this. Anything she said would be bent and twisted until it no longer resembled her words at all. She quickly changed the subject.

"How is your son doing these days?"

Mrs. Brenner was clearly disappointed not to receive any worthwhile gossip, but she couldn't resist the chance to talk about her son, Christopher.

"Oh, my Christopher is doing just fine, honey. He got another promotion after the holidays and the family had to move to New Jersey, of all places. Sara wasn't too happy about that. But the kids are young enough to adjust and he assured her this would be the last move for a while."

She continued on and on about him and his family while Laura gathered the flowers. She was always sure to include some of Mrs. Brenner's favorites, amaryllis, delphinium, and gladiolus.

Then she arranged the bouquet for Jake's mom. She remembered how much Mrs. Callaway liked gerbera daisies and was sure to include plenty of them in the mix.

As Mrs. Brenner went on and on, Laura couldn't help stealing glances out the window to look for Jake. Her concern over Sam was rising to near-panic levels, as she tried in vain to squash it down. She quickly finished tying a bow on the bouquet for Mrs. Callaway, gathered all the flowers and placed them in the special bags she used that protected the blossoms and made them easier for her customers to carry.

"Okay, Mrs. Brenner, here you go. Now this one is for Mrs. Callaway. I've included some of her favorites." She carefully handed the bag over to her.

"Thank you so much, dear. They look lovely. Now, how much do I owe you."

In her haste to finish, Laura almost forgot to charge for her work. She tallied up the bill, collected payment and tried politely to hurry her customer out the door. But when she spotted Jake running toward the barn with Sam in his arms, all manners were forgotten. Laura ran out towards them, her panic no longer contained.

"Jake, oh my gosh, what happened!" She tried to take Sam from his arms but decided he was better off there, as Sam weighed about 100 pounds and Jake was moving at a much faster pace than Laura could.

"I found him way out in the yard, eating something." Jake was slightly out of breath from his trek with Sam in his arms, but he continued with his story and kept moving toward the barn.

"When I got to him, it looked like a hunk of meat, but it was tainted or something. Smelled funny, had a gray powder or something on it."

He laid Sam down on the grass in front of the barn.

"We need to get him to the vet, Lars. When I pulled him away from the meat and went to inspect it, he started choking, then vomiting. Then he started having a seizure or something. Scared the hell out of me. I grabbed him up and ran back as fast as I could."

As Jake told his story, Laura crouched down to Sam and tried to feel his heart rate. It had slowed considerably and his breathing was labored. Suddenly, his entire body seized up and he began to convulse. Laura wrapped her arms around him to try and control it while speaking as calmly and lovingly as she could.

"It's okay Sammy, honey. I'm here. It's okay. Try to relax. You're going to be fine, baby, my big fuzzy baby."

"Laura, I'm getting my Jeep. I'll bring it around here. We gotta get him help, fast."

Laura's eyes began to tear now and a lump formed in her throat. She couldn't lose Sam. Couldn't bear it. He was the only male companion who'd shared her bed in years. He was her loyal, devoted friend, protector of her and her girls. She could not lose him. A soft, gentle voice interrupted her thoughts.

"Laura, honey, what can I do?"

She had forgotten all about Mrs. Brenner, who must have been standing by her the whole time with her flowers in her hand.

"Oh, I'm sorry, Mrs. Brenner." She answered with a shaky voice. "No, no nothing. I just have to take him to the vet. Thank you though."

Laura tried to wipe her eyes and gain her composure. Jake's Jeep approached the yard so she tried to gather Sam in her arms and stand with him, but he was dead weight and almost slipped from her arms. She began to cry openly. He could not die!

"Come on Sammy, hold on for me, hold on, baby."

Jake lifted Sam effortlessly and carried him to the Jeep. Mrs. Brenner hurried over to open the door. She helped Jake maneuver the dog into the back seat and then helped Laura climb in next to him.

"You keep me posted, Jake. You take care of them both," Mrs. Brenner instructed.

"That's my plan. Thanks for your help."

Jake jumped into the driver's seat and hurried in the direction of town.

# Fourteen

Laura was physically and emotionally exhausted. It had not been a good day. She was finally home after spending hours at the vet while Sam teetered between life and death. All she wanted was a warm bed and solitude.

What she got was Jake insisting on coming into the house with her to make sure she was safe, especially since Sam was not here to protect her. Jake was inspecting the house while she put on a pot of coffee in preparation for the long night ahead. The Cavanaugh wedding was tomorrow and she would be up most of the night completing all the work she didn't accomplish today. No warm bed for her.

The good news was that Sam would hopefully make a full recovery. This was the only thing that enabled her to keep going.

The town veterinarian, Mike Simon, or Dr. Mike, as he was affectionately called, conducted blood work that concluded Sam had eaten some sort of poison. He had seen this before since field mice were common and homeowners would strategically place rodent poison around their properties to stop them from getting inside. All too often, the family pet would ingest the poison first and end up in his office.

Fortunately, Jake caught Sam before he had ingested too much and the vet immediately administered charcoal tablets, the standard treatment for arsenic poisoning, the poison of choice in this area.

Meanwhile, he ran tests to rule out other poisons, while Jake returned to retrieve the offending piece of meat that Sam had been sampling. Once arsenic was confirmed as the only poison, Sam was admitted to an overnight stay to receive continual doses of the charcoal, which would help to rid the poison from his body.

By the time Laura was forced to leave Sam for the night, he was doing much better and she felt as comfortable as she was ever going to feel leaving him.

The house was too quiet and Laura wondered what her girls were up to. Earlier, Mrs. Brenner, upon leaving the scene of the crime this morning, went to Jake's mother's home to deliver the bouquet along with the blow-by-blow of the morning's events in vivid detail.

Jake's mom was immediately on the phone with Jake offering her help. It was decided that she and Jake's dad would go to Laura's house. Jake convinced Laura that someone should be home when her daughters returned from school to explain what was going on with Sam and she reluctantly agreed. But Laura had no idea where everyone was now.

Jake had just finished his inspection of the house as Laura was about to search for the girls.

"Any sign of Ella or Brooke during your search?" she asked a bit sarcastically.

"No. But there's a light on in the barn, which is where I was headed next."

"Why on earth would they be in the barn? And where are your parents?"

"I'm hoping in the barn with them. Maybe the girls wanted to show them around or something."

Laura grabbed a flashlight she kept by the back door to light the path to the barn. They were quiet as they walked, both too tired to talk.

Laura hadn't fully expressed to Jake how grateful she was that he found Sam and rushed him to the vet with her. She didn't want to imagine how much poison Sam would have ingested had Jake not been with her, or how she would have gotten him to the vet so quickly.

She shuttered to think of the consequences. Jake seemed to sense her thoughts and placed a hand reassuringly on her back.

"He's gonna be okay, Lars, he's in good hands. Dr. Mike and his staff are the best."

"I know…I just can't stop thinking about what would have happened if you weren't here, Jake. I mean, I would have been so busy working on the wedding centerpieces. Who knows how long it would have been before I thought to go looking for him? You saved his life, Jake. I don't know how to thank you."

"Oh, I'm sure I'll think of something." He put his arm around her shoulder and jostled her around teasingly. Part of her wanted to let go and enjoy his playfulness, but she continued to hold back.

"Things are just so complicated, Jake."

"They don't have to be, Lars. Life is short, honey, you need to start enjoying yours."

"I wish I had your outlook on life. But my life has been so different from yours. I don't have your faith and optimism."

"You did at one time. You just need to find it again. Get back to your roots."

"My roots have been strangled, Jake, repeatedly." She didn't mean for that to come out as it had. Especially after what Jake had done today. She was just so tired and felt so vulnerable. It would be so easy to fall into Jake's arms and let him take care of her. But she couldn't risk trusting him again. She had her girls to think of now. It wasn't just about her.

She sensed a shift in him, as he removed his arm from around her shoulders. She stopped walking and turned to look up at him. His eyes were deep pools of blue. Over the years she'd forgotten that sensation of deep connection his eyes created for her. She had felt it with no one else. No one.

"Jake…I didn't mean to sound like that, I'm sorry. I'm tired. It's been a long, crazy day." She searched for the right words, to explain all the feelings and thoughts swarming in her head, but couldn't find them.

"It's okay, I understand. It's just that I …" Laughter from inside the shop interrupted their conversation. She gave him a questioning glance then they both turned to enter the shop.

Ella's voice boomed from the back room. They headed in that direction. The scene that Laura witnessed as she entered her workroom brought tears to her eyes.

She found Ella and Brooke with Mrs. Callaway and Mrs. Brenner. The table was covered with all the centerpieces that it could hold. All the ribbons, silk pieces and ornamental bells were in place. Laura would just need to add the fresh flowers in the morning. She was overwhelmed with gratitude, which rendered her speechless.

Jake, again, came to her rescue. "What do we have here? A room full of beautiful ladies, laughing and having a good 'ol time. Having a party without us, are you?"

Mrs. Callaway turned and her face lit up when she saw them. "Jake, honey, you're back. How is Sam? Laura, sweetheart, you look exhausted. Come. Sit." Mrs. Callaway went to Laura and took her by the arm and guided her to the closest chair.

"I don't know what to say. What are you all doing here? How did you accomplish all this? How did you even know what to do?" Laura's voice quivered slightly as she spoke.

"First things first, dear. Tell us about Sam. Jake, how is he?" Mrs. Callaway turned her attention to her son.

"He's gonna be fine. Dr. Mike knew right away it was poison on the steak he was eating. Ran some tests to confirm it and began treating it straight away. He started perking up soon after the doc treated him. Doc wanted to keep him overnight. Had to pry this one off him." He gestured towards Laura. "But by the time we left, he was almost back to his old self. The overnight was just a precaution. We can pick him up first thing tomorrow."

After a collective sigh of relief, Ella and Brooke, whose eyes had started to fill, hurried over to hug Laura. Then, to Laura's surprise, they both turned to hug Jake as well.

"Thanks so much, Jake. Mrs. Brenner told us the whole story. How you set off to look for Sam and ran back carrying him. You saved him. He would have died without you." Brooke was always the more talkative twin. Ella began to cry openly, which started Brooke crying, which caused Laura to cry, despite her best attempt to control her emotions.

Jake tried to add some levity to the situation. "That's right, you will be forever indebted to me, ladies, and I already know what I want for my first gratitude payment — for the three of you to join me at the July 4th picnic. I want you all sitting on a blanket with barbecue sauce all over your faces. And Sam too, he can lick you all clean!"

***

As night encroached upon the happy scene, he sat in the woods nearby watching. He looked for the dog but only saw crying and hugging which lead him to believe the dog was most likely dead. He didn't like to harm animals. He much preferred to harm people.

He needed to report back to the Elders, but didn't want to risk disturbing the silence in the woods by making the call. Plus, the cell phone service was spotty in this area. He would wait until he hiked back to his car. He knew the Grand Master was anxious for a report, but he would have to wait. He was enjoying watching. It was one of his favorite pastimes. People were so predictable, which made them easy targets. He liked watching almost as much as killing.

****

Once Jake had gotten his mom and Mrs. Brenner into the car and on their way, he returned to the house to check on Laura and the girls. It had been an exhausting day and he had trepidations about leaving the three of them alone tonight.

He had no doubt that Sam had been intentionally poisoned. He didn't belabor the point with Laura since she was upset enough. And he certainly didn't mention it in front of the girls. But this heinous act continued to gnaw at him. Who would want to hurt Sam? Was it the same person who left the threatening note at his house? What had he and Laura stumbled onto?

Jake admitted he encouraged Laura's interest in this initially because it was a chance to be close to her. Now he was afraid he may have put her in danger. That was the last thing he wanted. He had caused her enough pain. His goal in returning home was to right those wrongs, not add to them. But if Laura was the same person he knew years ago — and he bet money she was — she would be even more determined to solve this mystery.

He let himself into the house through the back door. The house was quiet, with no sign of the twins, so he assumed they had gone to bed. He found Laura sitting at the breakfast bar with a freshly opened bottle of Merlot and two glasses. The pot of coffee was long forgotten.

"I hope that second glass is for me." Jake smiled his easy smile and sauntered over to her. "Or are you expecting someone?"

"I hate to drink alone. I was hoping you'd join me?"

"How can I resist an offer like that?" Jake chortled. "I would have preferred, 'Jake don't leave me alone, stay, have wine with me, you big, gorgeous man.' But I'll settle for you hating to drink alone. What can I say, I'm desperate."

"I didn't mean it like that. I'm…forever grateful to you for saving Sam. I am. And right now I want you to stay. You're growing on me. But I don't want you to jump to any incorrect conclusions …"

Jake stepped towards her and put his finger to her lips to stop her from going on.

"Don't finish that sentence. Let's just have that glass of wine. We certainly earned it today, and let's not worry about all the other stuff. Deal?"

"Deal."

He reached for the bottle to pour them each a glass, all the while grinning mischievously.

"So, I'm growing on you? Really?"

"Jake!"

"Okay, okay I'll just pour the wine and behave like a proper guest. Just don't try to get me drunk and take advantage of me."

Laura rolled her eyes, "I'll try to control myself, I promise."

"Good, because I'm not that kind of guy."

He raised his glass, "To Laura…" *The love of my life, and the most beautiful woman I've ever known.* Several thoughts along this line came to him, but of course, he couldn't say them.

Instead, he continued with, "a fabulous mom and talented florist." They clinked glasses and slowly let the dry, fruity wine pass their lips and warm their tired souls.

Since they'd barely eaten all day, the second glass had them fondly reminiscing about the good old days. They remembered old friends and laughed about some of their escapades. It didn't take long to reach their third glass.

"How about that baseball game against the Bears? I had to sit out because of that damn knee injury."

"I know, I felt so responsible for that, considering how you injured it." Her laugh at the memory reached right up to her eyes, which met Jake's and their gaze held.

He was flooded with so many feelings for her. For too many years he had waited to touch her again. Today in the barn he couldn't wait any longer. He felt her respond. He sensed she wanted him as much as he wanted her. If only she would let herself go.

He reached his hand up to brush the hair from her eyes and slowly moved in for the kiss he had waited a lifetime for. It was worth the wait. Her lips were soft and moist and tasted of wine. She responded as he hoped she would, returning the kiss with a hunger he only imagined she possessed.

He stood and moved closer to her, enveloping her in his arms as they continued to kiss. She fell into him willingly, her body molding into his as if it were exactly where she belonged. Then he felt the shift. Her body stiffened and she slowly pulled away.

"Jake...I can't, I'm sorry."

He tried to gently pull her back into his embrace as he murmured into her hair.

"You can, Lars, it's right, you know it feels so right."

"But it's not right. I married Bill and had his children. You choose Gwen..." She pulled away from him physically and emotionally.

"I didn't choose Gwen. You need to know the whole story, Laura. I've waited sixteen years to tell you."

"I know the story, Jake. It started that night at the game when you were benched. I was in the bleachers with...Bill." They both paused. "And you left the game that night to be with Gwen. I thought you were jealous about me sitting with Bill and wanted to get back at me. I had no idea you two had been seeing each other."

"Laura, we weren't seeing each other...I tried to tell you that..."

"Jake, stop, it doesn't matter now. It was a long time ago and too much has happened."

"But Lars, you never knew the whole story about that night. Everything got so messed up. I had to go with Gwen and after that night you barely talked to me. All we did was fight. Then it seemed like you and Bill were together. I didn't know what to think."

"As I said, it was a long time ago, Jake. It doesn't matter anymore."

Just one look at the hurt in her eyes and he knew it did matter. He'd waited so long to be able to talk to her and explain everything. He had rehearsed it a million times, and now, after three glasses of wine, he was sure he'd screw it up. But he might not get another chance, so he just blurted it out.

"Laura, the baby wasn't mine."

She jerked her head towards him so fast her whole body shook and she almost spilled her wine.

"Jake, don't lie about that now. That just makes it worse."

"It's not a lie. Lars, I swear to you, I was never involved with her, in that way."

"What do you mean?" She looked so vulnerable, so confused. He wished that night after the game had never happened. How different their lives would have turned out.

"Lars…Gwen and I were friends, you knew that. Something happened to her that night, something terrible, and I was the only one she could confide in."

"I'll bet you were. Just stop, Jake. I don't want to go there. Just let it be." She got up and put her glass in the sink.

"No, Laura. I waited too many years to tell this story, please, let me tell it and you can throw me out when I'm done if that's what you choose. At least give me a chance."

She didn't respond, didn't even turn to him, just stood at the sink staring out the window. Finally, she turned. Her eyes no longer twinkled, her body now straight with purpose.

"I need to check on my daughters. It's been a long day. You should go." She turned to leave the room.

"Laura, please…don't leave things this way. I didn't imagine that kiss just now. I know you felt it too…" He walked towards her.

"Jake, I have two daughters who depend on me, solely on me. I don't have time to get involved with someone like you. I can't risk that again, being destroyed. I need to be strong for them. The past is the past. It's over, what's done is done. Let it be."

"I can't. Not until you know everything. Hear me out. If you decide to throw me out, I promise I'll leave willingly and never bother you or your daughters again."

She exhaled, and her body seemed to relax a bit, and her voice softened.

"I don't have the energy tonight, Jake…I just don't. I have a wedding to decorate for tomorrow and it's so late as it is. I'm exhausted. I can't go back there…can't go back all those years tonight. But I am grateful to you for saving Sam and thinking of the twins' safety today. I owe you for that. I promise I will let you tell your story, but not tonight."

Jake's heart lightened a bit. She wasn't completely refusing him. He felt hope and he would cling to that.

"Okay. I'll go for now. But I won't forget your promise." *I love you more than you can know, Lars.* "I'll just wait here until you check on the girls. Once you're sure they're safe, I'll go."

"That's not necessary. I'm sure they're fine."

"Humor me."

"Fine," she said with a sigh. "I'll be right back."

She left him standing in her kitchen. He may have lost this battle, but he would win the war. He was determined. He took this time alone to check that all the windows and doors on the first floor were locked. He didn't want to scare her, but he still felt uneasy about the events of the day.

"Okay. The girls are fine, I'm fine, and you are free to go." Her face had softened, the anger completely gone now.

"Promise me you'll lock the door behind me and call me at any time of the night if you see or hear anything suspicious."

"Jake, I've been on my own now for a while. I'll be fine."

"I'm just concerned with what happened to Sam today and the fact that he's not here tonight. A lot of odd things happened today, Laura, and I want you and the girls to be safe."

"I promise to lock the door and I'll call if the bogeyman scares me in the middle of the night." She smiled hesitantly, with tired eyes.

He returned the smile, trying to convey all he felt in a single glance. He wanted to embrace her again, to feel her in his arms one more time before he left, but he was certain that would just push her further away. He would wait. He had already waited this long.

He finally said, "Good night then. I'll call you in the morning."

"I'll be out early to prepare for the wedding, then I have to bring Sam home from the vet."

"I have a great idea. You'll be busy all day. Why don't I swing by here, pick up the girls and take them to the vet to get Sam?" He didn't think she'd be able to resist this plan. She would be busy all day and she didn't want Sam to stay at the vet a moment longer than he had to. Plus, the girls would be eager to bring Sam home as soon as possible. He watched her weighing all these points in her head.

"I hate to impose, you've already done so much…"

"Laura, I'd love to take the girls and bring Sam home…it would be the highlight of my day."

"Alright. I'll tell the girls you'll be here in the morning. Thanks…again."

"Don't mention it…you can be sure I'll collect it back in spades." He joked, the mood lightened from before.

"That's what I'm afraid of. Now go, before I collapse right here on the floor and you have to carry me to bed." She realized the double entendre of her words as soon as she spoke them.

Before he responded, she laughed and shook her head, "Go...now!"

"I'm going, I'm going. Good luck with the wedding tomorrow." *I love you.*

"Will he really be okay, Dr. Mike?" Ella looked at the vet with her big brown eyes.

"He'll be just fine. Just keep an eye on him in that yard."

"But how was he poisoned in our back yard?" Brooke looked at both Jake and the vet with a confused expression. The two men exchanged a furtive glance, neither sure how to tackle that question. Dr. Mike attempted first.

"Well, honey, all kinds of things are found in backyards. With you being so close to the woods, perhaps another animal found the poison from a neighbor's house and carried it to your yard where Sam found it. This was a common poison that many people around here use to kill mice and smaller rodents they don't want living in their homes. Sometimes our pets ingest it accidentally and they end up here with me. Sam was lucky and he'll make a full recovery."

"Dr. Mike is right, girls. Sam's gonna be right as rain as soon as we get him back home. I'm sure he wants out of here as quickly as possible. No offense, Doc." Jake smiled at the vet.

"None taken. Most of my patients are eager to leave." A knock on the exam room door interrupted the conversation, and Dr. Mike turned to open it. "Excuse me a moment." He stepped out of the room, leaving Jake and the twins alone with Sam.

"Well, he does look okay," said Ella. She turned to Brooke for her opinion.

"Yeah. Maybe just a little skinnier, but we'll fatten him up in no time." They both turned to Jake.

"I agree. Sam will be in good hands with you tending to him." Jake smiled reassuringly just as Dr. Mike returned with another, younger doctor in tow.

"Jake, girls, I'd like you to meet my son, Cal. He's doing his internship here with me this summer. He stayed with Sam last night and took good care of him, didn't you Cal?"

"You bet." Cal was a younger version of his father. Tall, tanned with thick blond hair and broad shoulders, probably in his mid-twenties. "Sam did great last night. No more vomiting, drank some water and rested comfortably. He was the perfect patient. Just keep an eye on him. Check that he continues to drink and eat normally. If you notice any vomiting, diarrhea or anything else that concerns you, call us immediately. We have a 24-hour emergency line." He smiled, somewhat flirtatiously, at both girls. Jake, for some reason, felt the need to play the role of protector. He stepped in between the young man and the girls and made eye contact with him.

"Thank you, Cal. We appreciate all your help and we'll call with any concerns. Are we free to go?"

"Dad, are they ready for discharge?" Cal addressed his father, who then joined the conversation.

"You're all set. And, as Cal said, call if you have any questions or concerns."

Dr. Mike lifted Sam off the exam table and set him gently on the floor, as Cal bent down to connect Sam's leash to his collar. Jake observed Laura's daughters' exchange admiring glances regarding the handsome young man. Cal, aware of the effect he had on young women, gave them both a flirtatious smile. Jake, fully aware of all the tricks, was appalled that this guy would use them on children.

Even though the girls looked much older than fifteen, they were still Laura's daughters and Jake felt his protective instincts kick in. Jake gave the guy a "back off buddy" look as he elbowed his way in to take Sam's leash from Cal's hand.

"I'll take over from here, Cal," he said in the sternest voice he could muster. "Let's go girls. Thanks again, Dr. Mike." He shook the older man's hand on his way out the door while turning to give Cal one more of his don't-mess-with-these-girls looks. He realized he was being a bit over-the-top, but instincts were instincts.

Once safely in the car and on the road, both girls couldn't stop giggling and comparing notes on the gorgeous doctor-to-be.

"Oh my god, El, was he too hot or what?"

"I know, right? He looks like Ian on *The Challenge.*"

"Oh my god, I know. Looks like we'll be going to the vet with Sam from now on."

Jake couldn't take anymore. "Girls, that guy's old enough to be your...your...older brother."

"Yeah, so?" They replied in unison.

"Yeah, so, I just think...I mean I'm sure your mom would think he's much too old for you and he's a flirt. You have to watch out for guys like that."

"How do you know, Jake? Were you a guy like that?" This from Brooke, as Ella looked to him for an answer.

"Let's just say, I knew... know a lot of guys like that and they're nothing but trouble. Trust me. Steer clear. I'm sure your mom would agree. You want to go for the nice guys."

"Are you a nice guy?" This time from Ella.

"Yeah, I'd like to think so."

"Then how come our mom didn't marry you after high school?" Brooke asked.

This was a tough one. How did he answer this without disrespecting their father or enraging their mother?

"Well, I guess you'd have to ask your mom that question. But your dad was a nice guy too, so she had a tough choice to make. And since your dad gave her the two of you, I'd have to say she made the right choice. Unless you two keep giving me a hard time. Then I'll have to make you both walk home." He gave a wink in the rearview mirror.

***

At the wedding reception hall, Laura had completed the finishing touches on the last centerpiece. She surveyed the room to inspect all her hard work. She made a few minor adjustments to some bows, straightened a few candles, and secured a couple of flowers before being completely satisfied that her work was done. The wedding planner would be meeting her here in a few minutes to give her approval. As soon as she received that, Laura was free to go.

As Laura stood in the beautifully decorated room, she was filled with a sense of sadness. Weddings were supposed to be happy occasions. But to her, after becoming a widow, they were filled with memories of loss. Lost loves, lost opportunities, lost innocence.

Bill was always so sure of everything. He had been sure they were meant to be together, sure that marriage was the best thing for both of them. She was never sure of anything after Jake. She had thought he was her one true love. Look how that turned out. But Bill was there for her. He was her pillar of strength. When she told Bill she was pregnant, he didn't run away or tell her to "take care of it." On the contrary, he was thrilled at the thought of being a father and insisted they marry immediately. Again, he convinced her it was the right thing and that they would live happily ever after. And they were happy, at first. His parents weren't thrilled about her pregnancy or the impending marriage, but neither were hers. She and Bill assured his parents he would still go to college. And he did. In fact, his life changed very little after marriage.

Meanwhile, she stayed home with the twins doing all the things that new mommies do. She loved her babies and loved being able to have that time with them.

Then one morning Bill complained of a headache. He said it was the worst headache he'd ever experienced. Laura urged him to take the day off and rest, but he insisted on going to work. She got the call after lunch. Bill was gone. The result of a ruptured brain aneurysm.

In an instant, her life was thrown into a foreign fog of chaos. Who should she call first? How would she tell the kids? What immediate arrangements had to be made for Bill's body — Bill's body, not Bill, never Bill again. The first several months were a blur. Laura did what was required of her. Found an undertaker. Planned a funeral. Wrote an obituary. Consoled her children. Family and friends were her lifeline immediately after. But then, life continued and people got back to theirs. Laura was left alone to figure out the rest of hers.

She now knew "happily ever after" didn't exist. Having a happy ending depends on where you stop the story. That's why fairy tales stop right after the wedding. Because after that, real life kicks in and real life isn't always happy.

She wasn't able to realize her dream of college. She gave up all hopes of ever being the famous journalist she had aspired to be growing up. And whenever memories of Jake tried to surface, she'd push them back to the deep recesses of her mind.

Now here she was, years later, with a successful business, her babies now teenagers, and Jake back in her life. He had her so dazed and confused. If only she could read his mind and gain a clear understanding of his intentions. How many women wished for that power since the beginning of time, she wondered?

He had managed to stir up feelings in her that were dormant for years. Too many years. Jake seem determined to tell her his story and she wasn't sure she could handle it. What was he talking about the last night? Saying the baby wasn't his. She wasn't sure she could go back all those years to that night, even though she promised him she would let him tell his story. That one night altered the course of her entire life and now he was telling her she had it all wrong.

Her ringing cell phone interrupted her thoughts. She answered, "Hello."

"Laura? It's Karen Wentworth." Karen was the new mayor of Newbury, having been elected in November after beating the incumbent mayor by a narrow margin. It was quite an upset for the long-time residents of the town. They blamed all the newcomers who, according to them, didn't understand the workings of a small town. Karen had her work cut out for her trying to deal with the good ol' boys club that refused to accept her. Laura liked her and had been one of the longtime residents who voted for her. She had fresh ideas and concrete plans for the town that Laura agreed with.

"Hi, Karen. How are you?"

"I'm well, thank you. Laura, I wanted to touch base with you regarding the July 4th parade and picnic this year. I know you handled flowers for the picnic last year. I wanted to personally tell you what a fabulous job you did and ask for your help again this year."

"Thanks, Karen. I'd love to help out again. What's the plan?"

"Well, I was wondering if you'd be available to meet with me and Susan Callaway to go over the plans? You know Susan, don't you? She is the glue that holds this whole picnic together."

"Yes. I know Susan, Mrs. Callaway, quite well. She does a great job every year. Just say when."

"I'm actually meeting with her this afternoon. I realize this is short notice, so if next week works better for you, we can set something up then."

"This afternoon should work for me. I'm just finishing up with a wedding now, then I need to check on my girls, but after that, I'll be free. What time were you thinking?"

"I'm meeting Susan at three o'clock. We have a list of things we need to discuss, so anytime between three and four o'clock would work."

"Why don't you count on me being there? I'll reach out if anything changes."

"That sounds great Laura. We'll see you then."

It was good to keep busy. At least that's what she kept telling herself. Her work for the wedding was now complete and she was heading home to check on things. This afternoon she would meet with the mayor and Mrs. Callaway to discuss the picnic. Keep busy. Keep your mind off Jake. This was good, very good.

She repeated this mantra in her head as she pulled into her driveway, only to find Jake's Jeep parked by the garage. How was she supposed to keep her mind off him if he kept popping up in her life? This was bad, very bad.

She pulled her car around the side of the house and parked by the backyard. A blur of fur ran by with a ball in his mouth. Sam! He was okay, thank goodness. Also in the yard were her daughters and Jake playing with Sam. Sam looked fully recovered and the girls looked relieved and happy. As soon as Sam registered Laura's presence, he ran to greet her.

"Hey, Sam. Welcome home, buddy." Laura hurried over, knelt and gave him a big hug to which he reciprocated with wet sloppy kisses all over her face.

"Hi, Mom. How'd the wedding go?" Ella yelled from her spot on the grass. She, Brooke and Jake were sitting on the grass with several of Sam's balls nearby. They obviously had been playing fetch with him and knowing Sam, he was loving all the attention. Laura stood and walked towards them with Sam at her heels.

"Great. Everything went as planned and the room looked lovely. How'd things go at the vet?" Laura sat, joining them all on the grass.

Both girls began to giggle and replied in unison, "Great. Really great." Ella added, "We'll take Sam to the vet with you any time, Mom."

Laura, confused, looked to Jake for an explanation.

"Well, Lars, it would seem that Dr. Mike has a son who has been interning with him."

"Yes. Calvin. I met him last time we went in for a check-up. So?" Laura threw a ball for Sam.

"Mom...So?! So he is sooooo hot. Why didn't you tell us?" Brooke said.

"Because he's twenty-something and way too old for you." Laura shot a look at Jake to determine if he was encouraging this. Before she could say anything to him, Ella interrupted.

"Ugh...you sound like Jake! 'He's old enough to be your older brother' blah, blah, blah."

"And he's a flirt," Laura added.

"Did he flirt with you?" This from all three of them.

"Don't sound so surprised. I'm not that old. You've heard of the term, cougar, right?" Laura teased, "Some guys go for older women now."

"Moooom!!!! Now you're just being gross." At that, both girls stood and started walking towards the house. "We'll leave you to your fantasy world," Ella yelled over her shoulder.

Laura turned to Jake. "You let that guy flirt with my daughters?"

"You let that guy flirt with you?" Jake sounded rather jealous. "It's not enough that I had to stare him down over flirting with those two, now I have to take him down over you?"

Laura rolled her eyes. "You're not 'taking anyone down.' Did you really give him a hard time about the girls?"

"Damn right I did. I'm aware of his type. Not someone your daughters need to be tangled up with, literally or figuratively. Or you, for that matter."

"Oh please, I'm old enough to be his…older sister. And I'm old enough to know better. I, too, am aware of the type." She shot a knowing glance toward Jake.

"I am not like that guy and you know it."

"Let's not go here again. It's a dead end." Sam retrieved the ball so she threw it again. "Hey, thanks for picking him up today. Any discharge instructions from Dr. Mike?"

"Dr. Mike and Romeo both said he'll be fine. Just watch for any vomiting or odd behavior. Call them with any concerns. The girls asked how Sam managed to consume poison in his backyard. Dr. Mike answered as best he could. But you and I need to talk about that, Lars. I hate to think that someone would do that deliberately, but that's what the evidence seems to suggest."

"What do you mean?" Sam returned with the ball, dropped it and Laura threw it again.

"Well, think about it. I found a hunk of meat with arsenic smeared all over it. How else would that land in your yard? Dr. Mike told the girls that the poison might have gotten into their yard by another animal transporting it from a neighbor's yard. But I think he was trying not to scare them because that doesn't make sense."

"Why not? It could have happened."

"First of all, you don't have any neighbors that close. Second of all, it's unlikely a mouse or rat could carry a piece of meat that size all the way here. And thirdly, if a bigger animal had gotten a hold of it, they would have eaten it, not left it for Sam."

"Well, there has to be some other explanation, Jake. Who would want to hurt Sam and why?"

Jake reached into his back pocket and pulled out a plastic bag containing a pair of scissors.

"Do you recognize these?"

"Yes. They're mine. They're the scissors I misplaced in my shop. Where'd you find them?"

"A few feet from where I found the poisoned meat. They were buried. When I went to retrieve the meat for Dr. Mike, I noticed a small patch of ground that looked…disturbed. I started digging and found the scissors. I showed them to Dr. Mike and he was able to confirm traces of arsenic on the blades."

# Sixteen

Laura looked at him in disbelief. Sam returned with the ball and dropped it again. "That's just crazy. There must be some explanation."

"I've been racking my brain trying to think of one Lars, but nothing's coming."

"Who would want to hurt Sam? He's the sweetest dog." She wrapped her arms around Sam and gave him a big squeeze.

"I don't know and I don't want to scare you, but I want you and the girls to be safe. I'm gonna see if I can have these scissors checked for prints. In the meantime, I want you to be alert. Keep your eyes and ears open. Take your cue from Sam, he's a good watchdog. If he's barking at something, don't assume it's nothing. Okay?"

Laura just stared ahead, trying to absorb what he was saying. She threw the ball for Sam again as she pondered this information. This just didn't make any sense. Was Jake trying to scare her? Was this a ploy to ease his way back into her life? She certainly hoped not, because that plan would backfire on him. She had to ask herself, how well did she know Jake now? After all, she hadn't seen him for years. What if city living had changed him? He left this town amid controversy and now he was back claiming that controversy was a lie. Maybe he was crazy.

"Laura...are you listening?"

She turned to look at him. He had such concern in his eyes. Could he be crazy? She had always gotten lost in his eyes. And as they say, they are the windows to the soul. What did she see in those eyes? In that soul?

"Lars…what are you thinking?" His voice was calm and soothing as if he had scared her and now he was trying to make her feel better. He reached for her hand to pat it reassuringly. He didn't look crazy. He didn't sound crazy. He seemed to be the same old Jake. The same Jake she once had loved more than anyone else on the planet.

"I'm sorry. I didn't mean to scare you. I just want you to be careful." He spoke in a gentle voice as he continued to caress her hand. She forced herself out of her reverie.

"I'm okay. This just doesn't make any sense. My life is very quiet and predictable. Then suddenly, a car crashes in front of my home, details are shrouded in mystery, you turn up after all these years, and my dog gets poisoned. It's a lot to digest."

"I know. I've been thinking about all that too. I think we should just forget about the accident. It's probably just an accident and nothing for us to be concerned about. Let's just go back to our normal, predictable lives. Except that I'd like to be involved in yours and I'd like you involved in mine. And before you can protest, just take some time to think about it. We could be friends. Go out to dinner from time to time. That's all I'm asking. I'm gonna leave now. But I want you to know you can call me if anything seems weird, okay? Just be alert for a while and then we'll try to get back to normal. How does that sound?"

"Well, at the moment, I have to get to a meeting with your mom and the mayor about July 4th, so I guess it'll have to be okay for now. Let me put Sam in the house, tell the girls I'm leaving, and I'll walk you out." She did just that while trying to decide what normal would look like now that Jake was back in town.

***

Jake had no intention of forgetting about the accident. But he was damn sure he didn't want Laura involved in it any longer. He would pursue his investigation solo. His instincts told him everything was related somehow. He didn't know how yet, but he would find out and, in the process, would make sure nothing else happened to Laura or her family.

He had taken the scissors over to the police station and asked Jimmy if he could pull some strings and have them checked for prints. Then he decided to head over to his office at the *Tribune*. He hadn't explored that angle yet. Maybe one of his colleagues knew something. He pulled into the lot and realized by the lack of cars that not too many people would be there on a Saturday. Probably better that way. The fewer people he got involved in this the better.

He made his way to his office making small talk with those he encountered on the way. Since he was considered a big-shot reporter from New York, he was accustomed to receiving various reactions from colleagues. Some people held him in high esteem and worshipped the ground he walked on. Others were suspicious of anyone who would make it big in the industry, win prestigious awards, then chuck it all and move back to small-town America to work for the local rag.

His least favorite reaction was from the occasional jerk who was insanely insecure so, therefore, was jealous of Jake's success. Usually, this person would go out of his way in an attempt to sabotage Jake's work and try to make him look foolish. Here, at the *Newbury Tribune*, that jerk was named Pete Hartford.

Unfortunately for Jake, Pete was in charge of local news, including accidents and any resultant fatalities. Jake was hoping on a Saturday to encounter Pete's assistant, Julie, who fell into the category of worshiping the ground he walked on and who would be much more helpful than her boss. But today was not Jake's lucky day, because as he rounded the corner to his workspace, he encountered Pete's scowling face instead of Julie's awestruck one.

"Hey, Pete." Jake gave a casual wave as he walked into his cubicle.

"To what do we owe the honor, and on a Saturday too," Pete replied. Jake let this comment hang out there for a few minutes while he contemplated his game plan. Finally, he headed over to Pete's desk.

Jake pretended to be annoyed. "I've been out of this town for how many years now? I come back and it's like nothing ever changed. Everybody gets so worked up over this July 4th picnic and parade and now my mom is dragging me into this. It's like I'm sixteen all over again."

Pete took the bait. "It's ridiculous. They block off all the main roads for that damn thing. Causes traffic jams all over town and nobody can get where they're going. Stupid tradition."

Just the response Jake was hoping for. He assumed Pete wasn't a big picnic and parade man.

"Now my Mom has me running all over town checking out parade routes as if I care where the damn parade goes."

Pete chimed in, "I thought it went the same place every year. In fact, I count on it using the same roads so I can take my alternate route. Now, what are you telling me?"

"Yeah, I know, it's a pain in the ass. According to Mom, the number of motor vehicle accidents has increased around here lately, with all the new construction and new residents who aren't used to these roads, not to mention the deer population that's gotten out of control. Some of the roads are in desperate need of repair. The consensus is that crumbling road shoulders and damaged or missing guard rails, are conditions that would make certain roads unsafe for the parade. Anyway, she has me looking into recent accidents that might have damaged a road, maybe made it unsafe, that sort of thing. Hey, I just had a thought. Your team covers the local accidents around here, right?"

"Yeah. So."

"So, maybe we can help each other out. You could make my life easier by giving me easy access to the accident report files and I can fill you in on possible changes to the route. Even consider your input so if they have to change it, it won't be too much of an inconvenience for you. What do you think?"

He could see the wheels turning in Pete's head. Jake added, "Of course, I can just go through the old accident reports the hard way. Just thought we could help each other out." Jake wanted the reporters' notes and anything told off the record. He could get that only from Pete. Jake could see Pete thinking this over, probably wondering if it was worth helping a guy he disdained in exchange for information that would make his life easier.

"Yeah. I guess that would work. It's no sweat off my balls to hand over the files. But you better hold up to your end."

"You know it man, no problem." Jake waited for the coveted information. Pete gave him the stare-down as if to say, "you better not screw me on this." Finally, he opened his desk drawer and pulled out a set of keys, which he threw to Jake.

"It's the one labeled 'Julie.' Everything's in her cabinet over in her cubicle."

"Thanks, man. I'll reach back out as soon as I know anything on the route."

"You better."

Jake turned to leave as he searched for the needed key, then headed over to Julie's area. He changed his mind and decided to hit the soda machine first. It might take him a while to search through everything and find what he needed, especially since the *Tribune* was still in the dark ages and kept hard copies rather than digital files. Plus, he'd have to make notes about possible road problems in case Pete wandered over to check on his progress. He would need some help to keep him going through the next few hours. Thank goodness for caffeine

***

The Grand Master stood before the cross in his private quarters as he began preparations for the ceremony that would take place in a few weeks. He reflected on all he had achieved to attain the position of Grand Master of the Brethren. He always had handled any problems that arose with efficiency and expediency. The community he was in charge of here was a theocratic model for other sects around the country. His hard work and dedication insured this. His sect managed to survive and thrive in their secluded commune, hidden from the rest of the world and sheltered from its sins and impurities. Soon sects like his would outnumber the sinners and the theocratic state would become the model for the country. Government by divine guidance and a legal system based on religious law was the ultimate goal. This was always the plan and it was a long time coming. Finally, they were making progress.

Of course, certain members were required to live outside the commune and interact with outsiders. This insured that necessities were delivered, such as food they couldn't grow or raise in the commune, supplies, financial donations from wealthy philanthropists who shared their vision, and, most importantly, new members — especially those of child-bearing age who were needed to grow their population.

His patience was tested lately with members disobeying his commands. The Enforcer, the member who would handle problems that threatened to expose the existence of the commune to outsiders, was taking matters into his own hands and disobeying direct orders. The Chosen One, the one they entrusted to bring the young women to the commune, was also getting out of control.

He knelt before the cross and recited the prayers he knew by heart. Then he prayed for strength and guidance to continue the work before him.

he knelt before the cross and recited the prayers before him by heart. Then he prayed for strength and guidance to continue the work before him.

# Seventeen

Rain pummeled the windows as the earth seemed to shake violently from the roaring thunder. Lightning struck dangerously close as Laura watched through the windows of her flower shop. She knew rain was desperately needed, but the storm left her unsettled.

It was only the end of June, but the heat wave hit hard and held the town in its hot, steamy grip. Hopefully, this morning's storm would provide some relief.

The last few weeks had flown by in a blur. It was the busiest time of the year for her business. Once school ended, life was thrust into fast-forward. Preparations were made for the twins' annual summer trip to their grandparents' house in New England. Laura had to drive halfway to meet Bill's parents for the switch. She felt bad only seeing them for a quick meal at a diner and then handing over her daughters, but it was difficult for her to leave work this time of the year. She eased her guilt by committing to spend more time with them over the winter holidays. Always a bittersweet moment leaving the girls, she would miss them terribly, but would also enjoy her time alone.

Today was her first full day without them, always the toughest, so she busied herself with work. Now, watching the raging storm, she silently prayed power would remain on. The sound of sirens interrupted her prayers. She wondered if lightning struck something and ignited a fire. Would Jake be called to help?

She had been so busy the last couple of weeks she barely had time to see or think of Jake or anything related to him or the accident. She was caught off guard by the uneasy feeling in the pit of her stomach when she thought of Jake actually fighting a fire and putting himself in danger. She was so deep in thought that the ringing phone made her jump.

"Hello. Fleurs Du Jour. This is Laura."

"Hello, Laura. It's Susan Callaway."

"Hi, Mrs. Callaway. What can I do for you?"

"Well, honey I know how busy you are this time of year, especially with the work you're doing for the picnic, but I'm going to impose on you again with another request."

"You couldn't possibly impose. I appreciate all the business, honestly. And I'm thrilled to be a part of the picnic. So what do you need?"

"You're too sweet, dear. Here's what I need. I realize it's short notice so please decline if you can't do it. I will completely understand. My mother's coming up from Florida for the picnic. She arrives today. You remember Jake's grandmother, Elyse, don't you?"

"Of course. She was dear friends with my grandmother. I always thought of her as my surrogate Granny!"

"That's right, I'd forgotten you two were so close. It's been so many years now and Mom's been in Florida for so long that I almost forgot she used to be your grandmother's neighbor. You and Jake spent so many summers going back and forth between the two, remember?"

How could she forget? They were some of the best summers of her life. "Yes. I remember. I'll have to make it a point to say hello while she's here."

"Well, that's partly why I'm calling. I'm having a welcome-home dinner for her tonight and you know how much she loves fresh flowers. I was wondering if there was any way you could put together a few arrangements for me? I'd like one for her room, one for the kitchen and maybe one for the foyer. I thought it would make a nice welcome for her."

"Of course. I'd love to. Would you like me to deliver them?"

"Actually, I'd love for you to deliver them and then join us for dinner. Mom will be so thrilled to see you again. Please say yes, Laura. Jake will be here."

How could she say no? She didn't have any plans or responsibilities since her daughters were with their grandparents. "I'd love to. Thanks so much for thinking of me, Mrs. Callaway."

"Oh, I'm so thrilled! We'll see you tonight then, say around five o'clock? And I trust your judgment on the flowers. Whatever you think is best will be perfect."

"Sounds good. I'll see you tonight at five."

"Bye, dear."

Five o'clock arrived quickly and before she knew it, Laura was pulling into the Callaway's driveway with three beautiful floral arrangements and two bouquets, one for the hostess and one for the guest of honor.

The traditional two-story colonial had a brick front with black shutters, a two-car garage, mature landscaping and the requisite basketball hoop in the wrap-around driveway. She had always loved this house growing up. It was the kind of house used in feel-good movies, where the family gathered around for the holidays and mom and dad made everyone feel loved and welcomed.

She checked her reflection in the rearview mirror before exiting the car. She was sporting a nice tan from working in her gardens. This made her loose hair look blonder and gave the color of her eyes an added pop. She wore a simple white cotton sundress, which showed enough of her tanned skin to entice, but not enough to offend. She completed the look with white strappy sandals and diamond studs on her ears. Simple, yet sophisticated.

She grabbed the bouquets first and walked to the door. She noticed Jake's Jeep was nowhere in sight. Her heart sunk, thinking perhaps he wasn't coming. Come to think of it, she hadn't talked to him in awhile. Maybe he'd lost interest in her and moved on. It wouldn't be the first time. She found herself becoming annoyed; then realized, if she was honest with herself, she couldn't blame him for losing interest this time. She hadn't exactly given him much encouragement.

A crack of thunder in the distance had her ringing the bell quickly. She didn't want to carry the remaining flowers in a storm. The day had been filled with one violent storm after another. She was greeted by Mr. Callaway's big grin and even bigger embrace.

"Laura, honey. So good to see you. For me?" He took the flowers from her with a wink.

"One for the host and hostess, one for the lovely guest of honor." She returned the hug and then turned to retrieve the remaining arrangements. "There's more in the car. I'll be right back."

"Let me put these down and I'll help you."

They managed to get everything inside before the storm hit. Greetings were exchanged, and hugs and kisses given all around. Jake's brother, Rick, his wife, Kelly, and their two children were playing a board game on the floor. Rick also was a firefighter and ran his own computer repair business in town. Kelly was a stay-at-home mom. Jake's sister Addison, and her friend, Seth, were seated on the couch enjoying a glass of wine. Addi was a forensic psychologist and adjunct professor at a university in the city. Seth was her boyfriend de jour, whom Laura had not met before. Although Jake's parents and brother all lived in town, Laura's path rarely crossed with any of them, so it was like a family reunion for her. Laura and

Addi had been friends for years, but life got busy and they rarely had time to get together. She had grown up with this family and, being an only child herself, considered Rick and Addi like siblings. She hadn't realized how much she missed seeing them. The last time they were all together was at Bill's funeral, and there wasn't much time for catching up.

The inside of the Callaway house was as traditional and welcoming as the outside. Everyone gathered around the family room, which had a comfortable sitting area with couches and overstuffed chairs. The room centered around a stone fireplace with a television mounted above, flanked by built-in bookcases. The kitchen was off to the left, which led into the formal dining room.

An hour passed quickly as Laura got reacquainted with Jake's family, wine was poured, appetizers were served, and stories were told. Granny Callaway looked great for eighty years old and her mind was sharper than Laura's. The only thing missing from this picture was Jake. Laura couldn't stop the sinking feeling in her stomach, and she worried he wasn't coming. She just hoped her being here wasn't awkward if he didn't show.

Mrs. Callaway must have sensed Laura's concerns. "Laura, I'm sure you're wondering where Jake is. Don't worry, he'll be here soon. He was overwhelmed today with all the storms. There were several accidents, downed wires and a few fires. Joe wanted to help out, but Jake wouldn't hear of it. He said they had it all under control. So I'm sure he's on his way."

Laura felt guilty for thinking Jake's absence was personal. Here he was out fighting fires and saving the town and she was thinking it was all about her. The look on Mrs. Callaway's face had her concerned. Her words were comforting, but her expression showed worry. Laura guessed it had to do with having a husband who had put his life in danger for years and then having a son doing the same thing. Now Laura was worried too.

"Jake knows what he's doing," added Mr. Callaway. "He was trained by the best. He'll be here as soon as he can. Now, who needs more wine?" Joe Callaway tried to lighten the mood, well aware of his wife's concern and now Laura's. With that comment, the front door opened and in walked Jake. Much relief and fanfare followed. It did not go unnoticed how good he looked in his jeans and a simple black tee shirt with just-showered hair. Laura had forgotten how Jake could brighten a room. He was the golden boy of his family, which made the incident of that long-ago summer even more distressing for all involved. But his family stood by him and welcomed him home then as now, with open arms, hugs and kisses.

"Uncle Jake!" Taylor, his six-year-old niece, and Ryan, his eight-year-old nephew, ran toward Jake. He scooped them up together as if they were little sacks of potatoes.

"How are my two favorite Koala bears?" He planted a kiss on top of both heads, then gingerly set them down. "Where is she? Where's my favorite girl?" He spotted his grandmother across the room on the couch. With his signature stride and famous grin made his way to her and enveloped her in his bear hug embrace.

"Oh Jake, honey. I've missed you. You look good, but a little too thin. You're not eating right on your own. You need someone to take care of you." She shot a surreptitious glance at Laura as she returned Jake's hug.

Jake didn't respond to this but made his rounds through the room. A big hug and kiss for Mom. Handshake and hug for Dad. Handshakes, hugs and kisses for Rick, Kelly, Addi and Seth. Then he came to Laura. Suddenly, the confident man who had been in total control of his familiar surroundings, seem befuddled as to what to do. Laura, who was overwhelmed by feelings of relief that he was safe, combined with a warm fuzzy feeling for this family after witnessing the scene that had just played out, took control of the situation. She stood and embraced Jake in a bear hug and planted a kiss on his cheek.

"Jake, we're so glad you're here. I heard you had a rough day. We're glad you're safe."

"Hey, Lars. You look…incredible." He eyed her up and down. "Thanks for coming."

"How could I not?" For a split second, the rest of the world melted away. It was just Laura and Jake and the sparks they were emitting. Suddenly Laura became aware of the presence of the rest of the family, who were watching them with avid interest.

Laura brought Jake up to speed on the evening, "I haven't seen some members of your family in years. It's been great catching up with everyone. And how could I turn down a chance to visit with my surrogate Granny?" Laura broke her gaze with Jake and turned to look at the family, settling on Jake's grandmother, who beamed from ear to ear at the sight of them together.

"Laura, honey, it's been too long. If I wasn't so happy to see you, I'd give both of you a piece of my mind. You for not visiting me, and you, Jake, for not seeing to it that she did." Granny did her best to sound mildly annoyed, but it was clear she was bursting with joy.

The evening was the most fun Laura had in some time. The food was delicious, but it was the camaraderie of this family that made the night. They welcomed and accepted her as they had years ago. Laura realized how much she missed being part of this clan.

After all the food had been served, eaten, and the cleaned up completed, the women had gathered to chat. Granny Elyse pulled Laura aside.

"You belong here dear. You always have. You know it, Jake knows it, we all know it. Now let's get on with it."

"I wish it were that simple." Laura patted Granny's hand.

"What's not simple about it?"

"So much...I have children, for one. And a lot has happened over the years..."

"Nonsense young lady. Take it from me. Life is hard and filled with obstacles. But life is also short. If you find a person who makes you happy, you make it work. You do whatever you need to make it work. Don't waste precious time, my dear."

The rumbling thunder grew louder and the lightning closer as the rain, once again, beat down against the house. The power dimmed and threatened to quit several times, before finally giving out. Everyone scrambled for candles and flashlights. Taylor, who was afraid of the dark, began to cry. Meanwhile, Ryan, being her older and braver brother, began to tease her.

"You're such a baby Taylor. I can't believe you're still afraid of the dark. Baby, baby, baby!"

"Ryan. Stop teasing your sister this instant," his mother scolded.

Jake, after lighting several candles, came to Taylor's rescue.

"Come here, honey." He picked her up and sat her on his lap as she buried her face in his chest and cried. He patted her back soothingly.

"You know it's okay to be afraid, Tay. Everybody's afraid of something. You just have to figure out a way to conquer it. Take Grandpop and me, for instance. We don't like fire. It scares us. But we chose a long time ago to learn about fire and learn how to stop it, so we don't feel so afraid of it anymore. But it still scares us and that's okay because we know it scares us and we know what to do about it when it does. Most fears are like that. You can't run away from them. Sometimes you just have to face them. You may be scared and you may cry, but that's okay. And you know what? It helps to face them with somebody by your side to help you. You're with me now, and you're safe." He held her tight and her sobs began to subside.

"Sometimes you just need a safe place to fall, honey." He was speaking to Taylor, but his eyes met Laura's. Her body felt comfortably warm all over, and she knew it wasn't because of the wine. Seeing him with his family, watching him comfort his niece, awakened feelings she had tried so hard to keep dormant. She was treading on dangerous ground, leaving herself vulnerable to so many of her fears.

The storm raged on. As the night grew late, the party began to break up and Laura realized she too should be getting home. She said her goodbyes and promised not to stay away so long again. She searched for Jake and spotted him leaving the study with his father.

"Well, we've just got a call that this storm is playing havoc with the roads. More downed trees and wires, and roads completely washed out. I'm worried about everyone getting home tonight." Jake's dad addressed the group. "Rick, you've got the SUV and you don't live too far, so you should be okay. Addi, hon, appreciate it if you'd stay the night. You too, Seth. We've got plenty of room and all the roads you need to take are a mess. Laura, that van of yours just isn't good in this kind of weather. You'll be hydroplaning all over the place. You're welcome to stay as well, but I know you have Sam to care for at home. I'd feel safer if you let Jake take you home in his four-wheel-drive Jeep. It'll handle the road conditions better than your van."

Since Joe Callaway was not one to argue with, everybody agreed to his suggestions, except Laura. She began to hesitate, mumbling about not wanting to inconvenience anyone until Granny stepped in.

"Jake Callaway, you will see to it that this lovely young lady gets home safely and that's an order."

There was no arguing with Granny.

"Yes, ma'am. Laura, looks like I'm your chauffeur for the evening. Shall we, my lady?" He offered his arm to Laura in a gallant gesture.

Since left with little choice, she hooked her arm in his and let him lead her out to his Jeep. As they walked out the door, he turned to give a wink to Granny, whom he loved more than ever at this particular moment.

# Eighteen

The trip to Laura's house indeed was treacherous and she was glad she let Jake drive her. Their arrival was met with total darkness, a sign that Laura's house had lost power. Jake used a flashlight from his Jeep to guide them into the house and to help Laura find and light candles. Laura let Sam out, checked that the generator was working for the flower shop, and silenced the beeping alarm. She returned to see Jake sitting on her couch surrounded by candles he had lit.

"You don't need to stay, Jake. I'll be fine. Sam and I will just head to bed. I'm sure by the time I wake up the storm will be over and the power restored."

"You're going to make me drive home in this weather? After I gallantly escorted you to safety? What will Granny think?" He smiled mischievously and when she didn't reply he continued. "How about a short rest then, until the rain lets up a bit?"

"All right. Can I get you something then? Coffee, wine?"

"Do you have any brandy? A shot would be perfect on a night like tonight."

"I do as a matter of fact. I'll get some and be right back."

He rose with her and she left him standing by the fireplace. He called out, "Do you mind if I start the fire? It'll take the dampness right out of here."

"No. Go for it."

She returned with two snifters of brandy just as he got the fire started.

Laura handed a glass to him, "Here you go. It's fine French Cognac that someone had given me at Christmas one year. I never opened it till now." They each took a sip.

"Very smooth. Warms the whole body. Just what I needed, Lars. Thanks."

They sat on the couch in silence for a while, listening to the rain, and sipping their Cognac. Laura was the first to break the silence.

"I had a great time tonight. Your family is wonderful. I'd forgotten how much I enjoyed being at your house when we were younger. They're such warm, accepting people. You're very lucky to have them, Jake."

"I know. They're the best. They've always been there for me. They put up with me when all I did was complain about this town and how I couldn't wait to get the hell out of here. Then they welcomed me back with open arms when I couldn't wait to return. It broke my heart to see them suffer over the pain I put them through the summer of…well you know…that summer."

"It was really hard on them. I remember everyone thinking the worst of you, but they defended you to everyone and stood by you. They truly love you."

"I never wanted to hurt them…or anyone. I desperately wanted to tell them the truth, but I couldn't then. I finally told them the truth about what happened. It was such a relief. It righted so many wrongs for all of us. But not for you. I still couldn't tell you everything. You were married and had your own life. But now…it's time Lars. It's time I tell you the truth about that summer."

She didn't protest, didn't reply at all. She just looked deeply into his eyes. He must have taken this as her way of agreeing to let him go on, so he did.

"That was a crazy year. It was our last year of high school, we were all graduating and going off to college, work, or the military. It was frightening and exciting at the same time. Gwen was my friend, and that's all she was to me, Laura, nothing more. But that night… it was the last playoff game of the season, remember?"

Laura nodded, so he continued.

"I was pissed off because I couldn't play due to my injury and, to make matters worse, you were in the bleachers with Bill." Her body stiffened slightly at the memory. "That pissed me off even more. We both knew he was waiting for his chance to make a move for you. When he climbed the bleachers and sat next to you, it just pushed me over the edge.

"We were losing pretty badly to boot and my frustration continued to grow, so I just walked off the field. I just kept walking. I had to distance myself from the game, from you and Bill, from everything. That's when I spotted Gwen.

"She was limping, like she was hurt. I called out to her, but she didn't respond, so I ran to catch her, sensing something wasn't right. When I caught up to her, it was obvious she was crying. And when I reached out for her arm she jumped like a scared kitten. Lars, she was a mess. She was bleeding and crying and her face was bruised. I couldn't comprehend it at the time, couldn't wrap my brain around it. She just stared at me, bewildered, and then she seemed to recognize me and broke down crying. I kept asking her what happened, but she wouldn't answer so I just held her.

"We stood on the street, me holding her and her just sobbing and sobbing. I finally convinced her to let me walk her home. I kept asking her what happened, who had hurt her. She wouldn't talk, just kept crying.

"When we got to her house, no one was home. So I took her up to her room and helped her into bed. I sat with her for a long time. She finally told me what happened. Someone had raped her, Lars.

Raped and beat her. Right here in our town. I couldn't believe it. In our little safe, happy town.

"I wanted her to call the police, but she wouldn't. She made me swear I wouldn't tell anyone, not even her parents. She didn't want anyone to know. I was out of my comfort zone, with no clue what to do. Looking back now, of course, I should have told her parents. She needed more help than I could offer. But at the time, I didn't know...I just didn't know what to do. So I promised her I wouldn't tell anyone.

"When I left her house it was the middle of the night, but Mike and Matt Carson were having a party at their house across the street with the usual crew. They saw me leave and, of course, assumed she and I had hooked up. In their minds, why else would I be there? I just wanted to protect her. You should have seen her, Lars, so bruised and scared. I wanted to protect her, so I didn't deny the rumors.

"After that night Gwen was never the same. Since I was the only one who knew, we started spending a lot of time together. I tried to convince her to tell her parents, the police, a doctor, anyone. But she wouldn't.

"She managed to cover the bruises with makeup and no one suspected a thing. She just wanted to forget about it and move on, so I agreed to help her, to keep her secret. A couple of months later, she realized she was pregnant. I believe that's where you come into the story.

"You and I had been fighting a lot since that night. The rumor that I'd slept with Gwen found its way to you, and you didn't completely believe me when I denied it. It didn't help that I was spending so much time with her, but I couldn't abandon her with everything that had happened.

"She swore me to secrecy so I couldn't tell you the truth. You knew I was keeping something from you...we had known each other too long to be able to keep something from one another. You knew something was up and assumed I was sneaking around with Gwen. At the same time, Bill was moving in on you. He was giving you what I couldn't at the time. I hated it. Hated the whole situation. I felt trapped."

Laura's eyes were filled with tears. "Why didn't you tell me the truth then, I would have understood."

Jake shook his head, "It sounds so simple now, but it wasn't then. When Gwen found out she was pregnant, it got even more complicated. She didn't want the baby. She wanted to abort the pregnancy and the whole awful experience with it, or so she hoped.

"I supported her decision. She was adamant that was what she wanted, so I took her to the clinic. You know the rest. There were complications, she had to be rushed to the hospital, and her parents were called. Next thing we knew rumors were flying that Gwen had been pregnant, had an abortion, and that I was the dad.

"You refused to talk to me, my parents were crushed, Gwen's parents hated me. By then, you and Bill were practically a couple. I just wanted to get the hell out of this town. Summer ended and I packed up as fast as I could, left for college, and never thought I'd come back.

"But I never stopped loving you. After college, I settled in New York and tried to build a life. But, every girl I dated, wasn't you. I replayed our life before that night over and over and wanted it back. But you were married with a family, so I threw myself into my work, my career. I thought, I hoped, over time I'd forget about you. But I didn't.

"Then my mom called with the news about Bill's death. I wondered if I was being given a second chance with you. It may be wrong to admit that, but it's true. I tried to think of ways to reenter your life, but every plan I came up with fell short when I realized the reality of the situation. You were a young widow with two babies whose father just died. The timing didn't seem right. I want to be honest about everything now. No more secrets."

The tears spilled over and ran down her cheeks. "I thought you didn't love me anymore...that you wanted to be with Gwen. You had changed so much and I thought it was because you didn't want me. If only I'd known...but...no..." She wiped the tears off her face. "No. I believe things work out the way they're supposed to sometimes. If I'd never met Bill I wouldn't have my girls. It all worked out the way it was supposed to, Jake."

"I love you, Laura. I'm damn crazy about you, always have been, always will be. I just want a chance to start over with you. I want to be a part of your life, a part of your daughters' lives."

The light from the fire and flickering candles gave a soft glow to the room. When she didn't respond, he leaned in and, gently taking her face in his hands, kissed her softly, sweetly, longingly. This time, she kissed him back without reservations.

The ground shook beneath them as the thunder pounded along with their hearts. The rain continued to come fast and furiously as blood pumped through their bodies in equal measure. His kisses became more aggressive as the wind whipped the rain into the side of the house, pounding it against the glass window panes.

"Laura. I've waited for you forever, for this moment. I want it to be right, for you. If you don't want this, tell me now."

She could barely speak, her throat dry as the rain flooded the world around her. "I want this. I want you."

# Nineteen

At some point during night, the fire died. They had covered themselves with the blanket, but it wasn't enough once the heat from the fire was gone. The chill from the damp air awakened her.

At first, she was disoriented. Was this a dream? Was she really lying on her floor with Jake, having just had the most amazing night of her life? She thought about pinching herself to be sure, but was startled into reality by the sound of his voice.

"Good morning."

Laura turned to look at him, "It's still dark out, how do you know it's morning?"

"Because technically it was morning before you fell asleep."

"How long have I been sleeping?"

"About an hour. I've been laying here watching you sleep."

Laura groaned, "Great. Did I snore, slobber, make any embarrassing noises?

"A few." He laughed at her mortified expression. "I'm kidding. No snoring, no slobbering, no embarrassing noises. Although you moaned a few times and called out my name."

"Before or after I fell asleep?"

"Both."

She grabbed the throw pillow that had fallen from the couch and threw it at him.

"You were doing some moaning and name-calling yourself," she joked.

"I'm sure I was. You're incredible, Lars, you know that? That was just incredible."

"You're not so bad yourself." Laura cuddled into the warmth of Jakes body and they both drifted off to sleep.

The next time she woke, it was to sunlight and the sound of Jake peacefully sleeping beside her. She slowly slid out from under the blanket, gathered her clothing from the night before and took the liberty of throwing Jake's tee shirt on. She made her way to the kitchen, realized that power had been restored, and started a pot of coffee before hopping in the shower.

As she stood in the shower, hot water cascading over her body, she couldn't stop thinking about the night before. She was startled by the sound of the shower door opening.

"Hey. Want some company?" Jake stood before her, with messy hair and a sleepy grin.

"Only if you plan on washing my back."

"I'll do more than that."

"Then hop in."

***

Wearing only his jeans, Jake poured them each a cup of coffee. Laura, wearing yoga pants and a tee shirt, flipped the pancakes she was making on the griddle

"I feel selfish keeping you here so long. Won't they be looking for you to help with all the disastrous road conditions caused by the storm?"

"Nope," Jake answered. "There's a limit to how many hours we can work. I reached mine last night before heading to my parents. I'm not on again till tonight."

"Lucky for me."

"Besides if anyone needed me, my cell would be ringing." With that comment, his cell began to ring. "Told ya." He answered, "Hello, this is Jake."

Laura continued with the pancakes as she listened to Jake's one-sided conversation.

"Hey, Jimmy. How'd you make out?" Jake listened intently for several minutes. "Really? Okay... That's odd. No, nothing like that, just curiosity. Hey, Jim, thanks, man. I appreciate it. And do me a favor? I'd appreciate it if you didn't mention this to anyone. Thanks a lot. I owe you a beer."

Jake ended the call and returned to the coffee. Laura looked at him curiously, but he didn't volunteer any information. Finally, her curiosity got the best of her.

"Are you gonna tell me what was that about?" she asked.

"Nothing. Just a favor I asked Jimmy to do for me. No big deal."

The pensive, concerned look on his face told Laura he wasn't being truthful. She challenged him, "I thought you said last night no more secrets. Remember?"

"I remember. It's just that...I don't want to ruin this," Jake made a circular motion with his arms. "The incredible night, the shower, now breakfast. I don't want to bring up stuff that will kill the mood, bring us crashing back to reality."

"It's too late. I can tell by your face that something is bothering you and by not telling me you'll ruin this." She mimicked his circular arm gesture.

"You're right. But can we eat first and talk later?" He walked behind her as she turned to flip the pancakes, put his arms around her and kissed the back of her neck. "I'm not ready for reality yet."

"Okay. But you promise you'll talk after we eat?"

"Promise."

"Because I have ways to make you talk." She turned to face him, leaned into his embrace and kissed him. She felt him respond immediately. "Whoa…slow down. Pancakes first." She slipped out from his embrace and removed the pancakes from the griddle to their plates.

"Alright, alright. Pancakes first. But you might have to use extreme measures to extract information out of me later," he said with a grin.

"One thing at a time. Now eat."

***

Jimmy hung up the phone. It's too late for that, Jake, he thought. He already had reported the fingerprint request to his boss. He had no choice. He knew he was being watched, possibly bugged as well.

This wasn't what he signed up for when he joined the force and he resented the position he found himself in. That's why he decided to pass the true information he'd found onto Jake, rather than the bullshit story the chief wanted him to relay. Maybe his old buddy would be his ticket out of this mess. He decided he'd use a burner phone just in case his cell and home phone were bugged.

He just hoped Jake knew what he was getting himself into. He had to believe his friend, who'd made it big in the city, would know what he was doing.

He liked Jake and he'd hate for anything bad to happen to him. But Jimmy was out of his league on this one and he worried Jake may be too. That's probably why he'd been drinking so much. Too much pressure. And his buddy Jack Daniels was good at helping him deal with it.

He casually glanced around the parking lot. He had to go clear across town to buy the burner to insure he wouldn't be seen by anyone he knew. Plus, he had to check that he hadn't been followed. Yeah, definitely too much pressure lately.

He spied what looked like a nice bar at the end of the shopping center. Time to visit Mr. Jack Daniels.

***

"Okay. Now talk, mister." Laura began clearing the table and washing the dishes from breakfast. Jake rose to help her.

"What about your tactics for making me talk? I can be very stubborn and determined."

"Yeah, I remember. Now talk. I have a feeling it has to do with the accident. We haven't discussed it lately with everything else going on."

"Clever girl. You're right. Sort of."

"Sort of?" Laura continued to wash the dishes and griddle while Jake dried.

"I believe it's indirectly connected to the accident. Remember when Sam ate the poison?"

"How could I forget?"

"Remember when I went back to the yard to collect the meat for Dr. Mike and I found your scissors not far from the scene?"

"Yeah..." Laura stopped washing and looked questioningly at Jake. "And..."

"Well, I took the scissors to Jimmy to have them tested for prints. I figured it was a long shot, but apparently whoever took your scissors wasn't as smart as I gave him credit for. Jimmy not only found prints all over them, but he was able to match them with a name in the system. They matched a guy by the name of Phil Molino. Jimmy did some research into the guy. He has a record. Some small-time burglary. A statutory rape a while back. Then, apparently, he found God."

"Excuse me?"

"He found God. He was serving time for the rape when along comes some religious guy who hires an attorney for Molino. The attorney manages to reduce his sentence. Next thing you know, Phil becomes part of this religious sect and turns his life around, or at least so it appeared. Funny thing is, the name of the religious guy who converted him is Jonathan Laird, founder of the Hallowed Hills ministry. Sound familiar?"

"Hallowed Hills. That's the name of the retreat place where we followed that man from Betty Simpson's memorial service."

"That's right. And I'm willing to bet the name of the guy we followed is Jonathan Laird. Where's your computer? Let's do a search and see if we can come up with some information on this guy and maybe a picture."

"Great idea. Follow me."

Laura took Jake into an adjacent room off the kitchen, which, at one time, was her grandfather's den. Now it served as a study room for the girls and an office for her, complete with a computer, printer/copier and desk. The walls were covered with built-in bookcases, handmade by her grandfather many years ago. A variety of books lined the shelves. Some had been here since before she was born. Others were added by her or the twins. Long windows framed the computer center and were covered in plaid window treatments. The windows offered a view of the front of the house. An old brown leather couch and two matching chairs completed the décor.

Laura pulled an extra chair over to the computer.

"Here you go." She offered the main chair to Jake, assuming he was faster at this than she.

"Great. Let's see what pops up when we search his name first."

Jake typed in the needed information. The screen filled with data about Jonathan Laird. Jake read the information out loud.

"According to reports, he was an ordained minister who left mainstream religion years ago to join a somewhat questionable religious sect called The Saints of Our Lord. It was questionable, because by some accounts, certain sects within the group subscribed to polygamy. Some even were said to engage in ritualistic acts to demonstrate their dedication to their Lord. This sounds like my sister, Addi's, area of expertise. She teaches a class at the university on religious cults and the psychology behind them and their leaders. We should talk to her. Maybe she's familiar with Laird or this Saints of Our Lord group."

Laura and Jake continued to read page after page of similar information on Laird. Jake read, "To some, he was considered a savior, a prophet, almost God-like himself. To others, he was a dangerous zealot whose charismatic personality would entice others in a cult-like manner to join him and live by his strict doctrines."

Jake continued to read aloud, "He preached of a perfect existence in a theocratic utopia, where men were leaders and women were subservient, existing only to procreate and care for others based on their given roles in this society."

Laura interjected, "This sounds like a version of *The Handmaid's Tale*. So creepy."

Jake continued reading, "Communes were scattered all over the mid-western section of the country where members vowed to live by their own rules, keeping to themselves, and raising their families in isolation from the outside world.

"It was reported by some that The Saints of Our Lord sought to expand their movement to other areas of the country as well. Jonathan and others like him were sent out as missionaries to recruit followers and start communes throughout the eastern and western parts of the country. What does this sound like to you?"

Laura replied, "It sounds like Laird is running a cult. What do you think?"

"Agreed. And it makes me wonder what the hell is going on at Hallowed Hills. Let's do a search on that." Jake typed Hallowed Hills into the search engine. More pages of information appeared. They skimmed through them and Jake read the highlights.

"Hallowed Hills is described as beautiful, picturesque, tranquil, and serene. More than 1,200 acres, it is steeped in history, having been the home of the local Indian tribe, the Lenapes, who inhabited the area before the 1700s. Coveted by King Charles II, he claimed it for the English royalty. It passed hands several times to early colonial settlers and then municipalities until purchased by the religious sect, The Saints of Our Lord. It's now known as the location where they hold religious retreats throughout the year."

Jake commented, "Looks like a few of the members gave interviews. Let's read those." Jake clicked on links to the interviews. "They describe the retreats as family-centric. A time for several generations of families to unite and spend the week doing things such as studying scriptures, religious reflection and preparing and enjoying meals together.

"According to this woman, the retreat week is a time to revisit the past, living without modern distractions, such as television or other electronics, in a communal environment. Food is organically grown and meals are prepared from scratch with fresh ingredients."

"I wonder what she means by 'communal environment'?" Laura asked.

"I don't know. I wonder if this retreat idea has evolved into a permanent way of life for this group?"

Laura added, "I've been thinking that too. But wouldn't we have heard some murmurings about that? I mean it's a small town. Not much goes on around here without everyone knowing about it. You've just returned, but I've been here for years and never heard anything about the place."

Jake agreed, "Which is strange when you think about it. I mean, as you said, it's a small town and what do we really know about this place? Other than it holds annual religious retreats. Do you ever see the members during that time? Hear any noise from the place? Does anyone ever venture into town for supplies, that sort of thing?"

"Now that you mention it, no. I've never heard anyone speak of that happening. We all just drive by the place barely noticing it."

Jake stared at the computer screen, "Strange don't you think?"

"Yes…but what does this have to do with the accident and someone feeding my dog rat poison?"

"Good question. Let's see if we can find a picture of Jonathan Laird." Jake did an image search. Several pictures of Laird appeared, but most were taken from a distance and it was hard to get a good look at him.

"The man doesn't seem to like his picture taken," Laura surmised.

"Yeah, the best one we have must have been taken years ago, judging by the head of dark hair."

"I couldn't positively say if he was the man we followed or not. But take a look at his shirt in that picture."

"What about it?" Jake asked.

"That symbol on it. I've seen it somewhere before, on someone else, I'm sure of it. I just can't place it at the moment."

The symbol was a circle with a triangle inside and a cross inside the triangle.

"I think that symbol is on the sign to Hallowed Hills. I remember noticing it when we drove past that night. It was dark, but I'm almost sure that was it," Jake said.

"Could be." Laura pulled up the photos on her phone and found the picture she took of the Hallowed Hills sign and the symbol matched. "Look. You're right. But I know I've seen it somewhere else too, as a tattoo or piece of jewelry…something a person was wearing. I'm sorry, I just can't place it now. It'll come to me."

"Let's try searching Phil Molino." Jake first searched for data but came up empty. Then he tried images but struck out there too. "No luck. I may have better luck at the office. I can search the *Tribune's* database and see if they have anything on either of these guys." Jake's cell phone began to ring.

"Jake here. What's up? What? I'm on my way." Jake stood and simultaneously pocketed his phone.

"Looks like reality is crashing in on us, Lars. That was my dad. My house is on fire."

# Twenty

The waiting was agonizing. She couldn't seem to focus on anything but the waiting. Waiting for the phone to ring with news. Waiting for Jake to pull into her driveway unharmed. Waiting for any information on what happened.

After Jake got the call that morning he rushed to get dressed, as did Laura. But he refused to let her come with him. Too dangerous he said, and he wouldn't be able to do his job knowing she was there. In the end, she reluctantly agreed. Now she regretted her decision.

She tried to spend the day in her greenhouses, pruning roses. Then she returned to the shop and tried to concentrate on planning for the July Fourth picnic. Finally, she gave up and called the girls. If anything would take her mind off Jake, it was her girls. But they didn't answer. Probably at the beach, she thought. So, in the end, she was left sitting by the phone, waiting for it to ring.

Her mind oscillated between worrying about Jake and flashes of vivid images of their incredible night together. She was not sure how she ended up here. If someone had told her a month ago that she would be sitting in her shop daydreaming about her incredible night with Jake Callaway, she would have laughed them out of town.

She heard the front door of the shop open and rose to greet her customer. Good, something to keep me occupied, she thought. She hustled into the store area and found an unfamiliar man standing there. Sam, who normally greeted all customers with a wagging tail, instead had his tail straight up, was baring all teeth, and emitting a low threatening growl. Laura rushed over to them.

"Sam! No! Go lie down! I'm terribly sorry. He never does that. I think the heat must be getting to him."

"No problem. I'm more of a cat person, guess he can tell, huh?" The man half-heartedly laughed, but Laura caught him sneering at Sam and the hair on the back of her neck stood at attention. She was never afraid here. Even though she posted a sign advertising her store on the road, it was usually locals that came down the long driveway to buy from her, so she rarely had to worry about strangers.

"How can I help you?"

"Lookin' for some flowers for a friend. Nice place ya got here." His speech clued Laura to the fact that he wasn't from around here. As did his appearance. It wasn't so much the jeans and tee shirt, but he wore too many gold chains, a faded leather jacket, and shiny boots. All of which were out of place for this town and this time of year. His dark hair was slicked back. If he had been younger, gang member would have come to mind when she looked at him. She guessed him to be in his forties, probably too old for a gang. Maybe the mob would be more accurate.

"Thank you," Laura replied. "What kind of flowers are you looking for? Would you prefer a bouquet, flowers arranged in a vase, a plant arrangement?"

"Somethin' pretty, ya know, colorful. Something you would like." He nodded his head in her direction and his gaze traveled up and down her body and sent shivers up her spine. She just wanted to get him out of there. She was keenly aware of the fact that she was very much alone. Jake would be tied up for hours and Sam, while somewhat of a comfort, was just a dog after all.

"Do you know what kind of flowers your friend likes? Roses, daisies, tulips?"

"What do you like?" He inched closer to her as he spoke. She instinctively stepped back, only to be trapped by the counter behind her. He continued to come closer.

"What's a matter, you look afraid? I guess it gets lonely being out here all by yourself. Don't even have a close neighbor who ya could yell to, do ya?"

He was so close now she could see the whiskers on his chin and was assaulted by the overpowering scent of his cheap cologne. Her head throbbed with the sound of her beating heart. Because she was a woman, she was raised to be polite to others, so now her mind frantically searched for the proper behavior for this situation. Her body was telling her she was in danger. She needed to listen. *Think, think, Laura. Don't be a victim. Breathe, in and out, in and out.*

"You're such a pretty little thing too. I'll bet you're a real spitfire in the sack." He stepped even closer and his eyes had a soulless, evil glint to them. The adrenaline pumped through Laura's body screaming, 'Danger, Danger!' All at once he reached for her left arm as she withdrew the pruning shears from her right pocket. They were pointed toward him so she jammed them with all her strength into his arm as she screamed.

Sam jumped to attention and sprung at the man, knocking him to the floor as he bellowed in pain, grabbing his arm. Laura still held the shears in her hand. Without thinking, she went at him again, stabbing him in the thigh. He tried to grab her arm, but Sam attacked. She had never seen Sam so vicious. With Sam buying her more time, she grabbed a heavy glass vase she had on display and slammed it over his head. Then she ran, faster than she had ever run in her entire life.

She frantically yelled to Sam.

"Sam! Come! Come, Sam!" Her breath labored as she screamed and sprinted to safety.

Her first thought was to run to the garage since it was the closest structure to her. She had the ring with all her keys and all she could think of was escape. She turned to look behind her, terrified that he would be there, but he wasn't, only Sam following her lead. She must have knocked him unconscious, but she took no comfort in that and continued at full speed.

She made it inside the garage only to discover her van was gone. She had left it at Jake's last night. Bile rose in her throat as panic gripped her lungs and left her gasping for air. *Don't lose it now, Lars, deep breaths.* Bending at the waist, she forced herself to inhale deeply, exhale. *Think now!* Her van was gone, but Bill's old Mustang was still here and she had the key on her ring. She always loved that car and, thankfully, never sold it. She drove it from time to time. She opened the car door for Sam, then herself. She reached in her pocket for her keys. They were gone. *Shit! No!* Where were her keys? Did they fall out while she was running? Did she leave them in the shop? Think! Think!

The spare set. She kept a spare set hanging on a hook behind the girls' bicycles. *Hurry, Laura, hurry.* She hopped out of the car and raced to the bikes. She felt the keys behind them, but her hands were shaking so badly, she fumbled them and they fell. "God, no!" she cried out loud. Quickly getting on her hands and knees, she searched for the keys. Sam began to bark and she jumped, banging her head on the shelf above. "Shit!" Finally, she found the keys and forced her hand to settle, grasp them and pull them towards her.

Back in the car, she struggled to fit them in the ignition. *Breathe, God damn it, breathe.* She managed to start the car and maneuvered it out of the garage. Bang! She screamed and turned to see him there, banging against the trunk. Sam lunged at him, growling with exposed teeth. This startled him and he fell back. Laura quickly locked the doors, threw the gearshift from reverse into drive, and hit the gas pedal, causing the car to lurch forward and the tires to screech on the asphalt. *Go, go, get out of here.* She sped down the long driveway, slowing only once to check the rearview mirror. He was chasing after the car, but she was too far in the lead. She pressed on, not looking back, with her only thought of getting to safety.

# Twenty-One

Laura didn't know where to go. She didn't have her cell or her purse, just her dog and herself, both unharmed. She wanted to go to Jake's, but she couldn't. He had enough to worry about. She couldn't stop shaking and probably shouldn't be driving in this condition, but her goal was to put as much distance between her and that man as she could.

She wanted her mom, as crazy as that sounded. So she ended up with the next best thing. Jake's mom. Without even realizing it, she found herself in Jake's parents' driveway, not even knowing if Mrs. Callaway was home.

She needed a phone. Now. The police had to get to her house and arrest that lunatic. She forced herself to steady and made her way to the front door. It was hard to believe she was just here yesterday under dramatically different circumstances.

Within seconds, Mrs. Callaway opened the door.

"Laura, honey, what are you doing here?" And then, taking in the sight of her, she pulled her into the house.

"Laura, my God, what happened? Are you hurt? I see blood on you. Come in, let's get you cleaned up. Good God, what happened?"

"I need your phone. I need to call the police. A man, he came to my store. I was alone. He tried to….grab me. Sam…where's Sam?"

"He's right here, honey, he's okay. Let's get the phone immediately. You're absolutely right, we need to call the police."

Mrs. Callaway took control of the situation. She called the police and repeated Laura's story. She cleaned the blood from her hands and gave her a clean shirt. She made her a cup of tea and sat with her until the color returned to her cheeks.

"I'm going to call Jake. Tell him you're here so he doesn't worry."

"I didn't want to bother him….his house. Do you know what happened?"

Mrs. Callaway rubbed Laura's back, "There'll be time for all that later, honey. He'll worry if he tries to reach you, or goes to your house and finds the police. Or worse. We don't want him coming face-to-face with the intruder."

Mrs. Callaway reached for the phone again and called her son, but this time her call went unanswered.

***

Jake was exhausted. He couldn't remember the last good night's sleep he'd had. Now on top of the physical exhaustion, he was mentally and emotionally spent. He went from the exhilaration of the night of his dreams with Laura to seeing his house almost destroyed along with many of his personal belongings. He needed three things: a shower, a good night's sleep and Laura. Not necessarily in that order.

He pulled into her driveway and drove around back to the garages to park. He could see they were all open, but no cars were inside. Then he remembered she had left her van at his parent's house and wondered how she would get around today.

As he opened the Jeep door and prepared to exit, he was aware of that feeling in his gut that told him something was not quite right. It all seemed to hit him in slow motion as he walked towards the house. Blood on the ground. The back door was open. Broken glass. The shop door swung in the breeze. No sign of Sam.

"Laura! Laura, where are you?" His adrenaline kicked in. He ran into the house first, following a trail of blood into the kitchen. He frantically searched the house, screaming for her. He searched all the rooms before dashing to the shop. More blood met him there as well as a smashed vase. This was not a simple accident.

"Laura! Sam!" He reached for his cell and remembered he'd lost it while fighting the fire that threatened to consume his home. He looked for the shop phone, but before he could reach it a man's voice bellowed behind him.

"Freeze. Stay where you are. Hands in the air and don't make any sudden movements. I've got my gun pointed at your head." Jake did as he was told. He heard the crackling of a walkie-talkie.

"It's Jackson. I've got him, in the barn. Over."

"Sending back-up. Over."

The voices were familiar to Jake but he didn't dare turn around.

"Pete? Is that you?" Jake hesitantly asked.

"Keep your mouth shut and stay where you are."

"Pete, it's Jake. Jake Callaway. I just arrived on the scene and found the place like this. Laura's gone, Pete. You have to find her. I'm not the villain here, but something's terribly wrong.

"Jake Callaway?" Pete walked in front of Jake to make a positive identification. "Man, what the hell?"

"Can I put my arms down now? We have to find Laura, Pete. You have to help me."

"Shit, I'm sorry man. Yeah, put your arms down. Hold on, let me make a call." He grabbed his walkie-talkie and relayed the news that he did not have the perpetrator. He had Jake Callaway instead.

"Sorry about that, Jake. We got a 911 call for this address and rushed over here right away. Attempted assault and possible robbery."

"Who called? Was it Laura?"

"No. I believe it was your mom."

"My mom? Can I make a call?"

"Sure, go ahead. Listen I need to search the place. You watch your back in case he's still here, although I doubt it."

"I doubt it too. I already searched the house and only found blood and a broken window. Might get some prints though."

"I'll check it out."

Jake grabbed the phone and called his parent's house.

"Hello." It was his mom.

"Mom, it's Jake. Do you know where Laura is?"

"Oh thank goodness, Jake. Yes, she's right here with me. She's fine, just a bit shaken up. Someone tried to assault her in her store today. She fought him off and fled with Sam. I cleaned her up and she's having some tea while the police investigate."

"I'm on my way." He hung up without waiting for a reply.

***

The door flew open and Jake came bounding through. Laura was startled, at first, but when she turned to see Jake, his hair a rumpled mess, soot-stained clothing, and a look of fierce concern on his face, she relaxed immediately. He made his way to her in a few long strides as she rose to meet him. Their embrace said it all, as Laura saw Mrs. Callaway and Granny Elyse exchange a knowing glance.

"Are you hurt? Where did he hurt you? Tell me everything from the very beginning."

"Jake, honey…" His mom stepped in. "She's fine. Don't badger her right now."

"I'm fine, Mrs. Callaway, really, it's okay." Laura sat down with Jake and told him the entire story, from start to finish. Her voice cracked at certain parts, but she managed to stay in control.

When she finished, she was alarmed by what she saw. Jake's face was tight with anger and his normally serene blue eyes were filled with rage.

"Jake, I'm fine. He didn't hurt me at all. I did more damage to him. As did Sam." She reached down to pat Sam on the head as he lay by her feet. He hadn't left her side since she arrived at the Callaway house. "Now tell me about your house. How is it? I've been sick with worry for you all day."

"I'm fine. It's you we need to be worried about. He could have killed you, Laura."

"But he didn't. I'm sure the police will catch him and it'll be over." She tried to sound more confident than she felt, for Jake's sake.

"Speaking of the police, they need to talk to you and get your statement. Do you feel up to that? The sooner the better. They don't even have a good description of him."

"Yes. Let's just get it over with."

"I'll call them and have them come here once they're done at your house."

"They're still at my house?"

"Yes. I didn't want to tell you this, but it looks like he broke into your back door and rummaged through the kitchen, probably look-ing for some first aid supplies to stop his bleeding. The good news is, he probably left some prints. The police wanted to check the place out. You'll eventually need to go and see what's missing.

"Then let's go now. I just want it to be over."

***

Later that night Laura lay in the unfamiliar bed in Jake's sister's old bedroom. Mr. and Mrs. Callaway insisted she spend the night with them. Jake was down the hallway in his old room, since he had no home to go to at this point.

As the night wore on, Laura became more and more emotional thinking about the events of the day. She had retold the story sev-eral times to various people, but couldn't shake the nagging feeling that she was forgetting something about the incident, something very important.

She replayed the scene over and over, but nothing new came to her. She was only making herself more upset. She called the girls earlier hoping that would ease her mind and soul. She was so thankful they weren't home today, and she was careful not to mention the disturbing incident. Talking to them did help, but as she lay here now, her mind refused to shut down and sleep was becoming more and more elusive.

She couldn't help thinking of what could have happened to her today. What if she hadn't had the shears in her pocket? What if Sam hadn't been there to help her? All the what-ifs continued to bombard her thoughts until the reality of the situation slammed into her. She began to cry and shake in her unfamiliar surroundings. What had happened to her simple, uncomplicated life? Was the universe sending her a message? Maybe being with Jake was a mistake.

She tried to get control of herself. The last thing she wanted was to wake anyone else in the house. The Callaways had been so kind to her, but in truth, their kindness was a bit overwhelming. She wasn't used to people doting on her.

Then there was Jake. Everything was happening too fast. It seemed as if overnight he had become such a significant part of her life and that frightened her. Her old life suited her just fine and she realized that she missed the security and continuity of that life. She was safe there. No one could hurt her.

She continued to cry, but softer now and her body began to still. She forced herself to take deep breaths, which helped her to settle. She decided that tomorrow she would regain control of her life, one way or another.

The morning arrived with rays of abundant sunshine gleaming through the window and Jake sitting on the edge of her bed with a cup of coffee in each hand.

"Good morning. How'd you sleep?" He offered her one of the steaming mugs.

"Fine. How about you? Thanks." She accepted the mug and took a long sip.

"I collapsed. I guess I was totally exhausted after the events of the day. I did think about sneaking down to your room though." He grinned mischievously. When Laura didn't respond he took a more serious approach, and asked, "How are you feeling today?"

"Okay. I just want things to be back to normal. I'll need to get into my shop today. I can't afford to take any more days off this time of year."

"I'll come with you."

"No." The word came out sounding harsher than Laura intended and she saw the wounded look on his face.

"Jake, I appreciate all you and your family are doing for me. But I can't stay here forever and you can't babysit me around the clock. I need to go back at some point and I'll need to work alone. As they say, there's no time like the present to get back on the horse...or something like that." She tried to force a smile but could tell he wasn't going to be that easy to shake.

"I get that, but not today."

"Jake, you're not my keeper. Plus you have your own hands full with your house and work. You're busy and don't have the time to follow me around."

"I'll make the time."

"No. I won't allow it," Laura snapped.

"Won't allow it?" He laughed as he said it, but his eyes betrayed him.

"That's right. Jake, it's too much for me. Too much for you. Too much, too fast. I mean, I've only known you were back in town for a month and already you've infiltrated my life, against my wishes and..."

"Whoa, hold on there. I infiltrated your life…against your wishes. Correct me if I'm wrong, but you seemed to be a willing participant the other night, or were your moans actually in protest?"

"No, of course not. I…enjoyed the other night very much. But it was just one night. It doesn't mean we're in a committed relationship."

"Oh, I see…I get it." His eyes flashed with hurt and anger. "Just for the record, that night meant everything to me. Thinking about it was the only thing that got me through yesterday as I watched my house and my fucking life go up in smoke."

He stood and walked towards the door. He turned to face her, his face hard, his glare penetrating.

"I guess you were right before when you told me I didn't know you anymore. I sure as hell don't. Enjoy your coffee." He turned from the bed and stormed out of the room slamming the door behind him.

***

Jake left the house without so much as a goodbye to his family. Laura had his head spinning. She thinks she's so damn independent, fine, let her handle things on her own. Besides, he knew the police would be patrolling her property today anyway.

He headed to the fire station to see how the investigation into his house fire was progressing. He had to navigate around tree branches and debris remaining on the roads from the storm. The road crews could only do so much and they would be concerned with the main roads first.

He decided he would check on the progress of his house fire, finish a story for the paper and then make time to help the crews with cleanup. Like the lady said, he was busy. And he knew he had to stay busy to keep his mind off her.

He was not surprised to find his dad already at the station. Retired or not, he knew Joe Callaway would be involved in his son's house fire.

"Hey, Dad. Any news?"

"Oh, hey Jake. Been waiting for you to get here. How's Laura?"

"She's fine. What's the word on the fire?" Jake's response was abrupt and he could tell it didn't go unnoticed by his father. He hoped he wouldn't call him on it.

"The fire is still being investigated. You know these things take time. However, based on the evidence I'm looking at so far, it's looking like arson."

"Arson? Who the hell would want to burn my house down?"

"Don't know. Was waiting to ask you that question."

"What makes you think it's arson?"

"Several things. First of all, there were multiple points of origin, which as you know is a dead giveaway. Secondly, some sort of accelerant was found and is being tested. Probably gasoline. Looks like amateurs to me, maybe kids fooling around. You know, summer vacation, too much time on their hands, then somebody has the bright idea to burn a house down."

Joe shook his head in disgust as he walked over to a table that held some of the evidence collected from Jake's house. He picked up a clear plastic bag that contained a discolored piece of paper. He handed it to Jake.

"What do you make of this?" Jake took the bag and turned it over in his hand. The paper had writing on it that looked familiar, although it wasn't Jake's writing. The words he could still decipher read, "Mind your own business...second warning."

"Where was this found?"

"It was stuck in the bushes by the house. Must have blown away before it burned. Got wet though, that's why it looks the way it does. Look familiar?"

"I'm not sure, but it's not the first one I've gotten. A few weeks ago I found one pinned to the porch post. I figured I pissed somebody off with one of my stories, although I haven't been working on anything I would consider controversial. But sometimes what I consider controversial and what someone else does, are two different things."

"Well there's no telling if the notes are connected to the fire, but it's a heck of a coincidence, don't you think?"

"Yeah, it sure is." Jake continued to study the note, then handed it back to his father. "I need to get into the office for awhile. You okay to handle things here?"

"Sure. I'll call you if anything else turns up. Meanwhile, you keep thinking of anybody you might have pissed off enough to want to torch your house."

"Yeah, that reminds me, I need to get a new phone. I'll text you when I do. Thanks, Dad."

# Twenty-Two

None of the Elders were happy about the recent developments. Their directive was to cause a distraction, not burn a house down and assault a woman. This would cause too many questions and more investigations. Exactly what they were trying to minimize.

The four elders were assembled at the table, demanding answers from their leader.

"It looks like your man needs to be reined in." This comment came from the malcontent. He continued, "He seems to be having trouble following orders. What do you plan to do?"

The Grand Master returned his piercing glare and replied, "I take offense at you describing him as 'my man.' He was chosen by everyone at this table as being competent to carry out our orders. If he is having a problem with that, it is a problem we all share. However, since I am the elected leader, I can assure you the problem has been addressed. As is customary, he will be given one more chance to prove his loyalty and obedience. If he fails, he will be terminated."

The usually quiet man with dark-rimmed glasses offered his opinion. His voice was soft, but he spoke with authority. "Can we risk giving him one more chance? His most recent error in judgment will cost us much-unwanted attention. And let us not forget that there is still a chance evidence may link him to the fire, in which case he needs to be terminated immediately."

"That goes without saying. I have our friend at police head-quarters on alert for any news. He will notify us immediately of any problems," said the Grand Master. He continued, "I already have met with our man to discuss his behavior. He was remorseful and understands the position we are in. He understands the consequences of his behavior and knows what will happen in the unlikely event that he displeases us again. I don't believe we will have any more trouble from him.

"Now we should move on to more important business, such as our plans for the Fourth of July...."

***

Laura still had to figure out logistics of getting two cars home from the Callaway's house, but for now, she decided to take her van and leave the Mustang for later. She said her goodbyes and thank-you's to Mrs. Callaway and Jake's grandmother and was on her way home with Sam by her side.

As she neared the house a feeling of dread came over her. She could feel her heart beating a bit too fast. Her palms felt clammy and she had to force herself to breathe normally. She wondered if this was the beginning of a panic attack. She really didn't want to have a panic attack. She had survived thirty-some years without one and didn't want to start now.

She read somewhere that by concentrating on breathing and her surroundings she could prevent an attack. So that's what she did. She breathed in and out as she approached her house and admired the trees, the colors of the flowers, and the smell of fresh air. In and out as she turned into her driveway. In and out as she made her way around the side of the house to the garage. And then gasped as she saw a strange van parked there.

Her heart began beating out of control as her breathing reverted to shallow bursts. She forced herself to focus on the unfamiliar van and realized there was writing on the side. *Breathe.* In and out, in and out. She managed to read the writing, Newbury Windows and Doors.

She let out a sigh of relief. It was probably Steve Bruso, the owner of Newbury Windows and Doors here to fix the broken glass in the back door. She wondered who called him.

Feeling somewhat better, she parked her van. As she got closer, she could see it was Steve.

"Hi, Steve." Laura hopped out of the van and opened the door for Sam who, at first, began to growl protectively until Steve crouched down and told Sam it was okay.

"Hey, Sam. It's just me. Hey, Laura. Sorry about the break-in here. It's the talk of the town. Newbury rarely has a crime like this. Everyone's in shock and wondering how you are." Sam no longer sensed danger and allowed Steve to scratch him behind his ears.

The Bruso family had owned the window and door store for as long as Laura could remember. Steve took it over from his father years ago. He was in his mid-fifties, about five-foot-nine, a little soft in the middle, with salt and pepper hair and a round, happy face. He had done work for Laura before when she needed windows replaced or screens repaired. He always was kind and friendly and Laura immediately relaxed in his presence.

"That's kind of everyone to worry, but I'm fine. Please pass the word or you know I'll be inundated with calls and visitors checking on me." Laura smiled as she said this, but inside she dreaded the prospect.

"I'll be sure to tell everyone you're doing great. I won't be long here, just about done. Anything else you need while I'm here?"

"Gosh, Steve, I don't even know. I haven't had the time to survey the damage. How did you know to come out anyway?"

"Jake Callaway called me. Said you needed the back-door glass replaced and some glass clean-up here and in the shop."

"Oh. You didn't have to do the cleaning up, Steve. What do I owe you for all this?"

"Nothing. Jake already took care of everything."

"Really." It was hard to suppress her irritation and Laura was sure Steve heard it in her voice.

"I hope that's okay, that I'm here and all?"

"Of course it is. I'm just a little out of it today. Still trying to wrap my brain around this whole situation." She knew Steve would think she meant the break-in situation, but she meant the whole situation, including Jake taking over her life.

"Understandable. You must have been pretty shaken up."

"Yeah. But I'm fine now. Please make sure you report that back in town, okay?" Laura smiled to emphasize the fact that she was indeed just fine.

"You bet. Don't let me hold you up. Do you want to take a look around before I go in case you need anything else?"

"Yeah, that's a good idea." Laura had to admit she did feel more comfortable checking out the place while someone else was here, just in case.

***

Jake was having trouble focusing on the piece he was writing for the paper. His mind kept going back to the note found at his house. The note, the possibility of arson, and the fact that he was now homeless. They had to be connected. He believed they all were connected to the accident investigation as well, since he wasn't working on anything else contentious enough to cause such an extreme reaction. At least he didn't think he was.

He decided to quit racking his brain on the newspaper article and to do more research on Hallowed Hills instead. His previous search through Julie's files on local accidents came up empty. Literally, empty. No file on the accident on Wagontrail Road existed. So he had to proceed with plan B.

He headed over to the old archives room. Sometimes the paper had files on pieces that never made it to print for one reason or another. It would be unlikely that the information in the files would be available on the web, so he had a bit of an advantage over the casual researcher.

The archives were kept in a large room in the basement, filed alphabetically. Hard copies were kept on the last five years, with older data having been stored electronically. Jake figured he'd start with H and see what that produced, although he doubted he'd find a file labeled "Hallowed Hills" that contained all the information he needed.

He opened the file cabinet for HA and began the search. As he suspected, nothing on Hallowed Hills. He then moved on to the L cabinet to search for Jonathan Laird. Again, nothing. Next, he moved to the M's for Phil Molino. Strike three.

Well, he didn't think it'd be easy. Research rarely was. It was time to approach this from a different angle. What other topic could contain the information he needed? He spent the next few hours brainstorming names and events hoping to hit a home run. When he ran out of ideas, he began going through each drawer and skimming the file names hoping something would jump out at him.

It was during his search of the L's that he finally hit that home run. A file labeled Lenape Lake caught his eye. He remembered from his earlier research at Laura's house that Hallowed Hills had originally been the home of the Lenape Indian tribe. He pulled this file and began to read.

Some of the information was a repeat of what he had learned previously, that the land, now called Hallowed Hills, was during the 1600s inhabited by the Lenape Indians. Once the English settlers arrived in the late 1600s King Charles II took claim of the land for the royal family. The land passed hands many times over the years and, at one point, was referred to as Lenape Lake.

What Jake didn't learn from the internet articles was that the owner before The Saints of Our Lord was a local family, the Magils. He knew the Magil family as a kid. Years ago they owned Magil's Ice Cream store in town. They had a son, Albert, and a daughter, Helen, who were close to his parents' age, although he didn't remember his parents being particularly friendly with them. That was odd in itself since his parents were friends with almost everyone in town. If he remembered correctly, the ice cream store closed during Jake's senior year and the parents moved the summer after graduation. He wasn't sure what became of Albert and Helen. He made a mental note to ask his parents about them.

He continued to inspect the file. His best guess was that someone had gathered information on the Magils and the property for an article, but either the author decided against writing it, or as often happens, some other pressing story surfaced and the fluff piece got pushed aside.

He couldn't be sure from the information what the article's purpose would have been. An educated guess had him thinking it was an angle on the sale of the property. There was information regarding the death of both the Magil parents and how the land was passed to Albert and his sister, Helen.

Jake remembered the family as being very religious. Not being an overly religious person himself, Jake was unsure which denomination they followed. He doubted it was an unorthodox one or he would have remembered the gossip. He needed to talk to his parents about the Magil family.

He took notes on pertinent information in the file, including the name of the reporter who was working on the article, Kevin Malloy. Jake had never heard of him, but maybe if he could track him down, more of his questions could be answered.

# Twenty-Three

Laura spent the last week working on plans for the Fourth of July parade, tending her flowers, making deliveries, cleaning the girls' rooms and organizing closets. She even cleaned out the lint collector in the clothes dryer, which most people didn't realize, was a fire hazard if left to accumulate. Basically, she did anything and everything to keep her mind from obsessing over the events of the last few weeks, including, most notably, Jake Callaway.

She was determined to get her life back in order and to return to the woman and responsible mother she had been before Jake's intrusion. So she busied herself with the most mundane, but responsible, tasks she could find (hence, the dryer vent). If someone had been watching her from afar, she would have resembled a squirrel in autumn, frantically gathering nuts to prepare for the tough months ahead. She hoped, in her zest for normalcy, she wouldn't dart in front of a car with her mouth full of acorns and end up as road kill.

Now and then, a thought of Jake would intrude, and when it did, she found herself annoyed that he could so easily extract her from his life. Granted, she had pushed him away, but with all his talk about loving and missing her, she would have thought he might have pushed back a little harder.

She never should have gotten involved with him in the first place. She knew this would be the result. Jake would simply go about his life, while she was left to put the pieces of hers back together. Of course, her grandmother would have accused her of creating a self-fulfilling prophecy, but just because she had the insight to foresee the outcome of a situation, didn't mean she created the outcome. Did it?

Now here she was obsessing again. Time to get back to work. The problem was, she had done everything that needed to be done for the day. Except for one thing. Something she had been dreading.

There was still the unresolved issue of the accident and the possibility that the attack at her shop was related somehow. She had avoided delving any further since it only reminded her of Jake. But she still felt the need to investigate, if for no other reason, than to feel safe in her home and shop again. Although she continued to force herself to be brave day after day and night after night, the uneasiness she felt since the attack was undeniable.

She tried to avoid thinking about the awful incident, but the memories would surface in nightmares. Each time, she was left with the feeling that she was forgetting something vitally important. She would try consciously to focus on it. But that only left her anxious and fearful. It seemed to be a vicious cycle.

She decided to gather up what few notes she had made on the accident and the attack and head to the library. She hoped to find more local history there than she could find online. Maybe something would jog her memory or shed more light on Hallowed Hills and the strange religious group.

As she stepped outside, the heat and humidity of the day hit her immediately. She had dressed appropriately in a yellow tank sundress, with gold thong sandals, but she knew the library would be freezing. So she ran back inside to grab a sweater.

While she was inside, she noticed the keys to the old Mustang on the hall table. She had thrown them there when she retrieved the car from the Callaways and had barely given them a second thought. On a whim, she grabbed the keys and decided today would be a perfect day for a drive in a convertible, so she took the Mustang and put the top down.

As she zipped along with the wind whipping through her hair, listening to Taylor Swift sing about Romeo and Juliet, she thought of Jake. She wondered what he was doing, how things were going with his house and if he had been called to other fires recently. And, of course, she thought of her passionate night with him. Again, she was amazed at the experience. She had never felt like that in her entire life; so whole, so complete, so damn fantastic. She wondered if he thought of that night as often as she did and if he felt the same about it. But obviously he didn't or he wouldn't have dropped out of her life so easily. Maybe she was really bad at sex? It had been a long time for her and it wasn't like she had a lot of experience. He was probably used to being with sophisticated city women with sexy lingerie and moves to match. How could she compete with that?

At least one good thing came from her encounter with Jake, she was closer to his family again. It seemed not a day went by without some contact with a Callaway. Mrs. Callaway and Jake's sister, Addi, were always calling or stopping in to discuss the picnic plans. Mr. Callaway stopped in almost daily for fresh flowers for Granny Elyse, who called almost every day, just to chat. Even Jake's brother Rick took to coming in frequently to pick up a bouquet for Kelly or his daughter. It was great for business, but even better to feel like part of their family again. And it made the days without her own family easier to bear.

Her girls were scheduled to come home next week, in time for the big picnic, but they had called yesterday to ask for a continuance. Apparently, there was a big event planned in New England that they were invited to by 'seriously cute guys' according to Brooke. Ordinarily, Laura would have refused, but since she was still shaken from the assault, she thought it safer to keep them with their grandparents longer than usual. Hopefully, that would give her and the police the time they needed to solve the case.

***

Jake finally managed to finish the article for the paper just in time to meet his deadline. It was a mindless piece, in his opinion, regarding competition among the waste management firms in the county. But having it finished gave him peace of mind and time to continue with the investigation into Hallowed Hills.

He hopped into his truck and blasted the air conditioning. The day was one of the hottest so far, and the walk through the parking lot had his black tee shirt clinging to his chest. He headed over to the library to do local research. He had to establish a connection between the accident, the attack on Laura, the burning of his house, and Hallowed Hills. He knew there was a connection, he just needed a break to help him see what it was. He thought the library might have more on the history of the property.

Meanwhile, he had to continue to keep his mind off Laura. As much as he wanted to see her, to have some contact with her, he knew it was in her best interest if he kept her out of all this. To prove his point, nothing bad had happened to her since he had been keeping his distance.

His family had been a big help to him. They each took turns checking on her every day and reporting back to him, so he could concentrate without worrying too much. Of course, this meant he had to fill them in, somewhat, on what was going on. He kept the explanation simple, limited to the fact that he was working on a story that had possible long-reaching repercussions and he had reason to believe that Laura could be in danger if it was thought that they were a couple.

His family learned long ago not to ask too many questions about his work and agreed, without hesitation, to keep an eye on Laura. However, he knew it pained everyone involved to see the hurt his absence in her life was causing her. Not being able to explain the circumstances to her, frustrated them. But Jake swore them to secrecy, explaining the truth of the matter, that Laura could be stubbornly independent and would not allow him to protect her in this way if she knew the reason behind it. He assured them it would all work out in the end.

He only wished he could convince himself of that. He realized he was taking a great risk excluding her this way, but it was better than the alternative. His biggest regret was that he didn't have more time with her after their incredible night together. He never got the chance to convince her how amazing that night was for him and how he wanted to spend the rest of his life with her. It seemed that fate had different plans.

At first, he was shocked by her reaction the morning after the attack. But Addi helped him see it made perfect sense for her to push him away. She explained it was a healthy response considering Laura's personality. She needed to take control of a situation that seemed out of control. If she allowed Jake to take over, it would have impeded her healing. Hadn't he learned all those years ago with Gwen that being an enabler was not healthy for anyone involved?

So he gave Laura the space she needed, while having his family watch over her. This gave him the chance to dig deeper into this convoluted mess while keeping her out of it. He believed it was the best course of action for now. He needed to keep telling himself that, because every inch of his body wanted nothing more than to be with her, to keep her safe in his arms, in his bed, in his life. It required a tremendous amount of self-control.

He turned into the library's parking lot and a flash of blond hair caught his eye. Self-control was going to be difficult when Laura was flitting around in a convertible with her hair blowing in the wind and that tight yellow dress clinging to her body. She shot in front of his Jeep and parked, without seeming to notice him. He pulled into the spot next to her, put down his window, lowered his sunglasses and turned on the charm.

It only took her a second to feel his gaze. She turned in his direction and froze. For about two seconds. Then she grabbed her purse, flipped her hair, hopped out of the car and headed into the building without giving him the slightest acknowledgment.

Damn, she was gorgeous. He was doing so well keeping his distance until now. But she was impossible to ignore within this proximity. In that dress. With that tan. Damn.

He hopped out of his Jeep and ran after her.

"Laura, hey, wait up!"

She continued to walk, ignoring him.

"Lars, hold on."

Jake caught up with her, strode past her and blocked her path.

"Hey. How're you doing? I've missed you."

"Yeah, I noticed." Laura attempted to step around him, but he mirrored her move.

"You're mad at me. I'm sorry. I just thought it was better…"

"And it is, much, much better. Now, will you please get out of my way?" She maneuvered around him as her icy tone cut straight through his heart. He didn't know how to handle this situation. If he tried to explain, she would be angry with him for trying to protect her, for assuming she needed protection.

If he let her go, let her continue thinking he didn't care, he may not be able to repair the damage. It was a lose-lose either way.

"Laura, come on, give me a chance to explain." He caught up with her in two long strides. She didn't stop, just continued towards the door to the library.

"There's nothing to explain, Jake. I've lived most of my adult life without you in it, I'll continue without you in it as well. No biggie." She approached the door and reached for the handle, but he beat her to it and opened it for her. She shot him an annoyed look as she walked through.

"Lars, come on. Give me a chance..."

"I've given you enough chances, Jake. Just leave me alone, stay out of my business." She continued into the library with Jake on her heels. The library had been modernized over the years and the inside resembled a wheel with spokes coming out of the center. In the middle sat the reference desk and librarian. Each spoke represented a different section: Children's Literature, Popular Fiction, Non-Fiction, Reference, Computers and Archives. Shelves of books lined each spoke and each area had tables with sturdy chairs. More comfortable cushioned chairs and sofas were peppered throughout the space.

"And stop following me!" Her tone attracted the attention of the librarian, who shot her the 'please be quiet, you're in a library' look. Jake took advantage of the situation by grabbing her arm and turning her towards him.

"Laura, give me five minutes to explain," he whispered.

She lowered her voice to match, but her fury was still evident. "You're beginning to sound like a broken record, Jake," she mimicked him in a sarcastic voice. "'Just let me explain, Lars... let me tell my side of the story...give me five minutes'...blah, blah, blah. Give it a rest. Just go about your business and I'll go about mine. It's a small town, but I'm sure we can manage to stay out of each other's way if we try hard enough. I mean, take the last several days, for instance. We were able to completely avoid each other..."

"Which took a lot of work on my part, Lars. I thought that's what you wanted. Space. From me. You made that clear, remember?"

"Yes, I do, as a matter of fact. And you did a great job giving me space. Now all you have to do is continue with that. Right now for instance." She shook her arm free from his grip and stepped around him. He followed from a safe distance. When she found the area of the library she was searching for, the Archives, and claimed a table, he joined her.

She shot him a look of annoyance and got his signature grin in return.

He quipped, "What? I can't help it if you decided to go to the library on the exact day, at the exact time as me, and then go to the exact section where I need to be. Maybe we're looking for the same thing, Lars? Did you ever think of that?"

She ignored his question and simply took out her notes and went about her research. He did the same, aware of a small flicker of interest from her. He pretended not to notice, and they both left the table simultaneously to search through materials in the Archives.

They continued with their individual research, extracting various documents, books, and periodicals from the shelves. Each spent some time with the materials at the table before returning them and selecting another. This continued for over an hour, with neither one speaking to the other until, at one point, Laura was searching a shelf as Jake was returning a book, the exact book she was searching for. She reached for the book, their hands touched, they froze, their eyes met as they realized they were most likely searching for the same thing.

"Okay, Jake, I give in. What are you doing here?"

Jake smiled and waited a few beats before answering.

"Looks like the same thing you're doing. And if you ask me, I think we should do it together. Save time and energy, and it'll be a whole lot more fun." He refused to break the eye contact and she seemed incapable of breaking it, so they stayed there, at the shelf, hands touching, eyes burning into each other. Finally, Laura pulled the book free, along with her gaze, and returned to the table with Jake on her heels.

"Oh, come on Lars, admit it. We're both here for the same reason and we'd make a hell of a lot more progress if we pooled our information and our talents to figure this out together."

"Why are you even interested in this, Jake? It doesn't concern you and I'm sure you have bigger fish to fry?"

"Laura, what do you think I've been doing the past few weeks? I've been trying to get to the bottom of this because whether you want to believe it or not, I believe everything is connected somehow. The accident, the poison Sam found, the attack at your shop, my house, all of it. I just don't know how, but I'm pretty damn sure it comes together right there." He pointed at the book she held, titled, 'Hallowed Hills – A History.'

Laura stared at him in silence, so Jake continued.

"Do you really think I'd just let this go, let someone try to poison your dog, set my house on fire, then, knowing I would be busy fighting that fire, try to assault you? You know damn well that's not happening.

"I was trying to keep you out of it and, before you can chastise me for that, you have to see my point of view. You were attacked, Laura. You could have been seriously hurt or worse. How do think that made me feel? How am I supposed to explain that to your daughters, that you were hurt because of something I was digging into?

"I don't want you involved in this, but I can see you're still the independent, stubborn woman you've always been. Which is why I didn't tell you my plan to keep you out of this. I was hoping you'd just go about getting your normal life back and let me figure this out."

Jake paused to gauge her reaction, but as usual, Laura gave nothing away. Her face was as composed as always. When she finally broke the silence, her voice was calm and even, barely above a whisper.

"Well, how kind of you to try to 'keep me out of this' as you say. But did you ever think that perhaps it's the other way around? The accident happened at my house. I was the curious one who got us involved in this. You received a threatening note after asking around town for me, which then led to the suspected arson of your home. How do you think that makes me feel?

"When are you going to wise up, Jake? Didn't you learn your lesson fifteen years ago? You can't protect everyone. You can't take these burdens solely on your shoulders and expect everyone around you to simply go about life as if all is grand, while you set out to save the world.

"Grow up. Being an adult means realizing your limitations and asking for help when you need it. It means collaborating with others to get a job done. You're not a one-man band, Jake."

Instead of responding, Jake just pulled out a chair and sat. He knew Laura wasn't expecting that. She was expecting a fight, an argument in defense of his actions, anything but simple submission. She pulled out a chair and sat as well. They both sat, in the Archives section of the local library, staring at each other, neither knowing what to say next.

The mood was broken by Jake's cell phone vibrating, but he made no move to answer it.

"Shouldn't you answer that?" No response.

"Jake...your phone is ringing." Still no response. Jake just sat in the chair staring at her. Finally, the phone stopped vibrating.

"Jake, you should probably see who called. What if there's a fire or some other emergency? Jake... stop staring at me and say something. Look, I'm sorry...if I was...abrupt, or said too much. I just..."

Jake interrupted her, "You're right."

"What?"

"You're right. I do all those things. I assume I can do things on my own when I should ask for help. I wanted to swoop in and be your hero. I'm sorry."

They sat quietly until Laura finally broke the silence. "Okay, why don't we compare notes then? We're obviously researching the same thing. Let's see what we've each discovered."

"Now that's the best offer I've had in days." He snapped into action and began to lay out his notes on the table.

# Twenty-Four

Laura wasn't about to give up control, again, to Jake. She quickly interjected, "Slow down… hold on just a minute. I am willing to share information with you, but we have to have some rules."

Jake looked at her with disbelief. "What do you mean 'rules'? It was your idea to work together and I think it's a great one."

"My idea? I believe it was your idea and I'm just agreeing to it."

"Okay, Lars. I'll take the credit for the idea if you insist. Let's get down to it."

"Jake! You're not listening to me. Again. I don't care whose idea it is. What I am saying…trying to say, if you'll let me, is that we need to understand we are working together, not playing. I think it will be better if we just concentrate on this investigation, or whatever this is, and keep our emotions out of it."

"Sure, Lars. If that's the way you want it."

"That's the way I want it. I just think it'll make things less complicated."

"Okay. Let's get started."

"First you should check your cell phone to see who called."

"Right." He removed the phone from his pocket. "It was my mom." He pocketed it again.

"You should call her back. Maybe it's important." Laura stared him down until, rolling his eyes, he pulled the phone back out of his pocket and dialed the number. He smirked at her while he waited for his mom to answer.

"Hey, Mom, it's Jake. What's up? I'm at the library with Laura. Yes, with Laura. We just sort of ran into each other. I don't know. Okay, hold on." Jake moved the phone from his ear and turned towards Laura. "Mom wants to know if you're available for dinner? She called your house and left a message too. She wants to go over the final plans for July 4th."

"Sure. That sounds good. Ask her where and what time."

"Mom…Laura said that sounds good. She wants to know where and when? Okay. Yeah, I'll be there. Love you too." He ended the call and found Laura looking at him surprised.

"You're going to dinner too?"

"Oh yeah. It's a whole family pow-wow. The finalization of the July 4th plans. Big stuff in the Callaway household this time of year. The only way to get out of it is to become the black sheep of the family and move to New York. And that only works for a couple of years."

Jake dropped his voice to his best Al Pacino imitation, complete with arm and hand gestures.

"Just when I thought I was out, they pull me back in."

Laura had to laugh at that. The thought of Mrs. Callaway as part of a mafia family was worth a good chuckle. Jake continued in Pacino's voice, now channeling Scarface.

"She wants us all at the house by 6:00. Don't be late, or we'll be saying hello to her little friend.

Laura laughed even louder this time and drew more unwanted looks from the other library patrons. She quieted down and rolled her eyes at Jake.

"You're going to get us thrown out of here," she teased in a whisper.

He leaned into her to whisper back, "It's not my fault these people have no sense of humor." They found themselves inches from each other - face, lips, eyes. Laura cleared her throat and slowly backed to a safe distance.

"Well, it's four o'clock now, so if your mom wants us there by six, we better get busy. Do you think I should go home and change first?"

"Hell no. You look fantastic in that dress." He looked her up and down appraisingly and noted again how the bright yellow dress clung to her curves in all the right places and made her tanned skin seem to glisten.

His intense scrutiny made Laura blush, and she hated to blush.

"I should stop home first anyway to let Sam out."

"Okay, let Sam out, but don't change the dress." Now his eyes stopped roaming over her body and settled on her eyes. She wasn't sure which was worse.

Laura tried to get things back on track. "We should get started. We only have about an hour." Jake nodded his head in agreement but kept the eye contact.

"Jake, stop it."

"What?" he innocently asked.

"You are such a child." Laura broke the stare and turned to the latest book she brought to the table, 'Hallowed Hills – A History'.

"Fine. Let's get to work." Jake conceded with a sigh.

"And you seem to be forgetting my condition for working together. Just business. No personal stuff. Remember?"

"Yeah. I remember. Maybe you shouldn't wear that dress next time. Or that perfume." He subtly leaned in and smelled her neck. She could feel his breath lightly caress her skin and it gave her goosebumps. The good kind. This man was trouble with a capital T.

"Jake!" She tried to sound angry, but her throat had gone dry and his name came out sounding more sexy than angry.

"Okay, sorry. Work only, right. Let's do it." He turned to his notes and organized them as Laura continued to study the book.

"Oh my God, Jake..." Laura felt a cold shiver down her spine as she recognized something in the book.

"What...what's the matter?" Jake went into alert mode. He put his arm protectively around her and searched the book with her.

"What is it, Lars? Talk to me." He took her hand and rubbed it soothingly while she collected her thoughts.

"Jake, I remember something...from the attack."

"Good, that's good, honey. Can you tell me? Do you want to leave here and go somewhere? Tell me what you need."

"No, no...I'm okay. It's that mark." Laura pointed to the symbol on the page in front of her. It was the cross inside a triangle, inside a circle.

Jake followed her gaze and remarked, "It's the same symbol we saw on the sign to Hallowed Hills the night we followed the guy from Betty Simpson's memorial service. What do you remember?" He continued to hold her hand, rubbing it reassuringly.

"He had it, Jake. The man who attacked me...he had that symbol on a chain he wore around his neck. I remember it clearly now. I knew I was forgetting something important, and now I remember. He was so close to me and I was trapped by the counter behind me. He was taller than me, so that symbol caught my eye and I froze, staring at it before I had the courage to move, to react. Oh, God, Jake, what if I didn't move, what if I couldn't move? What if..." She began to shiver at the thought and Jake pulled her close, held her and rubbed his hand up and down her arms to warm her, and comfort her.

Jake spoke reassuringly, "But you did move, you did react. You can't think about the what-ifs. You'll drive yourself crazy. This is good…great actually that you remember this, Lars. It gives us the link we need to tie him to Hallowed Hills and that puts us one step closer to catching the bastard…one step closer to getting your life back. You did good, Lars, really good."

He continued to hold her and could feel her trying with all her might to regain control, but the sudden memory shook her to her core and she began to shiver at the memory.

"It's okay, honey. You're safe…he's not going to hurt you again."

She began to settle, took a deep breath, and pulled away from him. "I'm so sorry…I didn't mean to fall apart like that…it just hit me…"

"Lars, stop apologizing. You went through a traumatic experience and a memory snuck up on you. The important thing is that you remembered this. It's a good thing. It's going to help us."

Her heart rate and breathing calmed, then returned to normal. The shivers subsided. She reminded herself she was safe. She was okay. "Thanks, Jake. I think I'm okay now. What do we do with this information? We should tell the police, right?"

"I'm not sure yet. Let's keep it to ourselves for a bit and see what else we turn up."

Laura checked her watch.

"I really should go so I have time for Sam without being late. Plus, I'd like to bring some flowers for your mom and granny. Your dad didn't stop by today. He's been coming in almost every day, or someone from your family has …" Click. The light bulb turned on in her brain. "That was your doing, wasn't it?" She looked accusingly at Jake.

"What?" Jake looked at her innocently.

"You know what. You had your family coming by my place to check on me, didn't you?"

"What are you talking about?" He feigned innocence and glanced at his watch, "Hey, look at the time." He switched to Pacino again to lighten the mood, "We better get going or we'll be wearing cement shoes and swimming with the fishes."

Before Laura could say anything else, he gathered up their papers, replaced the books they borrowed, and began ushering her out the door.

He walked her to her convertible and opened the door for her.

"You shouldn't be allowed to drive around in this thing. All those heads turning and potential accidents. It's a hazard." Jake gave her a wink before putting his sunglasses on.

She rolled her eyes at him, took the stack of notes he carried for her, and got into the car.

"Thanks, Jake. I'll see you in a bit." She started the car and pulled out.

On the ride home, Laura found herself thinking about Jake and the way he made her feel. She had started her day feeling so in control of her life, so over him. Now, here she was, a few hours later with thoughts of him swirling through her mind. And her body. Even though he could be infuriatingly frustrating, he made her feel things she hadn't felt in a long time, if ever. And she couldn't deny how pleasant those feelings were.

Her mind wandered back to the night they spent together. Maybe he did enjoy it as much as she did. She wished she could just ask him. Why did this have to be so complicated? If two people were meant to be together, why couldn't they just be together and live happily ever after as the story says? Did it ever work out that way?

Laura was almost home when she glanced in the rearview mirror and noticed a white Jeep. Jake was behind her. Was he following her home? As she approached her house and signaled to turn, he did the same. Apparently, he was. A surge of excitement shot through her at the thought of being alone with him here again. But, of course, the responsible side took over and insisted she be in control of the situation and not let her heart overpower her head.

She pulled into the garage, as he pulled his Jeep behind her. She walked out to meet him.

"What are you doing here? I thought I was meeting you at your parent's house?"

"I had a great idea after you left. No sense in driving two cars over. So I thought I'd follow you here, then we can drive over together."

"Oh...I guess. But then you'll have to drive me home after dinner. I hate to make you go out of your way." Her mind flashed to the last time Jake drove her home after dinner, and she could feel her cheeks begin to burn. He appeared to sense her thoughts as he approached her, reached his hand to her hair and removed a small leaf that must have blown in during the ride home.

He gently smoothed her hair, smiled and replied in a soft, husky voice, "It's not a problem. I like driving you home."

She flirted back, "Really, how much do you like it?" What the hell was she doing? She should not be encouraging him.

"I really, really, love it," Jake replied, as he leaned in for the kiss she had been dreaming about since that night. It was soft and gentle, but at the same time filled with urgency. She let herself fall into it, as she didn't have any other choice. Her body screamed for it, for him, ached for him to touch her like he had before. How could she have denied herself this for so long? Then he pulled back.

"I'm sorry...lost my head for a minute. I know you said you want to keep it business between us and I agreed to that. I don't want to go back on my word. It's just that you look so good, smell so damn good, feel so damn good...sorry. I promise to behave."

Laura had stopped breathing, and apparently, thinking, so she was unable to respond at that point. She just knew that one moment she was feeling pretty fantastic and then the next, not so much. And, from what Jake was saying, she had wanted it that way. Right. She vaguely remembered saying something about keeping it business only. She tried to regain her senses and return to her responsible, level-headed self. It took a tremendous amount of energy to do so.

"Right. I did say that. Thank you for remembering and respecting that, Jake." She smoothed her dress and hair, then cleared her throat. "So, I guess I'll take care of Sam, gather some flowers, and then we can go."

"Great. Should I wait here or do you want me to come in?"

*I want you to come in and do what you did last time you were here,* she thought. But she said, "It's up to you. Whichever you prefer."

"I'll come in then. Could use a glass of cold water after that kiss. And I'm rethinking my apology, by the way. I'm not so sorry about the kiss. Kinda really enjoyed it to tell the truth. But I'll try to show more self-control like you asked."

Again, Laura wasn't sure how to respond. She did make the stupid rule. Didn't seem so stupid at the time but now, in the heat of the moment, it seemed ridiculous. Yet she had enough sense to stick to it. At least until she had a clear head and more time to analyze the current state of affairs. Plus, she was aware Jake was having a bit of fun with the whole situation. Two could play at that game.

"Yes. You're right. It's for the best. Come on in. Help yourself to a drink while I take Sam out and gather some flowers to go. And please, try to behave." She smiled sweetly as she held the door for him to enter.

# Twenty-Five

Dinner at the Callaway house was, as expected, warm, loving and delicious. They assembled in the formal dining room around Mrs. Callaway's beautiful, solid cherry table. The best china was used and placed on an antique white lace tablecloth. A mouth-watering roast beef was served, complimented by mashed potatoes, broccoli and a fresh summer salad. A full-bodied, cabernet sauvignon accompanied the meal.

No one mentioned Jake and Laura being together or not being together, or anything about them at all. The conversation centered exclusively on July Fourth. As Jake had explained earlier, it was a very big deal at the Callaway house, and Mrs. Callaway was one hundred percent in charge of the conversation.

"Okay, so to recap, everyone is clear on their duties? Jake, you'll help with the food deliveries from the establishments on your list and assist your father in insuring none of the vendors violate the fire code. Rick, you'll oversee all the electrical needs, also checking that everyone complies with the fire and electric codes. Addi, you're in charge of the volunteers, making sure we have enough to man all the food stations, game booths, and craft and bake tables. Laura, you'll deliver and arrange all the flowers and hanging baskets as planned and assist Jake with the food deliveries. Kelly, you and the kids are in charge of checking out the children's games

166

and activities, making sure they are safe and that the children are properly supervised. Any questions?"

Heads shook and murmured no's ensued.

"Good. This meeting is adjourned. I'll touch base with everyone Thursday night, before the big day, to do a last-minute check. Now for dessert. Addi, want to help me in the kitchen with that?"

"Sure, Mom."

"Mrs. Callaway, I'd be happy to help." Laura started to stand.

"Absolutely not. You're a guest here this evening. You just sit and relax with Jake…and everyone." It was obvious Jake's mom only cared about Laura spending time with Jake, but threw everyone else in to try and disguise her intentions.

"Okay, but next time you're all going to have to come to my home for dinner."

"That's a great idea, Lars. You and I could cook for everyone," Jake chimed in, very excited by the idea.

"Since when can you cook?" Laura shot him a surprised glance.

"Hey, I lived alone in New York for years. You learn things if you want to survive."

Rick snorted in disgust at that comment, "Yeah, like you really had to cook in the city, with all the restaurants to choose from and a different babe wanting to cook for you every week…" Jake's brother immediately realized he had inserted foot in mouth on that one. And by the look on everyone's face, so did the rest of the family.

"…ah, ya know, it's the city and all, there's so much to do and so many people to do stuff with…" He seemed to be digging the hole deeper and deeper and wished for someone to throw him a life-line, but his family just continued to stare at him in disbelief at his stupidity. It was Laura who finally came to his rescue.

"Rick, it's okay. I'm sure Jake had and will continue to have girlfriends. He and I are just friends…so no worries." That is what Laura said, but not at all what she felt. Rick had just confirmed her deepest fear about Jake. That he did indeed have women throwing themselves at him for the last fifteen years. City women too, with city looks, city ideas, and city sex moves. And, apparently, city cooking. Any elation she was feeling from the events earlier in the day had just been deflated.

Rick's wife, Kelly, seemed to sense Laura's pain and interjected, "Laura, just ignore my husband. He has always been jealous of Jake's adventure in the city and has always imagined it to be much grander than I'm sure it was. I mean, he spent most of his time working. He went there for his career and it paid off. You don't accomplish the kind of things he did by being the playboy Ricky imagines in his pea-sized man brain." She gave her husband a scolding punch on the arm. Rick began to reply, noticed the glare still coming from his brother and thought better of it. He was rescued by his mom and sister coming in with dessert.

Mrs. Callaway displayed a baking dish. "Okay, now in honor of summer, we have homemade peach cobbler with vanilla ice cream. Gran was kind enough to make the cobbler for us and it looks delicious."

"Where is Gran tonight?" Jake asked.

"Oh, tonight is her Bridge night. She'll be home later."

Mrs. Callaway began dishing out the cobbler, as Addi dropped a scope of ice cream on top and passed it to Mr. Callaway who passed it down the table. This continued until everyone was served.

Laura took one look at Mrs. Callaway and saw that she was keenly aware that something unsettling had transpired among the group while she was in the kitchen. When she finished serving dessert and sat down to enjoy her own, Laura watched as she took a moment to study everyone's face. It was obvious by the look on Ricky's face that he had said or done something to upset everyone. Everyone except Jake. Jake was not upset, he was furious. So furious the tips of his ears were red, as they tended to get when he was over-the-top angry.

Mrs. Callaway, apparently deciding it best not to rehash whatever just happened, did her best to start a new topic of conversation.

"So Jake, Laura, what were the two of you up to at the library, of all places?"

Neither answered immediately. Instead, they glanced a knowing glance at each other, then Jake nodded in agreement and responded.

"Well it's funny you should ask, Mom. Laura and I debated earlier whether we should bring that up tonight or not. But since you asked, it seems like a good time. Remember how I told you that I was working on a story that I feared was putting Laura in danger?" Laura could see Jake's anger at his brother began to fade as he discussed the new topic.

They all nodded in agreement.

"Well, it wasn't a story exactly."

Laura interrupted, "No, it was something that I got Jake involved in. Do you all remember that accident that happened in front of my house several weeks ago? Well, there were some circumstances surrounding it that I found odd, and I happened to mention it to Jake, and, long story short, he started asking questions around town. Next thing you know, he gets a threatening note on his porch, my dog gets poisoned, his house is torched and I am attacked in my store."

"And you think all these acts are related to this accident somehow?" Mr. Callaway asked.

"Yeah, Dad, we do. We've both been doing some research, together and separately, which is how we met coincidentally at the library today. We decided we could make more progress if we worked together...like business partners." Jake shot a sly glance at Laura before continuing.

"We realized today that you all might be able to help fill in some blanks as well."

"Of course, honey, whatever we can do to help. But what about Laura being in danger?"

"Mrs. Callaway, Jake tends to… overthink things sometimes. I don't believe anything he's done has put me in danger. I'm the one who got us involved in this, so if anyone put anyone in danger it was me. And quite frankly, I just can't sit this out, feeling like a victim, waiting and wondering if something else is going to happen. Especially since my daughters will be coming home from their grandparents' house soon. I have to do whatever I can to put these pieces together, see if there is a connection and make sure justice is served. It's the only way I can get my life back to normal."

"We'll do whatever you need, honey. Jake, tell us what this is all about and how we can help."

Jake and Laura spent the next hour filling the family in on all they knew so far. They started with the accident, Betty Simpson, Jonathan Laird, and Phil Molino, and concluded with Hallowed Hills, the Magil family, and possible ties to the religious cult.

Jake continued, "It's a lot to digest all at once, but all we really need from you right now is anything you can remember about the Magils. Addi, your input on religious cults can help as well. Let's start with the Magils. We know they owned the ice cream store in town, which they sold a while back. Can you tell us about them, their kids, where they are now?"

Mr. and Mrs. Callaway glanced at each other, then Mr. Callaway began.

"Well, you're right, Jake, the elder Magils opened the ice cream shop years ago. Heck, it was there as long as I can remember. The parents ran it mostly, the kids didn't have much interest in it. They only had two kids, at least that I knew of, Albert and Helen. Helen was older, close to your mother's age, right Sue?"

"She was a few years younger than me, although I didn't know her that well. She was quiet, in an odd way. And you know me, I talk to everyone. But she made it clear she wanted to keep to herself. Albert was the same way, but even stranger, wouldn't you say, Joe?"

"Didn't know him well either. As you said, Jake, they were extremely religious, but in a strange, zealous kind of way. Not even sure what religion, one of those off-shoots of the mainstream. They always make me suspicious. Anyway, as far as the parents go, they closed the store a while back and retired somewhere warm, I believe. Then I heard they'd passed away shortly after. If memory serves, they were in some sort of accident or something. I remember everyone talking about how it was such a shame that they worked in the store their whole lives, finally retired and then, bam, dead. Helen ended up marrying Bob Caully..."

"Bob Caully, at the post office, the deputy mayor?" Jake asked.

"One and the same. But it didn't last long. Like your mom said, she was odd, kept to herself and Bob's so friendly and outgoing. Probably doomed from the start."

"Did either remarry?" Laura asked.

"Not even sure Bob and Helen were ever officially divorced. Just heard rumors that she left town and he's still here. To my knowledge, he lives alone. Never seen him with another woman, have you, Sue?"

"Can't say that I have. That's surprising, too. Bob's such an outgoing fellow."

"What about Helen, no one knows what happened to her, where she went? Or Albert?" Jake asked.

"No. Never heard anything about Helen other than she left town." Mr. Callaway answered. "Now Albert, he was a strange one. Gave your mother the creeps. We stayed away from him. Then, I guess it was around the same time you left for New York, Jake, the family put the store up for sale, the parents retired and Albert took off as well. Never heard anything about him after that. Could be dead for all I know."

"Mom, what does Dad mean 'he gave you the creeps'?" Jake asked.

"Oh, you know, a woman gets a certain feeling from a man. The way he looks at her and other women. Sometimes it's flattering and flirtatious. But sometimes it's uncomfortable, frightening. Albert was like that. I didn't like the way he looked at me or other women, for that matter. It wasn't just me. A lot of the women steered clear of him and were happy when he left town."

"And you never heard where he went or where he might be now?"

"No, honey, nothing. Sorry I can't be more help. It's a shame Gran isn't here, she might remember something helpful. She knew the parents much better than your father and I."

"No, Mom, you're doing great. You too, Dad. Anyone else remember anything about the Magil family or Hallowed Hills or Lenape Lake?"

"Just that as teenagers we used to sneak into the lake to skinny dip." This from Rick, who had remained silent up until now.

"Ricky! I thought I'd raised you better," Mrs. Callaway said.

"You did, Mom. But you know...boys. We only did it a couple of times. I remember the last time. In fact, it was around this time of year. A bunch of us snuck in with some beers and decided to take a dip.

"Johnny Moore was there and he had to take a ...go to the bathroom, you know, from drinking all the beer, so he went off into the woods. Came back all out of sorts, yelling the Ku Klux Klan was after him or something. Claims he saw a bunch of people in black hooded capes coming after him. We told him the Klan wore white hooded capes, but he was still totally freaked out. I think he was doing more than drinking beer that night, if you know what I mean. But he managed to scare the heck out of us and we all took off and never went back."

"When was this, Rick…how old were you?" Jake asked.

"Let's see…you were living in New York…it was summer…I think it was the summer before my senior year. So that would make it about a year after you left town."

"Do you remember if it was called Hallowed Hills at that time?"

"No, I don't remember. Sorry, bro."

"How about this?" Jake held up a piece of paper with the religious symbol on it that Laura recognized on her attacker's necklace. He passed it around so everyone could get a good look. "This symbol is on the sign at the entrance to Hallowed Hills and today Laura remembered seeing it on the man who attacked her."

"Oh, Laura, honey, are you okay? It must be so difficult to keep remembering things about that day," Mrs. Callaway said.

"I'm fine, thanks. I'm glad I remembered because it helps to connect the attack with everything else. For some reason, that gives me comfort…like it wasn't just random but has to do with something bigger. Does that make sense?"

"Of course, honey. I just worry about you staying at that house alone. I wish you'd stay here with us until this situation gets straightened out. You know you and Sam are always welcome."

"I know, and thank you. But Sam is a pretty good watchdog and I can't live my life in fear."

"I understand that, but the offer stands if you ever want to take us up on it."

"Thanks, Mrs. Callaway. I do appreciate it."

"So, anyone else recognize the symbol?" Jake refocused the discussion. Heads shook around the table. Then Addi chimed in.

"It could be a religious symbol. Many religious organizations, mainstream or not, often have symbols to identify their sect."

"Thanks, Ad. I'm going to make of copy of this for everyone and I want you to keep it in your mind as you go about your business. If you see it anywhere, I need you to call me right away." They all nodded in agreement.

"Ad, since you're our psychology expert what else can you tell us about religious cults, cult leaders, that sort of stuff?" Jake turned the conversation over to his younger sister.

"A lot," Addi chimed in. "But I'll focus on the highlights. Basically, cult leaders seek to form cults primarily to meet their specific emotional needs. Most leaders suffer from one or more psychological disorders, but few, if any, subject themselves to psychological tests or prolonged clinical interviews that allow for an accurate diagnosis. However, researchers and psychologists who have studied them agree most exhibit traits consistent with being narcissistic, psychotic, and sociopathic. Many also suffer from a personality disorder, often narcissistic personality disorder. This is a disorder in which people have an inflated sense of their own importance, a deep need for admiration and a lack of empathy for others. They often have a 'God Complex' believing they are God-like and should be worshipped as such.

"These 'leaders' attract those who are searching for a purpose, security, a sense of belonging. The cult offers them this, but in return, they must go through a process of 'thought reform' brainwashing in essence. This process attempts to isolate members from the outside world, including their friends and family, while reprogramming the way they see the world. Willing members are so desperate to belong to a group they easily succumb to the beliefs, desires, and demands of the leader and other cult members. Others, who are forced to conform, take longer to 're-educate.' First the cult has to 'break them' to get them to comply. It's similar to Stockholm Syndrome, which I'm sure you've heard of, where kidnapped victims develop positive feelings for, or begin to worship, their captors. You've all heard the horror stories of sexual abuse, group suicides, and other atrocities. This is often the result."

Mrs. Callaway expressed her concerns, "Jake, I don't like this. This sounds too dangerous for you and Laura to be involved in."

"I agree, Jake. What about getting the police involved?" Mr. Callaway asked.

"They are, Dad, to some extent. I talked to Jimmy at the station, but apparently, no one is all that interested in a car accident with no known fatalities and they've hit a dead end on the man who attacked Laura."

"What's your next step then?" Mr. Callaway inquired.

"Jimmy's been helping me out here and there with research and I've got some angles to follow up on at the *Tribune*. Laura's going to be talking with some of her long-time customers to see if she can get more information on the Magil's and Hallowed Hills. And, thanks to your information, I may pay a visit to our friendly postmaster."

"What can we all do to help, son?" Mr. Callaway asked.

"Right now, just keep your eyes and ears open. We've got the big picnic coming up this weekend and most of the town will be there. This gives us the perfect opportunity to gather some information. If everybody can keep that in mind while you're working your shift on the Fourth of July, that'd be helpful."

"We all can do that. You both be careful, now, you hear. And I want us all to make sure we have each other's cell phone numbers programmed in case of emergency. Especially you, Laura. We need yours and you need all of ours. And don't be shy about calling any of us, any time of day or night."

Laura nodded in agreement, "Yes, thanks, Mr. Callaway I won't."

They pulled out their cell phones and began trading and checking current numbers for cells, home, work, and pagers.

After some lighter chitchat at the dinner table, the group started to disperse from the dining room. Jake went to the office to copy the picture of the symbol for everyone. The other men followed.

Jake's dad voiced his concerns, "Jake, I'm more concerned about Laura now that I'm aware of what's going on. You need to convince her to stay here or to let you stay with her until this mess is figured out."

"Dad, I couldn't agree with you more. But you know how stubborn she is. She won't hear of it. The best we can do is continue our surveillance of her house like we've been doing."

"But that's not a fool-proof plan and you know it."

"If anyone has a better idea I'd love to hear it because she won't move in here or let me stay at her place."

The men began to brainstorm ideas for protecting Laura without her knowledge. They finally settled on an idea.

"That would make me feel better, but she can't know about it."

"Who can't know what?" The men turned to see Kelly standing in the doorway.

"I'll fill you in later honey. Ready to go?" Rick quickly changed the subject. "We really should pick up the kids from your Mom's."

"Yep. I'm ready. Funny how our nights without the kids seem to fly by, don't they?"

"Sorry, Kel. I kept you longer than intended with all this stuff. You didn't even have time to yourselves." Jake smiled at his sister-in-law.

"Don't worry about it, Jake. That's what families are for," Kelly replied.

"How'd you ever score such a cool wife, Ricky? I don't see what you see in him, Kel." Jake put his arm around his sister-in-law as they walked back towards the kitchen to find the others. Jake's mom, Laura, and Addi were finishing with the last of the pots and pans.

"Hey, Lars, ready to head out?"

"Sure, let me just finish with this." Laura reached for another pot to dry.

"No, no, you go on honey, it's getting late. I'll finish this up," Mrs. Callaway insisted.

"Okay, but only because I feel bad that Jake has to take me home and it's getting late."

The party began to break up, with everyone agreeing to do their part for the picnic and for the investigation.

***

It was a warm night and the humidity had lessened, so Jake drove with the windows down. They rode along quietly, listening to the radio play "Take It Easy" by the The Eagles. Laura could feel her nervousness increase with the proximity to her house. She wasn't sure what was going to happen once she and Jake arrived. More importantly, she wasn't sure what she wanted to happen.

The glorious afternoon had been followed by Rick's comment regarding all of Jake's other women. She had to admit, that made her very unsure of herself where Jake was concerned. Was she just another notch on his headboard? Did he compare her to all the others? If so, how did she measure up? Too much pressure. She should just stick to her earlier plan to keep it platonic, figure out what was going on with Hallowed Hills and get her life back to normal.

"Can I walk you in, just to ease my mind?" Jake's voice startled her from her thoughts.

"Oh, we're here already, huh? Sure. That'd be fine."

They both exited the Jeep and Laura unlocked the back door. Sam met them, excitedly wagging his tail as he greeted them.

"I guess he needs to go out. I'll take him and then you can lock up when I leave." Jake offered.

"Okay. I'm going to text the girls. They texted during dinner."

A few minutes later Jake was strolling back with Sam at his side. He found Laura in the kitchen typing on her phone.

"He should be good for the night. I threw his ball a few times to tire him out for ya," Jake said.

"Thanks, Jake. I appreciate it."

An awkward silence hung between them, as Sam stood looking from one to the other.

"Everything okay with the girls?"

"Yep. They're having a great time and are excited about the July 4th party there. Of course, they're also excited about the boys who will be at the party. It's always about a boy, isn't it?" Laura smiled, happy to be talking about her daughters.

"Or a girl, depending on who you are." Jake smiled back. Their eyes met for the first time since that afternoon. The evening at the Callaway's had been all business, no time to think about what was going on between them.

"Laura, look. I'm gonna be honest with you, I'm worried about you staying here alone..."

"I'm not alone. I have Sam." She reached down and scratched Sam behind the ears.

"I know you do. But...he's just a dog..."

"Just a dog! He saved my life when that creep came to my shop. If it wasn't for Sam...I don't know what would have happened." Laura turned and walked towards the sink. She got a glass from the cabinet and filled it with water.

"I know he did. He's a great dog. But, Lars, come on. You're out here all alone and..."

"And nothing. Jake, I've lived here alone, with my girls, for a long time and I will continue to do so. I can't let some creep take that away from me. Don't you understand, if he does that, then he wins? I can't let him win." She took a long drink of water. Jake lowered his voice to a softer, more soothing tone as he walked towards her.

"Can't we just make a compromise until we figure out what we're dealing with here?"

"What kind of compromise are you talking about?" She turned to look at him.

"Well, I know you'll never consider moving into my parent's house."

"No. Absolutely not. As kind as they were to offer, I just can't."

"And I understand that. But, what about…and I swear I'm completely on the up and up on this…what about letting me stay here, on the couch, until we get more information about whatever is going on?"

Laura began laughing. "I bet that's what you tell all the girls, huh? Especially those city girls, 'I can't leave you all alone in the big, bad city. Just let me sleep here on your couch, baby.' Is that how it works?"

"No. That is not how it works." He approached her, took the glass from her hand, took a long drink himself, then set the glass on the counter. He was inches from her now and she could feel her heart rate increase as she inhaled his clean musky scent. He spoke very softly and deliberately. "I am not going to stand here and deny I met other women in the city. I lived there for fifteen years. Of course, I had girlfriends. You were married, remember?

"I will tell you in absolute honesty, that none of them were serious girlfriends. And by serious, I mean anyone I wanted to marry or even bring home to meet my family, for that matter. They were in my life to fill a void. And I know that sounds harsh, but at the time I believed I was trying to move on with my life. I thought if I looked hard enough, I would find the right one. Someone I'd want to marry and spend my life with. But I never did. And now… well here we are."

He very slowly took her face in his hands and, looking her directly in her eyes, said, "I've found the one I want to marry. The one I've always wanted to marry." He leaned into her and placed one soft, gentle kiss on her lips. He slowly moved back, keeping her face in his hands.

"But I can't compete with them, Jake. I don't have what they have."

"No, Lars, you've got it all wrong. They couldn't compete with you. They never had a chance."

This time, she leaned in to kiss him, but her kiss was hungrier, needier than his had been. She knew she needed him, wanted him, had to have him and she let him know it. He responded in kind, pulling her closer and letting his fingers get tangled in her hair as he let her devour his mouth, his heart, his soul. Laura gently pulled back.

"Jake, I want you to stay, but I'm scared. I don't want to get hurt. You scare me."

"Honey, I would never hurt you. I love you. And the night we spent together here, was the most amazing night of my life. I want that to be my life, forever. I want to be with you forever."

"I love you too, Jake. I just have to be careful. I don't want to confuse the girls and…"

He put his finger to her mouth and whispered, "Shhhh, it's okay. We can go slow. As slow as you want. But I really would like to stay here tonight, even if it is just on the couch."

"It's just that I'm afraid to…get used to you…you know, being here for me, in case one day you're not."

"Lars, I'll always come back to you, for as long as you'll have me.

He leaned in to kiss her again, just as the sound of his cell phone pierced through the moment. He groaned as he reached for the offending instrument, squinted as he read the message, then sighed.

"Well, it looks like I'm being called to prove my last statement to you. I have to go check out this fire call. But if you'll have me, I'll come back as soon as I'm done. And I meant what I said. Slow…nice and slow. I can sleep on the couch, on the floor, I don't care. I just want to be here with you. Plus, I am homeless, so you'd be doing a nice thing…taking in a homeless person." He flashed his impossible-to-resist grin. "What do you say?"

Laura rolled her eyes, "How could I be so cruel as to turn away a man so down on his luck?"

"That's my girl." He gave her a quick kiss on her forehead. "I'll be back as soon as I can."

# Twenty-Six

Laura wasn't sure what to wear. She didn't have the proper nightgown or pajamas for a sleepover with Jake, and there certainly wasn't time to shop now. So she settled on her usual bedtime apparel, pajama bottoms with a cami top. Laura got into bed, turned off the bedside lamp and heard Sam plop on the floor beside her. She lay in bed knowing that sleep would not come. Her mind was reeling with thoughts of Jake. Could this be happening? Was a happy ending truly in store for them? Her pessimistic nature wouldn't allow her to be too overjoyed by the thought. But she refused to dwell on all the problems that could interfere. This was progress, she thought.

She wasn't sure how long she had been lying there when she heard the sound. At first, it sounded like scratching. Like an animal trapped and trying to scratch its way out. Sam heard it immediately and was standing at attention, with tail up and ears perched high.

Laura sat up abruptly as ideas of what to do raced through her mind. Her first thought was to grab the phone to call 911. She hesitated, fearing sounding like a hysterical female. What if it was just an animal trapped in the attic? Or maybe it was Jake, returning already. But she doubted he'd be back so soon, plus she had given him a key. Her second thought was to grab a weapon in case she had to defend herself against an animal or worse.

The scratching sound intensified and, with it her fear. She leaped out of bed, threw on a robe and grabbed the baseball bat she kept in her closet. Her hands shook as she tried to grasp it tightly. Heat overtook her body, as the pounding of her heart collided with the scratching sound in the distance. She inhaled and exhaled in rapid bursts while trying to clear her mind to think, but it was impossible with her body betraying her. She needed to gain control before she could act.

She remembered to control her breathing. With that accomplished, her pounding heart eased up enough for her to hear the scratching sound more clearly. It was coming from downstairs, perhaps from the back of the kitchen, by the door, and it was more of a grinding sound then a scratching. Not from an animal, she thought. Panic again. Shallow breathing. Pounding heart. A dash for the phone to call 911 as Sam growled and darted towards the bedroom door.

"Sam! No! Come!"

He listened, halted in place and growled ready to attack.

"Come on, answer, answer," she mumbled into the phone.

Then she heard the sound of breaking glass and knew in an instant she was in trouble.

"911 emergency. Please state your emergency."

"Someone's in my home. You need to send help immediately." With that Sam's instincts overtook his obedience, he began barking and bolted through the bedroom door. BANG! Laura heard the shot, dropped the phone and ran without thinking to Sam.

"Sam, no!" She flew down the stairs towards the sound of breaking glass and heard another gunshot. She rounded the corner, bat in hand to see two figures wrestling on the ground in her kitchen. The dim light from the kitchen stove made them impossible to identify. Sam stood nearby barking, apparently not sure what to do either. The sound of metal sliding across the ceramic tile floor, then more breaking glass diverted her attention. A gun, on her floor. She ran dropped the bat, grabbed the gun, not sure what to do, who to shoot. She fired a warning shot at the ceiling, Sam howled, a moan surfaced from the scuffle on the floor, then a dark figure retreated out the back door.

Not sure who remained, friend or foe, Laura steadied her hands, gripped the gun and pointed it in the direction of the figure on her floor. She saw Sam move towards the figure, not growling, tail wagging, no longer on alert, but Laura's body refused to calm. She stayed in position with gun pointed, ready to fire if necessary. She vaguely recognized a familiar voice through her fear. She blocked it and stayed focused on the potential danger. The figure rose from the floor, Sam by his side, and began to approach her. Hands shaking, she knew she would shoot if she had to defend herself, but something held her steady, kept her focused on the man approaching, his voice, the way he walked, his familiar scent.

"Laura, honey, it's Jake. Put the gun down. It's okay. You're safe. He's gone. It's just me and Sam. Honey, put the gun down."

He was getting closer, the sound of his voice beginning to register. Her adrenaline still pumping, but starting to wane; her heart still pounding, but quieting; her breathing still rapid, but air filling her lungs; her arms still taunt with fear, but loosening; lowering the gun to her side, her legs shaking, shaking, collapsing, falling to the floor only to be saved by Jake's strong arms around her.

***

An hour later, Laura entered her kitchen and heard Jake retelling his story to the police.

"And then I entered the back door and saw a guy with gun raised, ready to shoot. It was like slow motion, I saw Sam, heard his bark, realized this man was going to shoot him and I just lunged at him."

One of the officers asked Jake, "Did you notice a vehicle on the scene when you arrived?"

"No. The first thing I noticed was the back door opened. Then instinct took over and I just flew in the door and before I could even yell for Laura, I spotted the guy with his gun aimed at the dog. I just reacted…just jumped on him." Jake turned to see Laura enter the room.

"Hey, how you feeling?" He rose from the table to get her a mug. "How about some coffee?"

"That sounds really good about now." She eased herself into a chair and greeted the two officers seated at her kitchen table.

Jake returned with mug of coffee for her and the pot in hand.

"Who else needs a refill?" Jake topped off the officer's cups, then filled his own.

Laura took a sip as she studied the police officers. The older one spoke first.

"Hi, Mrs. Delaney. I'm Officer Tom Burns of the Newbury PD and this is Officer Jim O'Neil." Laura thought the younger man looked familiar. He appeared to be about her age with reddish hair, and Irish fair skin. She couldn't recall ever seeing the older man. He seemed to be in his late forties or early fifties with graying blond hair and an easy smile. She smiled in return and nodded to both men as Jake returned to the table with a plate of cookies. Had the situation been different, she would have teased Jake about his excellent hosting skills.

"Laura, do you remember Jimmy, ah, Office O'Neil, from our school days?" Jake asked.

"Now that you mention it, yes. I thought you looked familiar. Please, call me Laura."

"Sorry to have to see you again under these circumstances," Jimmy said.

"Yes. Me too." Laura took another sip of her coffee and began to feel her brain slowly defog. "Can someone tell me what happened? I'm assuming I blacked out at some point. The last thing

I remember…I was holding a gun and pointing it…Oh my God! Where is Sam?" She jumped up to search for her beloved dog but became wobbly on her feet. Jake stood and quickly placed his arms on hers.

"He's fine, Lars. Relax. Nothing happened to Sam. He's out back in the yard and he's safe. Some of the officers are out there looking for clues. In fact, Sam suckered some of the guys into throwing his ball for him. So no worries there."

Her body relaxed immediately, and she let Jake ease her back into the chair.

Laura continued, "Okay…so the last thing I remember was pointing the gun and then nothing."

Jake took a seat, then recanted for Laura the story he had just told the officers.

"That's as far as I got for the official police report before you joined us. So if it's okay with everyone, I'll just pick up from that point?" Both officers and Laura nodded in agreement, so Jake continued.

"So, where was I? I had just jumped the guy, the gun went off, but missed Sam." Jake saw Laura flinch and looked for her approval to go on. She nodded, so he did. "My only thought at that point was that I had to get the gun away from this guy.

"I could see Sam was okay, but close, and then I saw Laura coming towards the kitchen…I had to get the gun…that's all I was thinking. I'm sure he was thinking the same thing because we were both struggling for it and then I heard it go off again. I heard Sam barking, so I had to assume he didn't get hit and I just had to believe that Laura was too far away, but the thought of her being shot kicked up my adrenaline, I guess, because I felt full of… I don't know… I guess fury is the best way to describe it, and I just started banging his hand with the gun against the floor.

"Finally, he dropped it and I swung my leg around to kick it away from him. I'm not sure what happened next, but almost simultaneously, I heard another shot, and something fell from above and hit us both. I heard him yell, then the next thing I knew, he was bolting for the door.

"I saw Laura holding the gun, shaking. In a split second, I decided to go to her, rather than chase him." Jake paused to take a sip of his steaming mug of coffee

Office Burns said, "You made the right choice. Unfortunately, we didn't get here in time to see him come out so didn't know to sweep the area until we came in and found you. By the time we did, he was gone."

Laura interjected, "I remember…that third shot you heard was me, Jake. I saw you on the floor with him, except I wasn't sure who was who, so I shot at the ceiling…like a warning shot I guess." Laura glanced over to the area of the kitchen where she had fired. She saw the hole in the ceiling. All three men followed her glance.

"Yeah, it looks like pieces of the ceiling fell. One must have hit the intruder. That combined with Jake overpowering him, and you in control of his gun, must have caused him to high-tail it out of here." Officer Burns explained.

"When I got to you Lars, you were out of it, not sure who I was, in shock. I convinced you to put the gun down, then you collapsed. The officers called for the paramedics. When they got here you were cognizant enough to tell them you were fine and refused to go to the hospital. They did a cursory check of your vitals and offered you a mild sedative. I sat with you on the couch until you dosed off. You were only out for about an hour."

"Okay…it's all coming back to me now."

"Mrs. Delaney, Laura, could you tell me what happened before you came downstairs?" Officer Burns asked.

"Yes, of course. I was upstairs in bed. Jake had been here and was called to a fire…Jake, how did you get back here so fast?" She turned her attention to Jake.

"Well…don't be mad at me now or my family. But we were all concerned about you staying here alone with everything going on. So after dinner tonight, all of us guys were brainstorming ways to keep you safe if you refused to let me stay here. Kevin suggested a sort of town watch, where we would take turns watching your house at night to check things out. I took it tonight since I was driving you home anyway, but the fire call came in and I had to leave. I called Ricky to take over the watch, figured he owed me anyway after his comment at dinner, but he offered to take the fire call instead, so I turned around and headed back here. Hope you're not mad we were conspiring behind your back, we're just all worried about you and know how you hate that so…"

"Jake, I'm not mad. I'm…touched, that you and your family would go to such trouble for me. I don't know what to say."

"Well now, you just raised some more questions for us, Jake," Officer Burns said. "What do you mean you and your family are worried about Laura with 'everything going on'? If something is going on that may impact this case, you need to disclose it."

Jake and Laura glanced at each other.

Jake answered, "Tom, Laura and I need to have a word alone. We're gonna step into the other room for a minute if that's alright with you?"

"That's fine, Jake. But keep in mind, we can't do our jobs to the best of our abilities if you aren't one hundred percent honest with us. We want to find this guy. We want our citizens to be safe in their own homes as much as you do."

Jake and Laura went upstairs to her bedroom to insure total privacy. Jake took her hands in his.

"How are you feeling, really?"

"I'm okay. Things are clear again. I'm not sure total reality has set in yet, that someone broke into my house, but there will be plenty of time for that later." She smiled and squeezed both his hands to try and reassure him.

"We have a decision to make here. How much information should we tell these guys?"

"Well, they are the police, Jake. I know we have some concerns about whether or not they have been handling the accident investigation on the up and up, but this has gotten much more serious now. That man had a gun tonight. You could have been shot." Her voice betrayed her and she began to shake.

"Hey, hey. If anyone is worried about someone getting hurt here, it's me worrying about you." He pulled her close and soothingly rubbed her back. She calmed a bit and he tilted her head up to his. "We're a team on this now. Whatever we decide, we decide together."

"Then I think we need to disclose what we know so far, about Hallowed Hills and the accident...everything."

"Okay. Let's do it."

# Twenty-Seven

"We're both fine, Mom. No, that's not necessary. The police are keeping an eye on the house and I'm staying here with Laura…for awhile. She's right here. Okay." Jake handed the phone to Laura, as he rolled his eyes.

"It's my Mom. She wants to hear your voice to reassure her you're okay."

"Mrs. Callaway, it's Laura. I'm fine. Yes, Jake is taking good care of me. Absolutely not. I am more than able to do my part for the picnic, don't be silly. I will report for duty on Friday as planned, and I'm looking forward to it. There's no need for you to worry. As Jake said, the police are keeping an eye on the house and Jake and I are safe inside with Sam. Okay, we will. Good night." Laura disconnected the call and sat on the edge of the bed next to Jake.

"Good morning is more like it. The sun will be coming up soon. I feel as tired as you look. Come here." Jake began to massage her shoulders.

"That feels so good. Every muscle in my body aches." Laura leaned into Jake's caresses. She couldn't remember the last time someone had given her a massage, or the last time she had needed one so badly.

"Jake?"

"Hmm?"

"Do you think we did the right thing, telling the officers everything we found out? I mean, your friend, Jim, kept looking at us like we were crazy. The other officer wrote everything down, but I sensed he thought we had a few screws loose too."

"Well, we made the decision, no sense second-guessing it. And Officer Burns had a point, the more information they have about this guy, the better chance they have of catching him. That's our ultimate goal here, to get him off the streets. I'm not sure the police will care much about what's going on at Hallowed Hills unless some sort of law is broken. As far as they are concerned, the accident was just that, an accident. They aren't going to waste valuable department labor and time unless we give them more evidence that an actual crime took place. That's the reality of the situation."

"I guess you're right." Jake's strong hands began to melt the stress of the night away. Laura felt herself becoming more relaxed with each caress.

Laura turned and reached for Jake's face. She ran her fingers through his hair.

"Jake…I could have lost you tonight…I could have lost you again, forever." Her voice was uneven as she spoke, and she pulled back to look at him.

"But you didn't…and you won't. I'm here…forever." He gathered her into his arms after they both settled into the bed then both slowly drifted off to sleep.

***

The morning arrived accompanied by stifling heat and humidity. The Grand Master again broke with tradition and abandoned his clergy robe, instead opting for shorts and a polo shirt. It was just too damn hot for tradition.

"It looks like we're all here and accounted for. Let's begin. As we are all aware, the Fourth of July is two days away and we need to finalize our plans. To recap for our younger members who are here today, the Fourth of July has special significance to our group here at Hallowed Hills. It was on this date, many years ago, that our people gathered here to discuss a better way of life for themselves and their families, an Independence Day, if you will, from the oppression of mainstream society. This tradition has been carried on ever since with a celebration of our commitment to this way of life and our everlasting faith. "Unfortunately, this year, our plans have been made more difficult by outsiders who do not understand our beliefs or our way of life. I received a call late last night confirming my belief that immediate action must be taken. These outsiders are a threat to everything we have created, to everything our founders have built throughout the years. We must take drastic measures to see that they do not hinder our intentions any further."

The second in command stood and interjected, "And, as many of you know, the Elders have debated several scenarios to take care of this problem. We are at odds, so now we come to you, our younger members, to help make the best choice for the future of Hallowed Hills."

The Grand Master now stood as well, refusing to be overshadowed by his subordinate.

"What my friend here says is true. We need your help and insight into a problem that is not only threatening the future, but is disrupting the current state of order within our group."

The two men, both standing, shot menacing glares at one another. It was apparent to anyone present that a power struggle was occurring and the outcome depended on what would be decided in this room today.

***

Jake and Laura had their agendas for the day. In addition to meeting Mrs. Callaway to finalize the plans for the picnic, Laura needed to stop by the post office and, while there, would casually pump Bob Caully for any information on his wife and her family.

Jake, after meeting with his mom, was going to do more research on Kevin Malloy and the story he was proposing about the Magil family and Hallowed Hills. If time permitted, he'd follow up with Jimmy at the police station and see if the investigation was progressing.

Jake got an early start, which left Laura alone to get dressed and ready for the day. She took comfort in knowing the police would be keeping an eye on her home. As she went about her morning routine, the realization that she was practically living with a man hit her repeatedly. That reality was evident as she had to make both sides of her bed instead of just one, as she did the breakfast dishes and washed two coffee mugs, as she straightened the bathroom and encountered two tooth brushes, two bath towels and men's clothing on the floor.

Each time a little thrill rushed through her stomach and she realized she couldn't remember the last time she had been this happy. But, of course, that feeling was always followed by the doom and gloom sensation that something would interfere with her happiness, as it had so many times before.

She did her best to shake it off and to try to remain positive, despite all the craziness going on around her. She tried to hum an upbeat song to herself and settled on Bob Marley's "Don't Worry About a Thing." So she hummed as she headed to her shop to get the workday started. She gathered floral arrangements, made deliveries, and ran errands all the while pushing down the memory of gunshots and the fact that someone had broken into her home with the intention of… of what? She didn't want to go there. She refused to go there. Instead, she hummed her happy song and went on with the day.

She hummed through all her morning deliveries and to her meeting with Mrs. Callaway. Now she hummed as she entered the post office to see Bob Caully. As usual, he was behind the counter singing to the oldies that played on the radio. He was wearing his official postal uniform, dark blue shorts, light blue short-sleeved shirt, which stretched across his ample belly, as he sorted letters and packages into their designated post office boxes.

"Hi, Bob."

Bob stopped his sorting and singing and turned to face Laura.

"Well, well, well. Look what the cat dragged in. Hello there, young lady. And to what do I owe the pleasure?"

Laura approached the counter and laid the package she was carrying onto it.

"I need a few things from you today. I have this package to mail to the girls. They're visiting their grandparents in New England and decided to extend their visit. I got an emergency text message, requesting more clothes be sent ASAP. So I need to overnight this please." She slid the package his way with a smile. "And also, I need a roll of stamps."

"My pleasure, my dear." Bob took the package, weighed it, stamped it and began gathering the roll of stamps. "And what's new with you these days? You're looking rather chipper. Does that glow have anything to do with a certain fellow I saw you with recently?"

Laura could feel herself start to blush, "Oh, now don't go spreading rumors, Bob, but yeah, I guess it sort of does."

"I'm glad. You deserve to be happy and Jake's a good guy. Always thought you two should be together. What have you both been up to?"

"Just getting reacquainted I guess."

"Ah, reacquainted, is that what they're calling it these days." Bob was enjoying toying with her and sported a grin from ear to ear as he handed her the stamps and receipts.

"What did I say, no rumors now. Actually, we've been busy helping Mrs. Callaway with the picnic plans. You know what a big deal that is. Has she roped you into helping yet?"

"Of course. She gets me every year for one thing or another."

"I'm sure. I mean, you are one of the long-standing members of the community, I guess you've been helping with this for years?"

"Oh yeah, since the beginning."

"That's right, I think I remember you dishing out ice cream years ago…from Magil's ice cream store, right? Didn't your wife's family own that?" She noticed a hesitation from Bob before he replied.

"Good memory. Yeah, that was probably me."

"That had to be a long time ago. You're divorced now, right?"

"That's right and Magil's ice cream store is long gone."

"Whatever happened to Mrs. Caully?" Had Laura not been looking for the reaction to this question, she might have missed it. But as it were, she was tuned into it and for a fraction of a second, she saw Bob's face redden and his mouth twitch ever so slightly before answering

"She's long gone as well."

"I'm sorry to hear that. She passed away, then?" This time the reaction was more noticeable with a hint of anger underneath the usually cool, jovial exterior. The reply was terse.

"Can't say that I know, to be honest. We lost touch and I never knew where she ended up. Why the interest?"

"No reason. Guess now that I've got Jake in my life, I've taken an interest in other people's love lives. I didn't mean to pry, sorry if I upset you."

"Not at all. Haven't thought about Helen for a long time, you just caught me off guard. Anything else I can do for you today?"

Laura got the impression she was being dismissed, which was unlike Bob. Usually, she dreaded a visit to the post office because Bob would bend her ear for twenty, thirty minutes if she let him. She normally had to pry her way out of there. Not today. Interesting.

"No, that's all for today. Thanks, Bob. I guess I'll see you Friday at the picnic."

"You know it. No way to avoid it." He was back to his usual, joking self. Laura gathered her stamps and receipt, threw them in her purse and turned for the door.

"Have a good day, Bob."

"You too. And say hi to Jake for me."

***

Jake needed a change of clothes, so stopped at his parent's house, which was also his house until he had more permanent living arrangements. He entered the kitchen and found Gran baking some sort of sweet-smelling concoction. He came up behind her and gave her a big bear hug and kiss on the top of her head.

"Hey, Gran. Whatcha cooking?"

"My famous brownies for the Fourth. And where have you been, young man?" She tried to sound tough, but the gleam in her eye told him she knew he'd been with Laura and nothing could have made her happier. He also surmised that no one told Gran about the break-in at Laura's and he wasn't going to be the bearer of bad news. No reason for her to worry too.

"Oh, you know, here, there, everywhere." He played it coy since Gran would expect no less.

"Is that right? Didn't I see you in those same clothes yesterday?"

"More or less. I think I left some of them at Laura's." He blurted this out for the shock value. Gran already assumed that, but she feigned shock, grabbed her dish towel and threatened to snap it at him.

"You bad, bad boy you!" Jake took his cue and dashed upstairs to change.

"Be down in a minute, Gran. Need some fresh clothes. Hey, how about having one of those brownies ready for me when I come back?"

"I'll do no such thing. These are for the picnic, not for ill-behaved young men." She yelled to him on the steps, but he knew there'd be a brownie and glass of milk when he returned. She loved to spoil him.

***

He sat at the table, enjoying the milk and brownie while making chit-chat with Gran.

"So we missed you at dinner last night. How'd you get out of the official Callaway pre-Fourth of July meeting?"

"I turned 80. I don't recommend it, but it does give you a certain leeway with all sorts of obligations." Gran joked.

"Well, in addition to mom's anal-retentiveness, you missed the history lesson on the Magil family."

"Honey, I lived with anal-retentiveness for over fifty years. You called him Grandpa. As for a history lesson on anything, I'm sure I could teach it, especially on the Magil's."

"Really. So you knew them?"

"Of course, I knew them, all of them. When you get to be my age, you know just about everyone."

"So you knew Albert and Helen and their parents?"

"I did indeed. Strange family."

"Really? How so?"

"Well, now don't get me wrong. I'm a church-going woman, always have been, but Erma and Albert, Sr., the parents, were oddly religious. The kind of people who scare you a bit. Always preaching the gospel and overly strict with their children. I know parents back then believed in, 'spare the rod, spoil the child,' but the Magils took it to a new level.

"Their punishments for those children would be illegal today. Not just spankings and the like, but locking them in their rooms for days, withholding food, crazy things like that, all in the name of God, you see. Once people start doing things like that in God's name, I get worried.

"As a result, those kids were just...different. The other kids were scared of them. Albert, Jr. more so than Helen. That boy was pure evil. I could never put my finger on why I believed that, but I knew it for sure. Just something about him. Poor Helen was just odd. Like a shy, scared little kitten, with no friends. Bob Caully took a liking to her and shocked everyone when they married. Didn't last long though."

"What happened to all of them?"

"Can't say that I know exactly. A lot of things happened around the same time. The parents were getting up there in years, so they decided to retire. Neither child wanted to take over the ice cream store, so they sold it and moved away. I never saw or heard from them again.

"I once asked Albert Jr. about them. He gave me a crazy look and told me they died in an accident. He didn't even seem upset by it. The news shocked me and, of course, I gave him my condolences. He just shrugged it off as if he didn't care at all.

"Helen and Bob had been married by this time. Nobody saw much of her though. Bob was as social as ever, just his nature, but she rarely left the house. We all felt sorry for Bob, being stuck with such an introvert for a wife, when he was the opposite. But he knew how she was before he married her.

"Then, as I said, a lot of things were happening at the same time. Your...scandal shall we say, was going on so I was mostly caught up in that. But I heard murmurings around town about a family feud between Albert and Helen. The parents owed a large plot of land that was passed to their children upon their death. Albert wanted to sell it, or something, and Helen wasn't cooperating. It was a pretty big feud, may have even been in the papers, but like I said, we had our own family drama taking place and I was sick with worry for you at the time."

"Sorry about that, Gran."

Gran waved her hand in a dismissive motion, "Water under the bridge. Anyway, word was that Helen finally gave in to Albert's wishes, apparently with much pressure from Bob. I guess there was a good bit of money involved in the sale and Bob was all for it. Don't know why Helen was against it, but she gave in. Shortly after she left town and Bob behind. I haven't heard anything about her since.

"Albert and Bob were awfully friendly with each other after that, which I always thought an odd combination. I mean, again, there's Bob who is so social and outgoing, with Albert, who was not. I used to wonder if we really knew the real Bob. Maybe he was like the sad little clown, laughing on the outside, but crying on the inside.

"Next thing I knew, Albert left town. Probably around the same time you did, Jake. Bob just went about his life like nothing ever happened, but his wife was gone and now his good friend. He never wanted to talk about it and people just stopped asking, I guess."

"Do you know where this piece of land was, the one Helen and Albert were fighting over?"

"Of course, it's the plot of land where the religious retreats take place. I think it's called Hallowed Hills."

# Twenty-Eight

Jake sat at his desk at the *Tribune* and debated his next move. He had narrowly made the deadline for his most recent article and tomorrow started a three-day weekend for him. No sense in getting started on his next project for work, might as well continue with his personal investigation.

Gran's announcement that Hallowed Hills was the parcel of land that Albert and Helen had been fighting over came as no surprise. What was surprising was the fact that they were in disagreement about selling it. Surely, Helen could have used the money. Perhaps she wasn't against selling the land, but selling to that particular buyer? Maybe Jake should try to find her and ask? Or perhaps Bob Caully knew the answer? That would be the easier route to take.

At the top of his list was Kevin Malloy. He needed to track him down and find out what he knew about Hallowed Hills. He might even know something about the feud between brother and sister.

Jake had already done searches for Kevin Malloy in Newbury and the surrounding areas, but came up empty. He did find a marriage announcement from ten years ago with a Kevin Malloy and Lisa Calcourt. So he searched for her, to no avail. Finally, after expanding the search to nearby cities, he hit a match. He found a Lisa Calcourt Malloy living in New York City. He had a phone number, but since he wasn't sure how to play it, hadn't called yet.

He debated about the best approach to take and decided on the truth. Sometimes honesty really was the best policy. So he picked up his desk phone and dialed. After four rings, voice mail picked up. A computerized message gave no personal information to indicate he might have the right number, such as, 'You've reached Lisa and Kevin.'

He decided to leave a message anyway and said, "Hello. My name is Jake Callaway and I work for the *Newbury Tribune*, a small newspaper in Newbury, Pennsylvania. I'm new to the paper and I'm researching a local story and found some information to indicate that a Kevin Malloy, who worked here previously, may have been interested in the same story.

"Anyway, I'm trying to locate him to ask some questions and was hoping to find him at this number. If I have the correct Malloy, or if you have any information that would help locate him, please call me at the following numbers." Jake left the phone numbers for his cell and Laura's.

The next option was to talk to Bob Caully, but he thought Laura might be doing that today so he decided to check in with her first. He reached for the phone to call her cell, noticed the time and figured she'd be home by now so he decided to do it in person.

He pulled into her driveway, saw her van was there and Sam was in the yard. He assumed she was in her shop, so headed in that direction, stopping to greet Sam and throw his ball a few times.

All the gardens were in full bloom and the sight was impressive. Rows of colorful roses, daisies, zinnias, and others he couldn't begin to name. It was remarkable what Laura had created here, alone. In a little over ten years, she had functioning greenhouses, outside gardens, irrigation systems and a profitable business all in her backyard. She was truly amazing.

He took a minute to, literally, stop and smell the flowers. Despite the traumatic events of the last few weeks, he realized his spirits were higher than they'd been in years. It was astonishing how the presence of someone special in your life could make that life so much more fulfilling and enjoyable.

He truly believed with Laura by his side, he could overcome any obstacle, including being homeless. Nothing was as important as having her with him, now and forever. Sam interrupted the moment by dropping his ball by Jake's feet.

"Okay, buddy. One more throw."

He tossed the ball high and right, then followed the path to the shop. As he approached, he noticed the place looked dark. Perhaps Laura wasn't working. He made his way to the door, pulled, and found it locked. Sam was back already with the ball.

"Last time, I mean it. Then you need to tell me where your mommy is, Sam."

Jake flung the ball toward the house, then followed in that direction. He reached the back door and knocked. No response. He tried the doorknob, but it was locked. He felt his heart begin to race ever so slightly. *Don't overreact, I'm sure she's fine.* He didn't think to bring his keys, so he knocked again, a bit louder. Still no response. She had to be home or Sam wouldn't be outside.

He decided to walk around to the front and ring the bell. Maybe she was upstairs and couldn't hear the knocking. Or perhaps she was in the shower and wouldn't be able to hear the bell either. He reached for his cell and decided to call her. If she was in the shower she might have the phone close by in case the girls called. He dialed her home number. No answer. He realized he was now running around to the front door as he dialed her cell phone.

He reached the door and began ringing the bell as the connection was made to her cell. The phone continued to ring and he frantically continued to push the doorbell. His next call would be 911, followed by his breaking down this damn door.

Finally, the door opened and Laura stood there with both the house phone and cell phone in her hand, and a look of panic on her face.

"What happened, what's wrong?" she blurted out.

Jake burst through the open door and grabbed her by both arms.

"What do mean, 'what's wrong'? What's wrong here? I've been knocking and calling and you didn't answer."

"I'm fine, Jake. You just scared me half to death. I was on the phone and I didn't hear you knocking. Then I saw on the caller ID that you were calling the house and my cell, but I couldn't end the call. Next thing I hear my doorbell ringing like crazy."

"I'm sorry. I didn't mean to scare you, but you scared the hell out of me. I hope that call was vitally important.

"Actually it was and you'll be happy I didn't cut it off."

"Really? Let me come in and calm my impending heart attack, then you can tell me all about it. A stiff drink might be in order as well since you scared me half to death." Jake continued into the house and made his way to the kitchen as Laura shut and locked the door before following. She had become the queen of door locking in the last several weeks.

"I suppose next you'll want dinner, too. It never ends with you." Laura teased with a smiled, more relaxed now, so Jake's adrenaline retreated as well. She waved her arm to indicate for him to take a seat.

"Dinner is the least you can do. Don't forget, I'm still homeless." Jake took a seat at the breakfast bar.

"Right. How did I get myself involved with such a needy man? My mother warned me about guys like you," Laura joked.

"Too late. You already fell for me. You're stuck now."

"In that case, would you like coffee, tea or wine, since it is almost five o'clock?"

"What happened to coffee, tea or me? I want that option." Jake stood from the chair and gave Laura a proper hug and kiss, now that his adrenaline had calmed down and his libido had revved up at the sight of her. "I am indeed a needy man." He kissed her again, more passionately this time, so there was no mistaking his intentions.

***

Laura realized she had fallen asleep. She was peacefully stirring as she lay comfortably ensconced in Jake's arms. She vaguely remembered ending up here, on the sofa in the office. It was all somewhat fuzzy. She remembered Jake kissing her in the kitchen, then her kissing him back, then being carried into the office. The rest is a blur of ecstasy that she hoped to remember more clearly, once the post-sex fog cleared.

Jake interrupted her reverie. "You're beautiful when you sleep."

"You didn't watch me sleep the whole time, did you?"

"No. I dozed off for a bit too. I missed you all day."

"Me too. You scared the heck out of me with the phone calls and bell ringing, though. Don't do that again."

"Well, we're even. You scared the hell out of me. Don't you do that again. By the way, have you heard from the girls today?"

"I did. They called earlier to check that I sent the package with the requested clothing. I'm sure they called to talk to me too, but the package was the top priority. They sounded great and are having a terrific time. I really miss them though."

"They'll be home soon."

"Jake?"

"Hmm?"

"How long do you think we'll have to live like this...being afraid, waiting for something bad to happen? It makes me not want the girls to come home. I mean, I'm handling all this as best I can, but if I have to worry about them... I don't think I can do it"

"I don't know, Lars. We have to make some headway in tying all these loose ends together. And don't forget, we have the police working on this now too. Oh, by the way, I tried to track down Kevin Malloy today and I left your phone number..."

"I know. That's who I was on the phone with when you couldn't reach me."

"You're kidding? Kevin called back?"

"Not exactly. His wife, Lisa did. Or I guess I should say, his widow."

"Widow?"

"Yes. I didn't get all the details. She seemed reluctant to discuss it. The only reason she called back is that she recognized your name from when you worked for *The New York Times* and was checking that you were the same Jake Callaway. Even when I confirmed that, she still seemed hesitant to talk to me

"Plus, I wasn't sure how much you revealed in your message or how much you want to reveal to her, so I'm sure I sounded suspicious. Anyway, she'd like you to call her back and said she would be home tonight. She's headed out of town tomorrow afternoon for the holiday weekend."

"Interesting. How about we jump in the shower, get dressed and go out to dinner? I'll give Lisa Malloy a call while you're getting ready."

"Sounds good to me." They both got up and gathered the blankets they grabbed from the basket next to the couch, and wrapped themselves up as they headed upstairs to the shower.

Showered and dressed, Jake now sat in the office and dialed Lisa Malloy's number. He wasn't sure what he was going to say, but figured it would come to him if and when she answered, which she did at that moment.

"Hello."

"Hello. Is this Mrs. Malloy?"

"Yes. Who's calling?"

"Hi, Mrs. Malloy. This is Jake Callaway, returning your call."

"Yes, Mr. Callaway. I've been expecting your call. Please, call me Lisa."

"Okay, Lisa. Please call me Jake."

"I understand you're working on a story that Kevin was possibly working on before he...before his...death."

"Yes. I'm so sorry for your loss. I had no idea when I made the call."

"That's alright. But to be honest, I would not have returned the call if I hadn't recognized your name. You are the same Jake Callaway that worked for *The New York Times* and did the investigation into the union scandal?"

"One and the same."

"I guess it's just hard to imagine why you would leave and go to the *Newbury Tribune*. Not exactly a step up, if you don't mind me saying?"

"Trust me, you're not alone in that question. Let's just say I made the move for personal reasons, not professional ones. And you happened to talk to her this afternoon."

"Ah, a woman. Now that makes more sense. She must be awfully special for you to give up everything you had in the city?

"What I gave up is nothing compared to what I gained."

"Then you're a lucky man, Jake."

"I am, indeed."

"I'm not sure I'll be of much help to you, I didn't know every story Kevin worked on, but he did talk about some of them, so you're welcome to run some questions by me."

"Thanks, Lisa. I really appreciate it. Basically, what I'm working on is a story about a place called Hallowed Hills and the family..."

"Mr. Callaway, you can stop right there. I won't be able to help you after all."

Jake was stunned. What had he said to elicit that response?

"I'm sorry...did I say something to upset you?"

"Mr. Callaway..."

"Jake, please."

"Jake, if you are as happy as you say you are in Newbury with your girlfriend, then you should forget you ever called me and forget about Hallowed Hills.

# Twenty-Nine

The train going into New York the night before the Fourth of July was practically empty. Jake's only company consisted of a few twenty-somethings, probably going into the city to visit friends for the holiday, and a few people dressed in business attire. He imagined the train leaving the city was jammed packed.

His conversation with Lisa Malloy did not go as smoothly as he hoped. It took considerable effort on his part to get her to agree to see him. She made it clear, there was no way she would discuss Hallowed Hills over the phone and she would only agree to meet him in New York, in a public place.

Since she was leaving for vacation tomorrow, Jake was on a train to New York tonight, even though he'd rather be having dinner with Laura. At first, he refused to leave her at night, but she convinced him he needed to go. The sooner they got to the bottom of all this, the better for them and her daughters. So he made a deal with her, he would go as long as she agreed to dinner and a movie with his sister, Addi. That way he wouldn't have to worry about her being home alone while he was gone.

Being overly cautious, he also called his brother, Rick, and Detective Burns to ask them to keep a watch on the house while he was gone. Rick agreed without hesitation. Detective Burns said he'd do what he could, but they might be short-handed with all the pre-Fourth of July firework mishaps. So much for the police doing everything they could to insure all residents felt safe in their homes.

Jake had mixed feelings about going back to New York. He had many good memories of his years there, but his journey into the city always brought back memories of his self-imposed exile years ago amid scandal.

The train approached Penn Station and Jake prepared to exit. So many memories of the city came flooding back. Good and bad. He left the station and strolled out into the July night. His senses were immediately assaulted by the city. The July heat; the smells of a myriad of restaurants, street vendors, delis, and coffee shops; the sights and sounds of traffic and people. These all competed for his attention and crashed into him at once. It left no doubt that he made the right decision to move back to Newbury.

He had agreed to meet Lisa at a neighborhood bar on 42nd Street, so he headed in that direction. The Lookout Bar and Grill was a familiar haunt. He'd spent many nights there with friends, drinking, eating and watching one sporting event or another on the numerous big screen televisions throughout the place. And, of course, he had met a few one-night stands as well. Hopefully, he wouldn't run into any tonight.

Lisa had described herself as petite, with a jaw-length bob of brunette hair. She said she would be at the bar closest to the pool tables. So Jake entered and began his search. The place was packed, it being the eve of a holiday weekend, so it was slow going making his way to the bar. He never realized how many girls had brunette hair. Being attracted mostly to blondes he had never noticed.

Finally, he identified a petite brunette at the bar who had locked eyes with him and finally raised her hand in an understated, hesitant wave. He nodded and made his way through the sea of people in her direction.

He began to appraise her immediately. She was younger than he imagined and had that sweet girl-next-door quality about her. But it was her eyes that were her most engaging feature. They were huge and dark and gave her a sense of innocence and vulnerability. This, combined with her tiny frame, caused one to want to protect her immediately, even though there was nothing to protect her from.

Her eyes watched him intently as he approached. He held out his hand and cocked his head slightly to the side.

"Lisa Malloy?"

"Yes. And you're Jake Callaway. I recognize you from a picture on the Internet. Nice to meet you." Lisa shook Jake's hand, then removed her purse from the seat next to her and motioned for him to sit.

"I appreciate you agreeing to meet me," Jake said.

"To be honest, I'm still not sure it's the right thing to do. Nor am I sure this was the right place to meet. It's so crowded and noisy." She glanced around at the throng of people.

Jake followed her glance. "It's funny, this place was one of my regular hangouts when I lived here. Now I'm not sure what the attraction was."

"Well, it's a great place to come if you're looking for a good time, or if you hope to blend in with the crowd, which is why I picked it. Maybe we could move to a booth in the back where we could talk more easily."

Jake agreed, "That sounds like a great idea. Shall we see what's available?"

"Sure."

They both stood and elbowed their way to the back room. More pool tables were in the back and a smaller bar. A couple was just vacating a small booth in time for them to grab it. A waitress appeared immediately, left menus and took their drink order, Chardonnay for her, beer for him.

Jake attempted to fill the awkward silence. "So how do you like living in the city? I assume you lived in Newbury before relocating here?"

"Yes. I went to college just outside the city, so spent a lot of time here. I met Kevin at school. We spent many of our weekends here with friends. But we wanted to put down roots in the country, raise a family, you know, the American dream." She looked down at her hands and Jake was afraid she would become emotional and wasn't sure how he'd handle that. But she quickly recovered and continued.

"So Kevin took the job in Newbury and we bought a small starter house in town. After he died, there was no reason for me to stay. My job is in the city and I was commuting every day. My sister has an apartment here. She works for a law firm in the city that sent her to their London office for a few months, so I'm staying at her place for now."

"Sounds like a good arrangement since it's so hard to find a decent place to live here."

"Yeah. She came to the rescue when I needed her. I just had to escape from Newbury after...Kevin. Jen took me in. When she found out she'd be out of town for a while, my staying there was the perfect arrangement."

The waitress appeared with the drinks and asked if they were ready to order. Jake motioned to Lisa to respond.

"I'm really not hungry. But feel free to order something for yourself."

"Not that hungry either. We'll just sit with the drinks for a bit. Thanks." He smiled at the waitress, who took her cue and left them alone.

Lisa sat staring at her wine while pensively running her fingers up and down the stem of the glass. Jake watched her for a few seconds before getting to the business at hand.

"Look, Lisa, I understand this is difficult for you. I can't imagine losing someone I love like you did, and so young. I'm sorry to bring up a bad memory for you. But I really do appreciate you agreeing to see me. I don't want to go into too much detail, but there are some circumstances surrounding this story that have become...I guess you could say life-threatening to someone I love. And you have alluded to the fact that you may be aware of some danger involving this story, perhaps relating to Kevin's death. It would be helpful if you could tell me what you know, what happened to Kevin...anything you can tell me about this story would be helpful."

Lisa looked up from her drink. She looked at Jake with her big, brown, pensive eyes for several moments before responding. He couldn't tell what she was thinking, what her look what trying to say.

"As I told you before, if you love your girlfriend as you say you do, you should leave this story alone." She looked around to insure she wasn't being overheard before continuing, then lowered her voice to a whisper. "The people involved in this Hallowed Hills place are sick, demented. They are also powerful and evil. Not a good combination. You seem like a nice person, Jake, and your girl-friend sounded nice on the phone. Take my advice and just leave it alone. Enjoy your life, and let this go."

"Lisa, I appreciate your concern for Laura and me. But I can't leave it alone. You know that. You read my work for the *Times*. I was an investigative reporter, I will always be an investigative re-porter. It's in my blood. If these people are as bad as you say, then they should be uncovered and brought to justice if they've done things against the law."

"They have done things against the law, Jake. But you'll never prove it and you could die trying." Her voice trembled, and the calm she had mustered all night, finally cracked. Jake reached across the table and held her trembling hands in his.

"Lisa, I can see you are scared. No one except Laura knows I am here talking to you. No one else needs to know the information you provide. But if that information can help bring these people to justice, to punish the people who, I assume, you believe are responsible for Kevin's death, then I am begging you to confide in me. Anything you say will be kept confidential by me. You know my reputation. You can trust me."

He felt her trembling begin to subside. He patted her hands, then took a swig of his beer while he waited for her to make her decision. She sipped her wine, possibly to help her muster the courage to continue. She looked around again, leaned into Jake and began in a whisper, even lower than before.

"Kevin stumbled on this story, an accident really. He was so excited at first. He thought it would be a career-maker." She snorted at this. "He liked to take early morning runs. We lived only a few miles from the Hallowed Hills property. We thought it was a campsite for disadvantaged children.

"One morning Kevin returned from a run and he was babbling like an excited child. It took me several minutes to calm him down so he could start to make some sense. He had been running by the Hallowed Hills property and decided, despite the numerous No Trespassing signs and blockade fencing, to take a run through the property. He found a small access area that led to a path, so he followed it. We believed that the property was mostly vacant except in the summer months when the children came for camp. However, more and more activity seemed to be going on year-round and Kevin, being a curious reporter like you, decided to check things out.

"It was early Spring, so normally the property would have been unoccupied, but that's not what Kevin found when he took the detour that morning. He was following a path through the woods, but he could see that many people appeared to be living there. He witnessed what looked like families, with children playing, laundry hanging out to dry, women cooking together and men working to build new cottages. But the strangest thing was the way they were dressed. He explained it as if he were witnessing a scene from colonial America. It was very strange and it bothered him, but his first thought, of course, was to do some sort of undercover investigation. After a few weeks of research, he began to receive notes warning him to back off the story. I begged him to listen. But the threats only served to encouraged him, corroborated his belief that he was on to something."

Lisa paused, shifted in her seat and took a long sip of wine. She seemed to become aware of her surroundings again, having been previously engrossed in her story. She glanced around to insure no one was listening, then continued.

"Kevin was found late one night in his car near the office. They said it was an overdose. Heroin. Which was ridiculous. Kevin never used drugs in his life. I told the police about my concerns, but they dismissed them. I am convinced what he discovered at Hallowed Hills ended his life."

Jake waited for her to continue, and when she didn't, he pressed on. "What did he discover, Lisa."

Her response was barely audible, "Disturbing things."

# Thirty

"So it looks like I'll be stuck here longer than I anticipated. Everything okay on your end?" Jake hated to be away this long, but he needed the information Lisa had to offer. He just wanted to make sure Laura was safe, then he could turn his attention back to the matter at hand.

"Yes. Everything is fine here. Your mom has us all working like dogs for the big day tomorrow. We never even got to the movie. Now I know why you had to run off to New York. This Lisa Malloy thing was just a cover, right?" Laura joked.

"Sorry, Lars. Mom can get pretty crazy about her July 4th festivities. But, trust me, I'd much rather be there with you."

"I know. What's going on there? Does Lisa have some good information?"

"Can't go into detail now, but I'm back at her apartment and she just went to get Kevin's personal files on his story. Stuff he didn't trust leaving in the office. She found it after he died and it's what's caused her suspicions about his death."

"So what does this Lisa look like and where will you be sleeping tonight?" Laura asked half joking.

"She doesn't even compare to you. And I don't plan on sleeping. I'm going to try to go through these files and then catch the train home as soon as I can."

"Good answer. Behave yourself. And be careful."

"I will, on both counts. Now about your sleeping arrangements…any chance you'd agree to sleep at my parent's house?"

"No chance. I've got Sam here. I'll be fine."

"How about a sleepover with Addi? Kinda like old times. You girls can catch up."

"Oh, Jake. I don't want to ask her to babysit me. She's exhausted. I'm sure she just wants to go home."

"You forget home for Addi tonight is at my parent's house, with the crazy Fourth of July lady, aka my mom. I'm sure she'd be thrilled to stay at your place. I'll run it by her."

"Jake, really…"

"It would make me feel better, which would help me concentrate better, which would get me home to you sooner. So no argument, please."

Laura acquiesced, "Okay, okay. I guess it could be fun. Like old times when Addi and I used to have sleepovers, but without you around to bother us."

"Yeah, yeah. But you'll miss not being able to sneak into my room for a make-out session."

"I'll try to power through. You do the same.

"Deal. I'll see you in the morning. I love you."

"I love you back."

Jake made a quick call to his sister to put the sleepover plans in motion. Lisa entered the room with a stack of files just as he ended the call.

"Let me help you with that." Jake took the stack from her arms and laid them on the table.

"Are there more? I'd be happy to lug them for you."

"That's okay. Only a few more. I can grab them while you start on these."

"Sounds good."

Jake had his work cut out for him. He began to organize the files into themes, but had no idea where to start. It was going to be a long night.

***

The plan was in place. The Brethren had voted, a decision was made, and now each person had a part to play in the drama that was about to unfold. As it turned out, the final vote was just what the Grand Master had hoped for. He proved yet again that he was in charge, and that his ideas were superior. And once this current threat was extinguished, he would deal with his second in command who continued to disagree with the decision of the majority. He was becoming a problem that would have to be dealt with soon.

The plan was nearly flawless. Getting the two women would be easy. It was the man who would prove more difficult, but with his girlfriend in danger, he would be more easily controlled. There was just one wildcard, two if you counted his second in command, which he did not. He knew how to control him for now. No, the only problem keeping him up at night was the disappearance of Phil Molino. He could be dangerous if he decided to go rogue. Hopefully, he was simply off pursuing more lucrative, long-lived employment.

***

The Fourth of July had finally arrived amid the expected, but still stifling, heat and humidity.

Laura was up early, disappointed to discover that Jake had yet to return from New York. She showered and dressed quickly so she could make her way to the kitchen to start breakfast for her overnight guest.

She and Addi had a fabulous time last night, drinking wine and reminiscing over summers past. She was again reminded how much a part of her life Jake and his family had been. She was amazed at the capacity of the mind to repress such memories, as hers did many years ago to protect herself from the void in her life caused by Jake's abrupt departure.

She had just finished whipping up a plate full of waffles when Addi entered the kitchen.

"Good morning, Ad."

"Morning. Yum, it smells good in here."

"How'd you sleep?"

"Great! Like a baby. A baby on half a bottle of wine." Addi joked.

"There's aspirin in the medicine cabinet if you need it. You will not survive this day with a hangover, so treat yourself as needed. And help yourself to a hearty breakfast. We'll need that as well." Laura carried the plate of waffles to the already set table, along with a big pitcher of orange juice.

"Gosh, Laura. You didn't have to go to all this trouble. But, thanks. It looks delicious." Addi sat down and helped herself to a plate full of food. "Any word from Jake?"

"No. I thought he might have arrived home early this morning, but he didn't. He's probably waiting to call until later, thinking we might still be asleep. He better get here in time for his picnic duties or your mother will be furious."

"As will the rest of us who will have to listen to her rant and assign us his responsibilities."

"Right. Maybe I should call his cell now and make sure he's on his way." Laura went into the office to make the call. The call went directly to voice mail. She left a quick message, then returned to the kitchen to inform Addi, "Well, his phone must be off because the call went right to voice mail."

"That's odd. He rarely turns it off, you know, because he needs to be on call for the fire station. Of course, I guess he has the pager for that."

Laura nodded, "Hm, I guess I'll wait a bit longer to see if he calls." Just then the phone rang. "There we go. I'll take it in the office."

After a few minutes, Laura returned to report that it was not Jake, but her daughters on the phone. She sat at the table and helped herself to some waffles and juice. "They're having such a great time. Today is the annual parade and fireworks there too. I'm glad they're having fun, but I miss them terribly."

"I'm sure you do. When do they return?"

"In a few days. On the one hand, I can't wait to see them. But on the other, I want this business with the break-ins here settled so I don't have to worry about them."

"Well, hopefully, Jake has gotten the information he needs to help with the investigation. In the meantime, you have the police force and our entire family looking out for your safety."

"I know, and I truly do appreciate all you and your family are doing for me." Laura was interrupted by the ringing phone again. "Maybe that's Jake." She left for the office again to take the call.

"Hello."

"Good morning. Sorry I missed your call earlier. How was your night?" It was Jake.

"Great. We had so much fun, staying up late and talking and laughing. You were right, Jake. We had a lot of catching up to do. How are things there? Where are you?"

"I'm at the train station. I was up all night going through all of Kevin's files. I still have a few more to go through. Lisa reluctantly let me take the last few with me since I had to get back and she was leaving town as well. Kevin amassed a ton of information over several months. I can't go into detail now because my phone battery is dying, that's why your call went right to voice mail. I turned it off to conserve power. I didn't think to bring a charger, not knowing I'd be here overnight. Could use a toothbrush and fresh deodorant as well. Anyway, like I said, there is a ton of information here that will help us put the pieces together to form, what looks like, a very disturbing puzzle."

"Disturbing how?"

"I'll explain it all in detail when I get there. But we are definitely on the right track. Remember our buddy Jonathan Laird? Well, apparently that name is an alias. He is aka Albert Magil, according to Kevin's research."

"What?"

"Yeah, I know, shocking. It looks like Albert left town and got involved in some sort of cult out west. Then he came back here to expand it at Hallowed Hills. There's a lot more, Laura. Twisted stuff, like kidnapping, forced marriages and child abuse. And the scariest part is that Kevin believed members of the community are involved, like they are living double lives. It's a huge story and we have our work cut out for us, but once we piece it all together, we'll have enough to go to the authorities. For now though, just stay safe, and don't go anywhere alone, okay?"

"Jake, you're scaring me."

"I want you to be scared if it'll keep you safe. You're going to be busy with the picnic until I get there right?"

"Yes. Addi and I are just finishing up breakfast and then reporting for duty. By the way, your mother is going to have a fit that you're not here yet."

"I know. Smooth it over for me, will ya?"

"I'll try, but Addi said she will not be happy and she'll start passing out your duties to others which will make them not happy, so it's not going to be an easy task."

"I know. I'll owe you. I promise to make it worth your efforts," Jake teased.

"Yeah, yeah, yeah. I've heard that before," she joked.

"Seriously though, Lars, stay with people today, okay? Keep your radar up and I'll be home soon. I'm going to turn my phone off to save the battery, but I'll check in when my train arrives."

"Okay. You be careful too."

***

Laura arrived at her designated spot on time with her van filled with flowers. She was assigned various locations around the parade route that she was responsible for decorating. The parade took the same route every year, and by now, Laura had it committed to memory.

The last spot was the toughest. She had to park a considerable distance from where the flowers needed to be. She quickly dropped off the pots, parked in a community lot, then hiked back to arrange the flowers properly.

By now the sun was approaching full force and the heat was oppressive. She had watered all the flowers before leaving her shop and hoped they would stay perky through the festivities. Once her work was done, she began the trek back to her car.

Her next assigned duty was to help Jake with the food deliveries, but since Jake wasn't here, she volunteered to take on the task alone until he arrived to assist her. This was her way of 'smoothing things over' with everyone for him. He'd better make it worth her while, she thought with a smile.

She got into her stiflingly hot van, consulted her list of food pick-ups, then mentally planned her route. She put the key into the ignition and turned it, but the engine refused to start. She tried again, but nothing. "This is just great. Just what I need today."

She got out of the car and walked around to the hood, opened it and looked inside. It all looked good to her — of course, she had no idea what she was looking at or for. She did know how to check the oil, so she pulled out the dipstick and inspected the oil level. It looked normal so she replaced it. Meanwhile, the heat continued to beat down on her and the sweat was starting to soak through her lightweight cotton sundress.

"I don't believe this, why, why, why." She cursed to no one in particular. After several more unsuccessful attempts to restart the car, she pulled out her cell phone to call the garage for a tow. Before she could dial, she saw a shiny, sleek, black Porsche convertible pull up next to her. The car was a head-turner for sure, as was the driver. It was Cal, Dr. Mike's handsome son and veterinarian-in-training. He shot her a big smile, which she returned, all the while thinking about the crush her daughters had on him and how protective Jake had been about the situation. He certainly was a good-looking kid, but much too young for her and much too old for her daughters.

"Having some trouble, Mrs. Delaney?" Cal said as he exited his car and walked toward her.

"What gave me away? The open hood on my car or the look of panic on my face?" Laura joked.

"A little of both. Let me take a look and see if I can help. However, I should warn you, cars aren't my expertise. I like to collect them, but don't know much about fixing them."

He smiled and held her eye contact a second too long, which caused Laura to wonder if he was flirting with her. She guessed it was just his nature. And why not, he was a rich, good-looking, soon-to-be doctor. I'm sure he had girls falling at his feet with one look at those pearly whites and azure blue eyes.

"Well, I don't see anything glaring at me like a loose hose or wire. Sorry."

"That's okay. I was just about to call Hank for a tow."

"I can save you the phone call. He's got both trucks down by Dilly's corner. Three-car accident needed to be cleared, so he'll be tied up for a while. Why don't I drive you home and you can call him later and tell him where the van is? It's too hot for you to wait out here."

"I just can't believe this is happening today, of all days. I'm supposed to be helping with the food deliveries, which I can't do without a car. Let me just think for a minute here...I guess you could drive me home and I could get my old Mustang and drive that to picnic central, where perhaps I can borrow a truck or van from one of the Callaways. That should work. Are you sure you don't mind?"

"Not at all. Grab whatever you need from your van and hop in." Cal held open the passenger side door to his convertible. "I'm sure Jake will loan you his vehicle." This time the smile and eye contact were harder to read. Not flirting, something else, but Laura couldn't decipher it. She grabbed her purse and itinerary from her van, locked it, and lowered herself into the passenger seat of Cal's car. He shut the door for her and then hopped in the driver's seat.

"I'm sure he would, but he's in New York for business and won't be back for a while. But I'm sure I can borrow Kelly's van or Mr. Callaway's truck. It'll work out. It has too. We need food at a picnic, right?"

"Right." Cal started his car and it roared to life. "So what's Jake doing in New York? I thought he left the *Times* and was working for the *Tribune?*"

"He did, he is. He's just doing some research for a local story and it took him to New York. He's on his way home as we speak." Cal had the top to the convertible down, and as he drove, the hot, sticky air whipped around them. It was not refreshing and Laura found herself wishing for air conditioning, but he was nice enough to drive her home so she wouldn't complain.

"You must be so hot, having been working out in the sun all morning." He handed her a bottle of water. "Here, get some liquids in you. I just picked that up on my way to work, but you take it. You need it more than me."

Laura was hot and thirsty, so she gladly took the bottle and a long swig of the refreshing liquid.

"Thank you, Cal. I'll replace it when we get to my house. So how is your Dad? He's been our vet for years. I think he was even the vet for my grandmother's little calico cat years ago."

"Dad's great. Wants to retire though. He's been at this a long time and I can tell he's eager to pass it all onto me."

"How do you feel about that?" Laura took another long, refreshing drink.

"Well, I feel fortunate to be handed a large, successful, thriving practice. That's a dream come true for any doctor. But to be honest, it's also quite frightening. I don't know how I'd manage the whole place without Dad around. I'd need a partner and it'd be hard to find someone I trusted with this business my father built over the course of his entire life. It's a big responsibility and I just hope I can live up to it.

The heat was starting to get to Laura. The water had helped at first, but now she felt worse. The wind whipping around her head seemed to be intensifying, causing her hearing to grow fuzzy. She felt as if she had heat stroke — dizzy, nauseated, and sleepy all at once. She was listening to Cal's story, but had trouble focusing on it or forming a reply.

"Mrs. Delaney, are you feeling okay?"

"I...don't know...feel a bit sick.

"You might be overheated. Have some more water. Try to finish it all. You need fluids in this heat." Laura followed the doctor's orders.

The world seemed to spin around her. The trees whizzed by in a blur. She tried to focus on the streets and buildings, looking for a familiar landmark. Somewhere in her brain was the realization that this was not the way to her house. Maybe Cal was lost. Did he even know where she lived? She realized something was very wrong.

She turned to him and tried to speak, to tell him the way, but her tongue was too thick and heavy to form the words. She watched as

Cal's hand shifted the car into high gear, and that's when she saw it. The symbol that was tattooed on the back of his wrist. It was a symbol she had seen before. Even in her fog she knew she was in trouble. It took all her will to speak, but she knew she had to.

"Cal, where…where…not way to my house, Cal."

"You just relax now Laura. There's no sense trying to fight it. And, no, we're not going to your house."

"Hallow…Hill…"

She tried to move, but her limbs were paralyzed. She tried to cry out, but no sound would come. Her head continued to spin until the sedation triumphed as she began to drift further and further into the fog that finally consumed her.

# Thirty-One

Jake was in desperate need of a shower and clean clothes. Since home base was technically still his parent's house, that's where he headed. He tried to reach Laura to assure her he'd be there to help soon, but wasn't getting an answer. He assumed she was busy doing her assigned duties, as well as his.

He found the house empty, which is what he expected. He grabbed a quick sandwich, charged his phone, showered, dressed and was on the road in no time. Since he couldn't reach Laura, he headed into town where the main festivities would be taking place.

He found his mother first. She turned, saw him and half ran in his direction.

"Jake, thank God. We've been worried sick. Where is Laura?"

"What do you mean? I thought she was here working?"

"She was supposed to be. She was scheduled to deliver the flowers and then begin with the food distribution, but no one has seen her. Your father and Ricky retraced the route and the flowers are in place, but no food and no Laura. We thought she was with you."

Jake didn't waste a second. He had his phone out and was dialing his dad.

"Dad, it's Jake. Any sign of her? What about her van? I'm on my way." Jake pocketed his phone, then turned to his mom.

"They found her van at the last flower stop in a parking lot. I'm heading over there now. Call me if she shows up here or if you hear anything. I'll call the police on my way."

"Honey, be careful. I'll make some calls as well and get everyone on the lookout. You call me if you find out anything."

Jake wheeled into the parking lot and immediately spotted his dad's truck next to Laura's van. He pulled in beside his dad's truck and hopped out.

"Police are on their way. Did you find anything here?" Jake said.

"Only some drops of oil down the front of the car and on the pavement. It looks like she might have been having car trouble, so she, or someone, checked the oil. I checked it myself, and it was fine. I don't have a key to see if it'll start. Don't suppose you do?"

"No. But I know where she keeps the spare at the house." The sounds of a police siren diverted their attention. The police cruiser approached, parked, and Officer Burns, the same officer who responded to the 911 call at Laura's house, exited the car.

"Well, I'm sorry to have to see you again, Jake. What do you have?"

"Laura's missing. She was supposed to deliver the flowers for the parade route and then start organizing the food delivery. I was in New York or I would have been with her, but she had to start without me. From what we can tell, she made all the flower stops. This would have been the last stop. She must have parked her car here and walked to the parade route. When she returned, we're guessing she might have had car trouble as evidenced by the oil spots in the front of the car."

Officer Burns, who had been taking notes, stopped and strode over to the front of the van to inspect the oil spot.

"Have you determined if the car will start?"

"No. We don't have a set of keys, but I can get a set if we have to. I'm more concerned with organizing a search for Laura."

"Have you considered that she may have called someone for a ride and is now with them having a cold drink or a bite of lunch somewhere?" Officer Burns asked

"She's not answering her phone and she wouldn't stop for lunch when she knows everyone's counting on her to make the food deliveries. She would have called someone in my family to tell them what was going on and to ask for a ride."

Office Burns looked around the empty lot then replied, "Well, she obviously called someone for a ride because she's not here."

Jake was losing his patience. Officer Burns clearly didn't see the urgency of the situation.

"Look, Officer Burns, Tom, you've been filled in on what's been going on here. You know there have been not one, but two, break-ins to Laura's house. Now we find her car abandoned and she is missing without a trace. We need to assume some sort of foul play going on here."

"No. You look, Jake, we don't routinely start a missing person's case for an adult until 24 hours have passed. The reason for that is that most people aren't missing. Like I said, she's probably out having lunch with a girlfriend."

"And I'm telling you, there's something wrong here," Jake said angrily.

Jake's dad could see his son's temper beginning to flare. He jumped in to the conversation, "Jake, we're wasting time here. Why don't you go on over to Laura's house? Check it out, grab the spare keys and meet me back here. Meanwhile, I'll finish up the police report."

Jake turned to his dad with the intent to argue, but the look in his dad's eyes had him thinking better of it. He knew he was right. Jake would get nowhere he wanted to be arguing with a cop. So, without a word, he turned, hurried to his truck, and took off in search of Laura.

***

The air smelled stale and musty. That was the first thing Laura realized. The second was that her arms and legs were shackled to a hard, cold surface on which she lay. The third was that she had been stripped of her clothes and was covered in, what felt like, a cotton gown or sheet.

The room, which was too dark to see, became slightly illuminated in the distance. Someone seemed to be slowly approaching and was carrying some source of light. She tried to remember what had happened, but her brain was too foggy to produce the details.

As the person moved closer, the room filled with more light and she could see this person was wearing a coat or robe of some sort and carried a lantern. The size of the silhouette appeared to be that of a man. The lantern was placed on some sort of pedestal and the person came to where she lay. She quickly closed her eyes and pretended to still be unconscious.

"You can open your eyes, Laura. I can tell by your breathing that you are conscious.

She recognized the voice, but couldn't put it with a face. She opened her eyes and standing before her was Calvin Harrison. Young, good-looking, flirtatious Cal, dressed in a black hooded robe. But yet it wasn't Cal. This Calvin had a sinister look in his eyes, not the friendly, flirty look that was usually found there. This Calvin looked evil.

She was aware that she was in some sort of cavern or cellar. There were no windows and the walls were made from stone. She was lying in the middle of this room, surrounded by large, pewter candelabras and more stone pedestals with smaller pewter candlesticks on top. Her vision was limited since she was bound to this stone table and could barely lift her head. But from what she could see, the room was mostly empty and there appeared to be a raised portion of the floor in front of her, like a stage. It looked like another body was placed on a stone slab on the stage-like structure.

Suddenly, images flooded Laura's mind. She saw herself out in the heat looking under the hood of her car and Cal with her, smiling. Then she was in his car, driving too fast with the wind whipping around her head. Next, she remembered the sickness, the water...ah, yes, the water. He must have drugged the water. But why? Then the tattoo. The same as the man who attacked her. The same as the symbol for Hallowed Hills. She had so many questions, but one took the forefront.

"Why?" Her voice was so thick with sedation, she barely recognized it.

"Why what, Laura? Why are you here, shackled to this altar? Why you and not someone else? Why indeed. I'll tell you why. Because you couldn't mind your own damn business, that's why. You and your boyfriend, Jake, couldn't leave things alone, could you? You want to know what happened in that accident outside of your house, Laura? I'll tell you what happened. Those damn winding roads happened and took control of my car, my beautiful car, and it hit that damn pole. It destroyed my car and broke my ribs. This interrupted our plans. The girl who was to be brought here and placed on this stone just like you are now died at the scene. Stupid bitch. She didn't fasten her seatbelt.

"It's not the first time something interfered with our plans, but it was the first time someone was stupid enough to die in plain sight. So it required more of a clean-up. First, we had to get my car out of there, then dispose of the girl's body. Oh yeah, we had to deal with that annoying woman who happened by and witnessed more than she should have. But everything was going well and would have been fine if you had kept out of it. But you couldn't do that, could you? So that is why, Laura. That is why you are here in this position, on this glorious day, our Independence Day. You'll be here for our celebration tonight. In fact, you'll be our guest of honor. Pity Jake can't be here to watch you die.

"Yes, it is a special night indeed. We will induct several new members into the inner circle and they will take their oath to our way of life. Then you, one who is not worthy of our way of life, will be punished and sacrificed to our God to insure another year of prosperity as we move closer to our vision of utopia. Then as our final act..." Cal grabbed his lantern and walked towards the body up front. Laura strained her neck to see as he removed the blanket to reveal Newbury's mayor, Karen Wentworth, bound, gagged and unresponsive.

Instinctively, Laura tried to jerk her arms and legs, but the shackles held tight and she was still too weak to put up a good fight. Cal found this amusing and his laughter echoed in the cavernous room.

He walked back towards her. "There's no use struggling against the restraints, Laura. You won't be going anywhere. In fact, tonight you'll get to witness the death of this non-believer so we may elect the rightful mayor to our town. A man of great vision with plans to move our way of life into the mainstream." He removed a piece of fabric from his robe and used it to gag her. "Let's both save our energy for tonight, shall we?"

***

Jake burst through the door of Laura's house.

"Laura! Laura! Are you here?"

Only Sam came running to him, wagging his tail. Jake ran through the house, searching room to room, hoping to find her safe, that he had panicked for nothing. His search came up empty.

He answered his ringing cell phone. It was his dad hoping Jake had found Laura here as well. He had finished the report with the police, but told Jake not to count on any help from them until 24 hours had passed. By then it could be too late, Jake thought.

He had another idea, and searched through his phone's contact list, then selected a number to dial.

"Hello."

"Jimmy, it's Jake. I really need your help, man."

Jake explained the situation. Jimmy offered to do whatever he could. He was currently on the duty desk, but would keep his eyes and ears open and, as soon as his shift was over, would actively help in the search.

Jake's cell rang again.

"Hello."

"Jake. It's Dad. I've got some news. I called Hank to come take a look at Laura's car and even without keys he can tell there's a problem."

"What's the problem?"

"Her alternator belt's been cut. He says it was deliberate, Jake. I've already called Officer Burns and reported it. He's taking this more seriously now, but it being a holiday and all, the station's stretched thin.

"Just so you're aware, Jake, your mom tried to cancel the festivities for today, but she couldn't reach the mayor. The deputy mayor won't make the decision without Karen's approval. He's not convinced this is an emergency and the town's got too much money invested in this to call it off. So the show must go on.

"I've pulled as much help as I can get and that includes the family of course. Everyone has delegated their responsibilities. We've sectioned off the town and we're sending out search parties looking for any clues we can find."

"Thanks, Dad. I've got some things to check out here, but let's keep each other informed."

"Jake, don't try to be a hero. The police are involved in this now, so go through proper channels for any plans you may have. You hear me?"

"Yeah, I hear you. I'll keep in touch."

The news of Laura's car, combined with the fact that she was nowhere to be found, confirmed Jake's worse fear. He thought he'd have more time to expose what he surmised was going on at Hallowed Hills. After reading through all the research from Kevin Malloy's files, he realized he had a hell of a story. But it would take more research and some clever undercover investigating to blow it wide open. That was no longer an option.

His current choices were now limited. He could go through proper channels, as his dad had suggested, and take his suspicions to the police. But there were several problems with that. For one thing, time did not allow for proper police procedures, such as getting a search warrant for the Hallowed Hills compound. For another, according to Kevin's research, there was a conspiracy involved here, which included key members of the community, including quite possibly, members of the police force. So tipping them off may put Laura's life in danger if she was being held inside that compound.

And that was a big "if." What if he was wrong and she was not at Hallowed Hills? Although he was certain the people involved there were responsible for her disappearance, the police storming in would tip his hand. Then he might never find Laura.

That left only one option. He had to go in alone. He had enough information about the place from Kevin's files, including a detailed map of the compound, that he could try to find his way around, try to go unnoticed. It was the only chance he had. He only hoped she was there and it wasn't too late.

# Thirty-Two

The sedation was lifting and Laura's brain was slowly defogging. Now panic was trying to set in. She had to think, had to plan, but how? She was fairly sure she was at Hallowed Hills, but had no idea what kind of room she was in. Was she underground? An old stone building? How would anyone find her?

Surely, she was missed by now. Someone would notice the food hadn't been delivered and wonder where she was. She wasn't sure how long she had been here. The lack of windows gave her no indication as to the time of day. She had drifted in and out of consciousness but now felt fully awake and alert. She jerked her limbs again to see if there was any way out of the restraints. They held firm. Her mind began to race as she worked to control her panic and steady her pulse. She thought of her daughters, then fought hard to push that thought out of her mind. She had to survive for them, but dwelling on that fact would not help her. She had to think, had to plan. The sound of voices diverted her attention. They were in the distance, but approaching.

She thought she heard chanting or singing, she couldn't be sure, but as the sound approached, she realized it was chanting. The room began to brighten and she was able to see a group of hooded figures filling the room, all carrying lanterns. Some hung their lanterns on hooks in the walls, others placed theirs on top of stone pillars. Someone lit the candles in the tall candelabras by her head. Her mind raced, searching for some prior knowledge, some information in her brain that would help her understand what was taking place here.

The throng of people now encircled her and continued to chant. All at once, they became silent as a lone figure moved to the raised platform in front of the room, and began to chant in an unrecognizable language. She saw some sort of pit in the center of the platform, in front of where Karen Wentworth lay. Then this solitary person, a leader of sorts, started a fire in the pit. The smoke rose to the ceiling and she could see a ventilation duct that allowed the smoke to exit.

The Grand Master addressed the crowd, "Welcome my brothers. We are here tonight to bring to fruition what we have worked years to achieve. The election of Karen Wentworth, a woman, to mayor of our great town set us back a bit, but tonight we take back what is rightfully ours. Once our man assumes the position of mayor of Newberry, our plans will be put in motion to slowly reeducate the town, punishing non-believers, and protecting our town borders from outsiders. Take comfort that our brothers-in-arms are pursuing similar measures around the country so that one day we can truly join as one nation, under God."

BANG! A loud sound echoed throughout the room. Laura's body jerked in surprise and she heard gasps from the crowd. She could see the others looking towards the entrance. Then she heard a familiar voice.

"Guess ya all didn't expect to see me here."

Laura strained her head to follow the voice. She saw a man dressed in street clothes, gun in hand, pointed at the Leader in the front of the room. The man holding the gun was Phil Molino, the man who had tried to assault her at her shop.

"This one's mine, chief." Phil pointed towards Laura. "I want her unshackled, now. Me and her have some unfinished business so she's coming with me. Now!"

BANG!! Phil fired another shot, in the direction of the Leader. More gasps from the crowd. Laura's head was pounding, her blood pumping even faster now. This was not good. If this man managed to take her from here, her chances of being rescued decreased drastically.

No one moved. Phil Molino kept the gun pointed at the Leader, approached him, then grabbed him from behind and demanded he order Laura released. Finally, the Leader spoke.

"Philip, you don't know what you are doing. You are welcome to be part of this ceremony. Please, put the gun down and join us."

"Yeah, right. Listen old man, you had your chance. You treat me like I'm one of your mindless minions who follow you without question. Those days are over. Now I've paid my dues, ten times over and this one's mine. Mine alone." He cocked the gun and held it to the Leader's head. "Now order her release or I'll blow your fucking brains out."

"Very well. Phillip. But you're making a mistake." The Leader's voice was a bit shaky as he spoke, but he ordered Laura released. A hooded figure from the side approached her and began to unlock the shackles from her ankles and wrists. She lay very still, realizing this was her best chance to escape, but also aware that if she moved, one of the hooded figures could grab her or Phil Molino may shoot her. She calculated her odds. She had a crazy man with a gun and a room full of even crazier people who would do all they could to prevent her from escaping. She needed a distraction, and she needed it now.

***

Jake parked his truck on a dirt access road that Kevin Malloy wrote about in his notes, grabbed his backpack and hiked to the compound at Hallowed Hills. He had prepared as quickly as he could for this trip, changed clothes and was now wearing all black to blend into the night. The backpack contained supplies he might need. He hated to waste a minute in the search for Laura, but his firefighter training kicked in and he knew he had to go in with the right clothing and equipment. This included a small hand gun he had holstered to his waist.

He found the breach in the fence that Kevin used to sneak into the property, slipped through, then followed the path in the woods until he reached the perimeter that lined the inner part of the compound. This is where the majority of the cabins and outbuildings were located. Kevin warned of armed militia guarding the property at times, but none could be seen from this vantage point. Now he had to figure out where Laura was being held.

The sun was beginning to set, alleviating the stifling heat from the day. Soon darkness would set in. He didn't know his way around here well enough to navigate in the dark. Of course, he'd be less likely to be seen in the dark, so that could work to his advantage.

So far, the compound looked deserted. He took out his binoculars and scanned the area. He noticed movement over to the far right and saw smoke rising from behind some of the cabins. He headed in that direction.

He was careful to move on the perimeter of the compound, being sure to stay hidden in the woods. It took him longer this way, but he couldn't risk being seen. The sun had lowered behind the trees and darkness was creeping in quickly. He could see movement inside some of the cabins, so he paused to take a look with the binoculars.

What he saw corroborated Kevin Molloy's research. The cabins were primitive, basic structures. There appeared to be limited electricity, evidenced by the fact that candles were being used for illumination. He saw mostly women and children, dressed as Kevin had described, in colonial-era style clothing. If he didn't know better, he would have thought he was witnessing a July Fourth reenactment scene of colonial times.

He put the binoculars into his pack and continued towards the far side of the compound. He wondered where the men were and thought his best bet was to head toward the smoke. Maybe there was a massive barbeque pit and the men were hanging around with beers, cooking burgers. Somehow, he doubted that, but he continued to follow the smoke.

If his directional instincts were correct, he was heading toward the main entrance of the property. He heard a loud bang in the distance that sounded like a gunshot. Jake tried to tell himself it was probably the fireworks getting started in town. He rounded the last of the cabins and headed toward the source of the smoke. It was not a barbeque pit, but an old stone building that resembled some sort of worship temple. A crumbling, stone chimney protruded from the center, which was the source of the smoke. Next to the chimney, a large, rusting cross was displayed on the front of the roof.

Jake was approaching towards the front of the building. The double doors were open, but he decided against simply strolling in. He scanned the vicinity. No one was in sight so he darted from his camouflaged spot in the woods to the back of the old building.

He found a few open windows and a closed door. He crouched down, pressed his body against the side of the building and made his way to one of the open windows. All was quiet, so he slowly raised himself high enough to peek in. The room he viewed was empty. He lowered himself again and slowly made his way over to try the door. Unlocked. He held his breath as he carefully turned the knob and opened the door a crack. He took a quick glance through the crack. Empty. He opened the door just enough to slip inside.

He had entered a kitchen, complete with a stove, refrigerator and sink. Apparently, this part of the building had electricity and a small light burned over the sink. Aside from the gentle humming of the refrigerator, the room was quiet, but the smell of smoke lingered in the air. Why was someone burning a fire indoors in July?

He carefully moved alongside the walls, through the kitchen and into a hallway. He continued and came to two closed doors on each side. Again, he paused to listen, but heard nothing. He had to check inside the doors, so once again he listened to the door on his right, silence, he opened it and looked inside.

It looked like a small library. The walls were covered with shelves of books and an antique desk sat at the rear of the room. No Laura. He shut that door then repeated the process with the door to his left. When he glanced inside, he discovered not a room, but a set of steps leading down.

BANG! Another loud blast rang out, much louder and closer than the last one. He thought it sounded like it came from below. Not fireworks. He moved quickly down the steps now, trying hard to keep the panic at bay. It would not help Laura if he lost his cool.

As he descended the stairs, he could hear voices and quickly followed in their direction. He assumed he was in a cellar of some sort. The walls were stone, the air damp with a musky scent that hung all around him mixing with the smell of smoke, which was getting stronger as he pressed on.

Lanterns hung at various intervals down the long hallway. He could hear a man's voice, but couldn't make out what he was saying. He had no idea what he was going to find at the end of this path, so had no concrete plan of action other than finding Laura and getting her out of here.

He came to the end of the hall with an opening to his left. He could clearly hear the voices. The smell and heat from the fire was overpowering. What was being burned? Some sort of incense or fragrant wood? He slowly, carefully poked his head around the corner. He tried to comprehend what was happening before him.

Two men seemed to be in a struggle at the front of the room, one with a gun. A large group of people dressed in hooded robes stood in a circle. And in the center of the circle was Laura.

***

Laura weighed her options as she surveyed her surroundings. Her vision caught something moving to the left. She refocused and saw Jake. Oh my God! Jake was here. Was he insane? That crazy man, Phil, had a gun. Jake was completely outnumbered and she had no doubt in her mind that Phil would shoot him if given the chance.

She had to act. Now! Taking advantage of the confusion between the two men up front, she jumped up, grabbed one of the pewter candelabras by her head, removed and threw the candles to create a distraction, then began wildly swinging the heavy object with all her adrenaline-fueled strength, at the heads of anyone who came near her.

BANG! BANG! Gunshots rang out. She refused to stop and kept swinging wildly while making her way toward Jake. She allowed herself a glance in his direction and saw that Jake had a gun and was prepared to use it, perhaps had used it. Her path to him was clear, so she darted, continuing to brandish her pewter weapon. Meanwhile, chaos ensued with Phil Molino being attacked by the remaining robed figures, while others lay on the ground, either shot or knocked unconscious by Laura.

"Jake!"

"Let's get out of here. Now!" He grabbed her hand and led her out of the room, down the long, dimly lit hallway.

Laura pulled him to a stop, "Jake, no. Karen Wentworth is in there. We have to save her!"

Someone fired a shot, which ricocheted above their heads.

"You'll never get out of here alive. Stop or I'll shoot again." A hooded figure now held a gun and was approaching fast.

"Laura, run. Get up the steps," Jake yelled as he spun around to return the gunfire. Laura did as she was told, taking the steps two at a time. She looked behind her and saw Jake a few feet behind her. They made it up the steps, ran down another hallway and found themselves in a kitchen.

Jake yelled, "Hurry. They're not far behind us."

"But what about Karen..." Laura cried out.

Jake replied, "We will get her once we get help. But if we don't get out of here, we'll all die!"

They ran forward, burst open the door to the outside and ran into the barrel of a gun.

# Thirty-Three

"Freeze. Hands up, down on the ground. Now!"

Jake was confused. The men holding these guns were police officers, one of them his friend. But they both did as they were told.

"Jimmy, for Christ's sake, don't shoot. It's Jake and Laura. They took her clothes, that's why she wearing this gown. We're the victims here. Can we get up?"

"Try it and I'll shoot you both." This was from a voice Jake recognized, but couldn't place. Since he was face down on the ground, he couldn't put a face with the voice. But it had to be a cop. Jake had the feeling these were the police conspirators Kevin Malloy theorized about. He wasn't sure he believed it until now.

"What the hell's going on here, Jim?" Jake asked his friend.

"You'll talk to me, boy. Jim takes his orders from me." said the familiar, voice.

"Who the hell are you?"

"You don't remember me, boy? Well, all you need to know is you put your nose where it don't belong, you and your girlfriend..." He stopped abruptly, interrupted by the sound of sirens approaching fast. "What the...who the hell called the real cops."

"I did, asshole." Jimmy turned his gun on his chief of police. "Now drop your weapon and get down on the ground."

"Who do you think you're talking to, boy."

"You. Now do as I say." The sirens grew progressively louder. It was apparent they were inside the compound now. "Sorry about all this, Jake. This scumbag has had me by the balls for the last couple of years. Sometimes I drink too much, had an accident on the job a while back. He covered for me and I've been paying for it ever since. I wanted to stop you when you first started asking questions, but then I thought, hell, maybe my ol' buddy Jake can help me end this thing once and for all. When you called today, I thought we might get our chance, but Chief Stark here was one step ahead of you."

BANG!! Several things happened at once. A gun went off, the door to the chapel burst open, and out came two men in hooded robes. Jake, who still had a gun tucked in his pants, rolled over on the ground and fired at the chief of police who was aiming a gun at him, hitting him in the shoulder. The chief's gun went flying as he fell to the ground. Next, Jake rolled on top of Laura and shot the men bursting out of the chapel. He acted fast and took them off guard. They both went down. He jumped up and pulled Laura with him.

"Go. Run towards the sirens. I have to help Jim." He nodded his head over to where Jimmy lay in a pool of blood.

"No. I can't leave you here!" Laura cried out.

"You're not leaving me here. You're going to get help and fast." He could see her quickly weighing this in her mind, then she took off to get help.

Jake rushed to Jimmy. He saw the wound in his chest and tried to stop the bleeding. His pulse was weak, and much of his blood was on the ground.

"Don't you leave me now Jimmy, you hear? Help is on the way, buddy."

"It's okay…it's over now…no one else hurt…Jake, make sure it's over… for me…"

"No, no...you're gonna make sure it's over with me. Then we're gonna have that beer I still owe you. Stay with me, Jim."

Jake heard vehicles screeching to a halt and the next thing he knew, emergency personnel were taking over, pulling him out of the way. He felt a hand on his arm and turned to see Laura.

"There's nothing else you can do for him, Jake. Let them do their jobs."

He knew she was right. He reluctantly let her lead him away to the awaiting police car driven by Officer Burns. By now, the whole compound was swarming with officers. Not just the local cops, but Feds too. Jake wasn't entirely sure what he had helped accomplish, but he knew it was something huge and a long time coming. He hoped Kevin Malloy was somewhere smiling down on the scene.

***

Laura was released from the hospital after a thorough examination. She was now safely at home with Jake, sitting at her kitchen table being debriefed on the entire situation by Officer Burns. It was determined that she had ingested GHB, commonly referred to as the date rape drug. It must have been in the water that Cal had given her since it is colorless, odorless, and soluble in water. She was lucky she recovered from it with no lasting side effects.

Jimmy O'Neil was not so lucky. Office Burns informed them that the paramedics did all they could, but the gunshot wound, fired by Chief Stark, proved fatal. Laura knew there was nothing she could say to comfort Jake. In his mind, his friend died saving their lives.

She only hoped Jake could take some comfort in the fact that Hallowed Hills had been busted wide open. Kevin Malloy's investigation had come full circle. Unbeknownst to any of them, the county police in cooperation with the FBI had the place under surveillance for months in an operation investigating a religious cult they believed had settled there. Office Burns was the Feds' inside man. But they were lacking a viable reason to storm into the compound. Jake had given them that.

Once Jake received the news that Laura's car had been tampered with, he called Officer Burns and reported Kevin's findings along with the suspicion that Laura was being held at Hallowed Hills against her will. That gave the police enough reason to request a search warrant. Refusing to wait for a search warrant, Jake entered the compound alone, believing Laura's life could be in danger.

Officer Burns continued, "The search warrant netted some big arrests. Jonathan Laird, aka Albert Magil, was the leader of this particular sect. He was shot by Phil Molino in the shuffle, but he'll recover enough to be charged for his crimes. His second in command was none other than Bob Caully, who Laura apparently knocked unconscious with her candlestick-turned-weapon. The FBI has believed for some time now that Albert or Bob had Albert's sister, Bob's wife, Helen killed, as she was becoming an obstacle to their vision for paradise. We're hoping for a confession from one of them any time now.

"This cult's vision of paradise consisted of kidnapping, polygamy, rape, child abuse, and murder, to name a few. And Bob Caully was not the only local citizen involved. As I'm sure you're already aware, Laura, Cal Simon and his father Dr. Mike, your long-time veterinarian, were trusted members of the cult. Cal, being so good-looking and charismatic, was given the task of luring unsuspecting young women to the compound, probably with the aid of the drug, GSB, that he used on Laura. A drug that is easy enough for a veterinarian to gain access to. Once at the compound, the young women would be re-educated, basically brainwashed, into accepting this way of life. If they refused, they would be used in their sick rituals.

"Cal, being the spoiled pretty boy that he is, has no desire to see the inside of a prison cell, so he's been spilling all the secrets, turning over evidence on everyone, including his own father. It was Cal who took out the pole in front of your house and, with his help, we were able to ID the girl killed in the accident. She was from out of state and has been missing since that night. He picked her up at a bar in the city, which was his usual MO.

"Meet them out of state, have a few drinks, gain their trust, then drug 'em and bring 'em back here. We're still not sure what they did with the bodies, but we'll find out. They're all cracking under the pressure, so it's just a matter of time.

"Phil Molino's in critical condition. He sustained two gunshot wounds, one from your gun, Jake, which hit him in the leg. The second proved more serious, a hit to the stomach, which did a lot of damage. We traced that bullet to a gun that had Phil's own fingerprints on it and those of Jonathan Laird, AKA, Albert Magil. Looks like your shot knocked him down and then Albert tried to finish him off. It doesn't look too good for him, so I'll keep you posted.

"What's harder to swallow for me and my fellow officers is the fact that the chief of police and a few long-time officers were a part of this. It turns my stomach sour. At least, in the end, Jimmy did the right thing. We have to take comfort in that, I guess."

Laura spoke up, "What about Karen Wentworth? Please tell me she's okay."

Officer Burns replied, "Yes, she was unharmed. Drugged, same as you, but otherwise unharmed. Her being elected mayor was not in the plans of this sect. They thought the incumbent mayor had the election hands down. It was a shock when Karen went on to victory. But Bob Caully, as deputy mayor, was prepared to step in and take over after her untimely death. It's not clear how they planned to kill her, but I'm sure it would be made to look like an accident.

"Well, I'm done for now, so I'll let you two get some needed rest. Just don't plan on leaving town for a while in case we need more information from you."

"No, we won't," Laura reassured him. "We'll help you with whatever you need. I just have one question. Is it safe for my daughters to return?"

"Yes, ma'am. Bring 'em on home."

# Epilogue

An early snowstorm blanketed the town. Jake was busy tending to the fire, while Laura and the twins sipped hot chocolate and sorted through the boxes of Christmas decorations.

"I think we're missing a box," Ella said. "I can't find the apple ornament we got in New York City last year."

"It'll turn up," Laura assured her. "And don't forget we still have the box of ornaments Jake and I received as a wedding gift." Laura couldn't remember the last time she had been so happy. She had everything she dreamed of right here in her family room. Jake caught her watching him as he threw another log on the fire.

"Whatcha looking at, gorgeous?" Jake said as he removed his fire-safe gloves.

"You, handsome," Laura replied then sipped her hot chocolate.

"Ew, gross. Guys, knock it off." Ella rolled her eyes, while Brooke pantomimed sticking her finger down her throat.

"Yeah, knock it off," Brooke agreed. But both girls were grinning from ear to ear, happy with the recent turn of events.

"Sorry, girls. I'll behave," Jake promised as he took a seat on the couch next to Laura.

"It's okay. We'll forgive you since you were kind enough to lug all these boxes up from the basement. Mom used to make us do it. So we decided you can stick around."

With that comment, Jake took a pillow from the couch and threw it teasingly at Ella, "I can stick around, can I?"

Ella threw the pillow back, but it hit Laura instead. "Hey. How'd I get pulled into this?" Laura threw the pillow at Brooke and the next thing she knew a pillow fight was in full swing. Then they all fell to the floor in laughter. Even Sam got in on the action, running around them barking playfully.

"Hey, you better take it easy, Mom. You don't want to upset my baby sister."

"Baby brother, you mean," Jake corrected, as he laid a hand on Laura's stomach, caressing her tiny baby bump. "I need more testosterone in this house."

"It doesn't matter. Unless there are twin boys in here, God help us," Laura rolled her eyes. "You'll still be outnumbered, Jake," Laura pointed out as she patted her stomach.

"Oh well, that's alright. There are certainly worse things a man can be forced to endure than living with four beautiful ladies. Now let's get this tree decorated before Christmas is over."

# Acknowledgements

The idea for this book was born one rainy Spring day when I was still the mom of young school-aged children. Rain was forecasted for the entire week and I was going a bit stir crazy. There was a story in the news about a religious cult that was discovered and it got my wheels turning. It was not unusual to have car accidents on the road in front of my home and power outages were the norm in our little country town. I put these elements together, sprinkled in a sweet romance, and The Devil She Knows was born.

Well, not quite. It takes a lot to birth a book! I had no idea when I began this process that it would take over 20 years. I started and stopped the process many times, until finally joining the Amelia Island Writer's Work-in-Progress group. I was invited to the group by fellow author, Julia McDermott, and found everyone to be helpful and encouraging. I could not have gotten this far without you all, and you know who you are.

Many thanks to my brilliant editor, Susan Bennett, and the readers who gave me helpful feedback along the way. Among those readers were Carrie Rodgerson, Tony Flor, and my daughters, Lindsey and Ashley, who were in on this project from its inception when they were still in elementary school. They are now thirty-years old, with successful careers of their own!

There are many others who have influenced me over the years, including all the authors whose books I have enjoyed.

Lastly, I owe much gratitude to the Women in Publishing group, run by Alexa Bigwarfe. This group offers an annual conference that is amazing. It taught me much about the process of becoming an author.